GUNS & HOSES

BRENDA COTHERN

GUNS & HOSES

By Brenda Cothern © 2014
Cover Layout: Nathan Archer
Editor: David Coyle

ISBN-13: 978-1500225650
ISBN-10: 1500225657

First Printing July 2014

Brenda Cothern Books, Inc.
136 E. 145th Avenue
Tampa, Florida, 33613 USA

OTHER TITLES

Shadows Series
Soul Stealer (FREE)
When Beasts Bite
Barely Restrained
Shadows Anthology (v.1-3)
Embracing Sin

Goddess of Fate
Fates
Destiny (coming soon!)

The Sapphire Tower Series
New Beginnings

Brothers by Bond

Cresting Tide

UNDERCOVER LOVE
Not For Sale
Highest Bidder
Undercover Love (v.1-2)

Mad Dogs
Sixth
Deployed

Coming Home (FREE)

Before There Was Beer Pong (FREE)

AUTHOR MESSAGE

Thank you for buying this book. As an author it means a lot to me that you are spending your hard earned cash to read my work! To show my appreciation, I make a promise to you, my reader. The first chapter of every book that I have ever written or will ever write will be FREE on my website for you to read. As an avid reader myself, I know there is nothing worse than purchasing a book only to discover it is not that good. So, please enjoy the sneak peeks at the end of this book and visit my website if you would like to 'try before you buy' my other books!

DEDICATION

To all my friends, family and fans but especially my husband who loves me even when the voices in my head take control!

ACKNOWLEDGEMENT

Special thanks to Bubba's Sport's Bar in Tampa for letting me treat the bar like my personal office.

My wonderful Beta Team, what can I say that hasn't already been said? I don't know what I would do without you. Thank you, Sparkles, Lora, Dave, and Shirley, for all your hard work on this novel!

CHAPTER 1

Present Day

THE parking lot was crammed full and this Saturday night was busier than usual at Guns & Hoses when Tig walked through the door at half past eight. As he stood just inside the door, he scanned the bar that had opened five years ago to cater to the city's police and firefighters. The interior was decorated to match the establishment's name. Police and firefighter memorabilia covered every inch of the ceiling and walls, with the exception of the back wall. That wall was a memorial to all those who served the city, who died while protecting or saving lives. Even the memorial wall was a combination of police and firefighters photos. If one didn't look closely at the uniformed pictures, one might not be able to tell which department the deceased had worked for.

Tig couldn't see the wall through the crowd from where he stood by the door. But he did not need to see it to know the faces of those who fell in the line of duty. Even though he had never attended one, Tig knew the fire department held wakes here, just like the police.

A waving arm above the crowd caught Tig's attention and he began the gauntlet of 'excuse me's' that would get him to his brothers on the force. He was half way to the table his squad had grabbed when he was shoved roughly from behind. Tig caught his balance but not before he had to pick up the petite brunette in front of him to avoid mowing her down with his six foot frame.

"Ohh!" the brunette squealed before Tig set her back down on her break-neck heels.

"Sorry," Tig smiled down at the smaller woman who looked like she wanted to climb him.

Not happening, baby.

Whoever had slammed into him had to be just as big as Tig to make him stumble. There were only five men who fit that bill and of the five, only one was another cop. Tig glared over his shoulder. His eyes landed on the white letters, TFR, in pirate script on the back of a gray tee shirt that was stretched over the broad shoulders of Tommy Flame.

Just my fucking luck. The bastard isn't on rotation this weekend.

Tig and Flame went way back, back to the sixth grade when Tig moved into the house across the street from Flame. They were the same age, the same size, in the same grade, and had the same competitive streak that ran a mile wide. They should have been friends, best buds, but they weren't. From the get go, they meshed like oil and water. There was never a definitive instance that caused their hatred of one another. It was just instantaneous. They took one look at each other and the rivalry began. Matters were made worse when their mothers became best friends. For years, he had to listen to the women talk about how alike he and Flame were, but Tig knew they were nothing alike.

Tig was half tempted to shove Flame back but the last thing he wanted to do would be ruin the Johnson's five year anniversary of Guns & Hoses with a brawl. He was still staring daggers into Flame's back when a hand grabbed his bicep. A dangerous move now that he was pissed off at seeing his rival. He pulled out of the grasp before turning his glare on the culprit.

"Whoa, down boy," his partner grinned up at him. "It was an accident."

"Nothing is an accident except that asshole's birth," Tig said just loud enough that he was sure Flame would hear him.

Tig watched Pat lean to the side to look behind his bulk while he spoke, "C'mon man, you need a beer."

Pat made a hole in the crowd for Tig to pass and he fell in behind him. Tig knew his fellow detective was covering his back. Martinez kicked an empty chair toward Tig and held out a mug of beer when he reached the table. He accepted the mug and took a long pull of the amber liquid before plopping his ass down into the chair. It did not escape his notice that his squad made sure his back was to the man that could make him see red by just existing.

Sixteen years ago.

"Winnie the pooh, Winnie the pooh.... Tigger, Tigger, where's your pooh?" Tommy Flame's voice sing-songed across the playground. "Shouldn't you be bouncing instead of walking?" Tommy started bouncing around like the fabled Tigger. "Boing, boing, boing."

Tig's face grew red even though he was used to Tommy's taunts. He stomped over to his enemy, with his fists balled at his sides, while he stared daggers into the dark haired boy's pale blue eyes.

"That hurt the ashes in your head, *Flame*?" Tig knew his reply was lame. "Why don't you go roll in some hay and burn so your body can catch up with your brain?"

Tig shoved Tommy hard in the chest. He was always better with his fists than words. Tommy shoved him back and their first physical altercation was on. Tig's balled fist came up and connected with Tommy's cheek at the same time Tommy hit him in the face, splitting his lip.

"Tigger Flint! Thomas Flame!" Mrs. Wooster's voice bellowed across the playground.

Both boys were wrestling on the ground by the time Mrs. Wooster and Mr. Lawrence were able to reach them. Each gave as good as they got. Split lips and blackened eyes were the result of their tussle. If the glares the boys gave each other could kill, neither boy would have survived the walk to the principal's office. No, they would have dropped dead on the spot instead.

Present Day

Flame knew he had knocked into someone roughly when Brostowski jokingly shoved him. He glanced over his shoulder to apologize and the words died on his lips. There was no way in hell that he would ever apologize to that asshat Tigger Flint. Instead, he pushed Brostowski back and laughed when the smaller man said 'ow.'

That's what the little shit gets for catching me off guard.

Normally, his five foot nine co-worker wouldn't be able to budge his six foot two frame. Flame wracked it up to the beers. They either made Brostowski stronger or he had had more than enough. He had been at Guns & Hoses since five so his bet was on how much he had consumed in the last few hours.

"Nothing is an accident except that asshole's birth."

Flame heard Tig's insult and braced himself for a return shove. He wouldn't put it past the bastard to retaliate while his back was turned. When he heard Patty O'Brian's voice, he relaxed. He was glad Tig's partner dragged him away because if his nemesis threw the first punch, Flame would be forced to ruin the Johnson's party with a fist fight.

"Don't fuck with the Flame unless you want to get burned," Flame shot Brostowski a wink and wasn't sure if he was goading his co-worker or Tig.

Yep, I definitely have had enough to drink.

"That's still the cheesiest thing I've ever heard!" His ladder-mate made a face and Flame laughed.

"I didn't come up with it."

"Yeah, yeah. It's left over from your high school football days but that doesn't stop you from using it. Shit. 'The flame will burn you.' 'Stay away from the flame.' Yadda, yadda," Brostowski mocked.

Flame had no control over the shit people came up with where his name was concerned when he was playing high school ball. However, he was sure his quarterback sack stats gave them plenty of fodder for the word play. Just thinking about playing football made him grin. His grin widened when he remembered all the pain he rained down on that asshole Tig during football practices in high school.

Thirteen years ago.

Freshman year of high school sucked. If it wasn't for the opportunity to try out for football, Flame would have been miserable.

Hopefully that jerkoff Tig will go for basketball.

It was bad enough that all through middle school they were stuck next to each other because their names fell alphabetically. Flame then Flint. There had only been two classes during the three years of middle school where another name had slipped between them. Thankfully, high school had more last names to fill the gap between A and I. But they were still stuck in the same honors classes. Who knew the shithead was as smart as him? Certainly not Flame.

With any luck, I can escape the asshole by playing football.

No such luck.

Flame joined the group on the field for tryouts and low and behold, there was that fucker Tig Flint standing with the other freshman hopefuls. The only thing Flame could hope for at this point was that the asshole didn't make the cut. And if he did, then with any luck, they wouldn't be on the same side of the line.

The tryouts were brutal. The coach had them run timed laps, suicide drills, crunches, and a bunch of other body aching maneuvers. Of course, Flame's only real competition was Tig. He couldn't even be surprised about that fact by the end of the day because he was just too damn tired to care.

By the end of the week when they returned to the field, Flame almost prayed Tig wouldn't make the cut. But he knew better. They both made the freshman team. Then the junior varsity team. Then the varsity team.

Flame's only consolation was that they weren't on the same side of the line. His slightly larger size over Tig earned him the defensive tackle position and Tig's arm granted him the star position of quarterback. For four years Flame tackled his ass in practice, ground him into the grass as if he could grind the guy's bones to dust. He loved every fucking minute of it, too.

Flame never had to look at Tig in the locker room to see the bruises his tackles left on the asshole. The evidence of the pain his enemy felt was in Tig's every move after practice. Every time he saw the dickhead wince or shake off a limp, his heart soared with twisted joy. Never once did Flame think or realize that his abuse made Tig a better quarterback than he may have ever been without the daily hits.

Present Day.

Tig was enjoying the company of his fellow cops. He didn't go out with anyone from work often except his partner. There were other bars that he frequented for entertainment and he was sure they weren't the kind his co-workers would appreciate. Inside the bedroom kind of entertainment. Guns & Hoses was on his list for 'outside the bedroom' entertainment and he enjoyed having drinks with his co-workers even if he did have to dodge personal questions from time to time or put up with that asshole Flame being in the same establishment.

For the most part, the police and fire departments didn't mingle. Even though the Johnson's, Paul who was a retired fireman and Julie who was a retired cop, created the bar to cater to both by mixing the memorabilia, the rivalry between the two departments could not be dismissed. There was not a designated section for either department and if Tig gave the matter any thought, which he didn't, there wasn't a single place in the bar he hadn't sat at one time or another.

"So, any new info on the Cortez case?" Stanson asked before she took a drink of her beer. The question pulled Tig back from his musings about the bar.

"Thought we agreed to leave work at work?" Wallace grumbled.

"No shit!" Tig agreed heartily.

"Okay," Stanson grinned like a cat that ate a canary. They all groaned at the look on her face because it clearly said she was about to drop a bomb in their laps. "You guys hear about the football league the county is trying to put together for the Big Brothers and Big Sisters Program?"

Tig tensed and did not even realize his mug stopped in mid-motion on the way to his mouth. Wallace spoke the words Tig thought.

"What the hell are you talking about?"

"It's on the bulletin board in the break room. Don't you guys ever look at the damned thing?" Stanson looked around the table.

"Who the hell reads that shit?" Pat grinned and continued, "Oh, I forgot. You do. Irene infomaniac!"

They all chuckled because it was true. Irene Stanson was always on the ball for any and all information the team needed. Whether it was for a narcotics bust or just shit around the station, if they didn't have Irene, they wouldn't know anything and every man at the table knew it.

"Well, I am sure the Lt. will be sending out an email this week due to the lack of sign-ups but the skinny is that TPD is looking for volunteers to play a few games against Tampa Fire Rescue as a fundraiser." Stanson continued to grin like she always did when she enlightened the team of men she worked with.

"Didn't you used to play ball, Tig?" Wallace asked nonchalantly and Tig tried not to grimace.

"Yeah," Tig replied before talking another sip of his beer so he wouldn't have to elaborate.

"That was in high school, wasn't it?" Wallace continued and it appeared he wasn't going to let the matter drop. "Weren't you a quarterback or something?"

"Yeah," Tig almost cringed at the admission. As much as he enjoyed playing football, he did not enjoy being the center of attention that being the star quarterback garnered him. "But that was almost eleven years ago. I haven't picked up a football since my senior year."

"So?" Stanson asked and her grin grew wider.

"*So*, that means I probably couldn't complete a pass if my ass depended on it. Plus, I am sure there are younger guys better suited to play." Tig took another deep drink of his beer and hoped Stanson would drop the topic. Of course, she didn't and Tig tried not to notice the gleam in her eyes.

"With as big as you are, Tig, I bet you were a bitch to tackle."

Tig pushed thoughts of all the brutal tackles his body had endured when he played high school football. The worst of which, were caused by fucking Flame in practice. Everyone was staring at him and waiting for his reply.

"I took my share of hits but I'm not a teenager anymore. I've no desire to be slammed into the turf to relive my high school days."

"Psssh. You're not even thirty yet. There are NFL players older than you who play every weekend," Stanson pointed out and laughed.

"Yeah but those bastards get paid millions to get their ass pounded into the field," Pat added in Tig's defense.

"True but this is for a good cause," Stanson countered.

"Don't hound him. Shit, Stanson," Wallace interjected even though he was the one who brought up Tig's football days. "Let the poor bastard enjoy his beer in peace without the work related bullshit."

"Alright, alright," Stanson held her hands up in defense. "I was just trying to give you guys the heads up.

'Cause you know the Lt. is going to demand volunteers." She looked at each of them in turn before taking another drink of her beer. "And I doubt any women will be on that field."

Tig watched her as she drank. She was an attractive woman, even if she wasn't his type. Her dark shoulder length hair fell loose down her back as opposed to the tight ponytail she normally wore at work. Stanson's lipstick was a brighter shade than she normally wore but the rest of her make-up was as minimal as he was used to seeing every day at the police station. She was not a beauty but attractive enough that someone wouldn't have to put a flag over her face to fuck her for old glory. Tig could admit as much and didn't feel guilty for the thought. However, the thought of Stanson fucking anyone was his cue that he had enough to drink, even if he hadn't been here that long.

Tig killed the last of his beer and set the mug on the table with a loud thunk. "Thanks for the heads up, Irene."

"That's what I do," Stanson shot the group a wink and smirked at her teammate.

"I'm heading out," Tig informed them. "See you guys on Monday."

His co-workers said their good-nights as Tig left the table and bee-lined to the men's room.

Flame was drunk. He wasn't drunk enough to think he wasn't drunk. He knew he was. He also knew that he should have left hours ago. That was impossible as his buddy's from the station kept rolling in and somehow Flame was still here.

The crowd had thinned out, for which he was grateful, as he stumbled his way to the restroom to relieve his screaming bladder. When he entered the hallway to the restrooms it began to tilt and he had to steady himself against the wall.

Fuck! I haven't been this drunk in awhile, Flame thought as he waited for the hallway to settle into a position he thought he could safely traverse.

Once steady, somewhat steady, Flame resumed his trek to the men's room. If he didn't piss soon, he would wet himself for sure. He pushed the door to the men's room harder than he intended and almost stumbled through the opening. He caught himself before face planting on the white tile floor. Waiting for his balance to return and the room to quit swaying, Flame became aware that he wasn't alone. As his drunken eyes focused, he realized Tig Flint was standing in front of one of the two urinals.

Just the fucking asshole I don't need to see me trashed.

The sight of his nemesis seemed to sober Flame enough that when the man he despised turned around, Flame was no longer using the wall for support. He had no problem returning the glare that greeted him, either.

"You going to move or do I need to move you?" Tig's deep voice echoed in the small bathroom.

The man hadn't changed much since high school. He still had the same sandy blond hair and eyes that were a brilliant shade of blue. If he hadn't been such an ass, Flame might consider him attractive.

"Well?" Tig growled.

It took Flame a moment to realize he was blocking Tig's access to the sink so the man could wash his hands.

Flame stepped away from the sink, toward the urinal that Tig did not use, and shot back over his shoulder, "as if you could."

As he relieved himself, Flame watched Tig step up to the sink, run his hands under the sensor to activate the water, and glare mutual hatred at him through the mirror.

"In your condition, a slight breeze could put you on your ass."

"Go fuck your Pooh, Tigger," Flame replied as he began to zip up while still holding Tig's gaze in the mirror.

Tig looked like he was biting back a scathing remark as he pulled towels from the dispenser. Flame turned and made his way to the sink, never once taking his eyes from Tig's.

"You're even more of an asshole when you're piss ass drunk." Tig put his hand on the door and stood for a moment. "I hope you drive tonight just so someone can cuff you and throw your ass in the drunk tank. Just the thought of you being someone's bitch gives me the warm fuzzies."

Flame didn't get the chance to reply before Tig opened the door and stormed out. By the time the door closed, he had thought of a witty reply, at least what his drunken mind thought was a witty reply, but Tig was already gone.

CHAPTER 2

MONDAY morning was like every other Monday for Tig with the exception of being called into his Lieutenant's office. He knew what was coming and groaned as he headed toward the Lt.'s door.

"Flint, you received the email?"

Tig hadn't even had a chance to check his email. Hell, he barely had the chance to grab a cup of coffee. However, Stanson's heads up gave him the insight he needed to fake it through the Lt.'s question.

"About the football league?" Tig asked even though he hoped his assumption was wrong.

"You played in high school, right?"

"Almost eleven years ago."

"It's like riding a bike, Flint."

"Hardly," Tig snorted.

"Look, the city commissioners want this. You know any funding we get is approved by them and to be honest, I don't want a bunch of fat fucks who don't know shit about football representing TPD on the field against TFR."

Tig gave his Lt. a hard glare as he spoke, "And the case against Cortez?"

"This won't take you away from that. If anything, the minimal you will give up is a few Saturdays."

"Most raids go down on the weekend, Lt." Tig reminded his superior as if the man didn't already know.

"The case takes precedence, of course," his Lt. paused. "Honestly, we don't have many officers, let alone detectives, that can play. I really want you to do this because it's a great cause, but I won't force you."

Tig sat in the chair across from his Lt.'s desk and knew everything the man said was true; the Big Brothers and Big Sisters program did so much for the community. Hell, every now and then one of the volunteers still visited one of the vice cops down stairs. Playing on a charity football team wouldn't take him away from the Cortez case or any raids so he really had no good excuse not to play.

"Alright," Tig agreed reluctantly.

"Great!" his Lt. grinned and Tig stood to go back to work. The Lieutenant's words stopped him in his tracks before he made it out of the man's office. "Now that you're onboard, I am appointing you the TPD liaison."

Tig turned around slowly and had to fight the urge to throttle his boss. It was bad enough the man pressured him into playing football again after almost eleven years off the field, but now he was supposed to be the go between with the fire department and charity.

"Seriously, Lt.? C'mon," Tig grumbled.

"You are going to be playing anyway and have the experience leading a team both on and off the field. You're the best choice."

"I fucking hate you right now."

Tig didn't fear reprimand for speaking to his Lt. in such a manner. The man wasn't just his boss, but also a friend. They had climbed the ranks together since joining the force and Brett Daniels wasn't going to take offense at his words.

"Yeah, yeah," Brett laughed and waved him toward the door. "Just do it Tig."

"Like I have a fucking choice," Tig mumbled under his breath as he turned and stormed back to his desk.

Patty O'Brian looked up from his desk and Tig knew by the look on his partner's face that a wise crack was forthcoming.

"So, All-star," Pat grinned at him with an evil twinkle in his eye. "You make team captain? When's your first practice?

Tig growled while he sat down before letting a slow smile appear. "You mean *our* first practice?"

"Oh fuck no!" Pat's amusement disappeared as he shook his head and waved his hands in denial. "I don't even know anything about the fucking game."

"You watch the NFL; you know enough," Tig smirked.

"That's like saying I can ice skate because I watch hockey!

Tig laughed at his partner's analogy. "You can play defense. I've seen you tackle perps. Just pretend anything wearing a TFR tee shirt is a suspect fleeing the scene and you'll be fine."

"I fucking hate you," Pat moaned echoing Tig's words to the Lt., causing Tig to chuckle.

"You'll hate me more on Saturday," Tig grinned sadistically at his partner.

Pat just groaned again as Tig picked up the file on his desk to get to work.

A two alarm blaze at a four story apartment building was a shitty way to end an otherwise routine shift. Still, nothing could wake Flame up faster than the adrenaline that came with fighting fire. It gave him a high that responding to medical emergencies did not.

Most rookies assumed they would be battling fire beasts most of the time when the exact opposite was true. Seventy percent of the time was spent at the station being beyond bored while they waited for the tones that signaled an emergency to blast through the building. Another twenty percent was spent responding to, and assisting, medical emergencies such as heart attacks and traffic accidents. It was the last ten percent that drove most men to become firefighters; the actual fighting of flames that consumed buildings and lives.

The fire that was currently overwhelming the apartment building in front of Flame spurred him and his fellow firefighters into action. Fire shot out of several windows on the second floor as residents, still in nightgowns and pajamas, staggered and coughed their way out of the building.

Controlled, efficient, chaos flowed around Flame as he cinched his SCBA tank and tested the airflow through the mask. Lines of hose were connected to hydrants and unrolled toward the building. Flat snakes that suddenly filled to look alive as men prepared to drown the complex in water. Thankfully the closest building was far away enough that it would not ignite.

"Flame, Brostowski," the Captain called out. "Third and Fourth floor."

Flame nodded as he pulled an axe from the side compartment of the engine. Brostowski was by his side and they cross-stepped the hose lines on their way to the entrance. While they walked, they pulled their masks over their face. Helmets cinched and face shields lowered, they gave each other a determined nod before entering the belly of the burning beast before them.

The smoke was thick and billowing on the first and second floors as they made their way up the wooden stairs. Flame only spared a brief thought that the way they ascended may not be the way they could descend after they cleared the third and fourth floors. It wouldn't be the first time Flame would have to find an alternative route out of a building that was ablaze.

As the men climbed the stairs, it was encouraging to see more residents passing them to flee the fire. The smoke was still and thick on the third floor as each man took a side of the hallway. They heard no cries of distress, which was reassuring, as they used the palm of their gloved hand to guide them down the wall to the first apartments. Flame's hand came to the doorjamb of the first apartment and found the door wide open.

Just because the door is open doesn't mean there is no one inside, the voice of Flame's instructor echoed in his mind as it did every time he encountered an open door in a burning building.

People panicked when there was a fire and adults frequently did not think of one another when they tried to escape. Only parents seem to think of the others in the house or apartment when the flames threatened to consume them.

"Tampa Fire Rescue!" Flame yelled through his mask as he entered. "Anyone in here?"

His left hand maintained contact with the wall, while his right gripped the axe when he moved through the apartment. Even though smoke filled the apartment, it was not thick enough to obscure his sight of the center of the rooms. Still, experience and training caused him to maintain the contact with the wall that was his lifeline if he needed to retreat from the room.

Flame cleared the apartment, and the next two, without finding anyone. Brostowski met him at the end of the hall where they found another set of stairs leading to the fourth floor.

"Third clear. Moving to fourth," Flame heard Brostowski report to the Captain through his earpiece.

Again, the men shared a determined look before they began the ascent to the fourth floor to repeat their search for potential victims of the beast.

Five hours later, Flame and the rest of his co-workers rolled into the station. Their shift ended over two hours ago and the next twenty-four hour rotation was awaiting their return. Every man was tired and wreaked of smoke. It was par for the course for the job that was their passion. There were reports to be completed but most of the men just wanted the stink of sweat and smoke off their skin before they did anything else.

Flame wasn't of that mindset. He enjoyed the smell of smoke that lingered in his hair and on his skin. It reinforced his love for the job. As he filled out his report, he was overwhelmed with a sense of pride and satisfaction at a job well done. There were no casualties and the injuries were few and minor. Paperwork complete, he turned it in to his Captain with the intention to clear out and shower at home.

"Flame," Captain Stevenson's voice halted Flame's exit from his office.

"Yeah?" Flame turned back to the man who had made him the firefighter he was today.

Captain Stevenson was almost more of an Uncle, though not blood related, than a boss. The man and his father had been best friends since before Flame was born. Everything Flame knew and learned about firefighting was because of the man who sat behind the desk before him.

"You're on the team, right?"

Flame knew his Uncle Bob was referring to the football team the department was putting together for the charity.

"Yeah. I signed up when it was posted. It'll be good to get on the turf again," Flame smiled tiredly at his adopted Uncle. He truly did hold affection for the man who stepped into the role of his father. Bob Stevenson didn't have to take his best friend's son under his wing when Flame's father died on the job six years ago but Flame was grateful that he did.

"Thought so. We need a liaison to coordinate with TPD and schedule the fundraiser games."

"Alright, send me the details."

"Will do, Tommy. See you in forty-eight," his Uncle smiled at him. "Give my regards to your mother if you talk to her."

"Sure thing," Flame replied before he left the office to head home.

Almost a week later, Tig was frowning as he watched his fellow cops approach the pavilion they were to meet at for their first day of football practice at Lettuce

Lake Park. He ignored the pile of Velcro belts and flags that sat on the picnic table behind him while he watched his co-workers greet one another.

The Lt. was full of shit. Not many fit enough to play, my ass.

Most of the men looked younger than him and he could appreciate the physiques of the men before him. But that cursory inspection was fleeting as he filed away their faces to the 'work related' men part of his mind. Tig focused his attention back to the reason they were all gathered on their day off. Football.

First things, first. Let's see who's good at what.

"Who's played football before?" Tig asked the men after they had all exchanged names and precinct numbers.

Several of the cops confirmed they had played before and stated their positions when Tig asked. He mentally assigned the men to the positions they were familiar with before he asked his next question.

"Who hasn't tackled a perp?" When no hands went up, Tig grinned. "Alright. From this point forward, I want you to consider anyone on the TFR to be a suspect you need to take down. I don't give a shit if this is flag football. If you can get close enough to take them down, you are close enough to grab their flag."

"Sweet! So we can put them on their asses," one of the younger guys exclaimed excitedly.

Tig chuckled at the kid's excitement. "Just don't be obvious about it but..." Tig paused as he handed out the belts and flags. "Do what you need to do in order to grab their flag."

He watched his fellow officers wrap the Velcro belts on their waists and attach the neon yellow and bright red flags to each hip. Once more, he reminded himself that these were his co-workers as he had to force himself to ignore the trim, lean hips and toned bodies before him.

Three hours later, he had the offensive and defensive teams for the TPD sorted and they were scrimmaging. Patty O'Brian turned out to be a great wide receiver and defensive tackle. Several times the man was able to grab Tig's flag. Even worse, but better for the team, he knew he would never live down the few times his partner planted him on his ass.

"Alright, next Saturday at two," Tig ordered the team. "I am meeting with the liaisons this week to schedule the first game. Hopefully, for next month so we have time to get our shit together. I'll let you know more next weekend."

All the men said their goodbyes as Tig climbed into his vintage '68 Camaro. He was feeling good about what they had accomplished that afternoon and was even surprised at how much he enjoyed being back on the field again.

Flame paid the three dollar fee to get into Lettuce Lake Park. Hopefully, it would be a good place to hold practice for the team he was compiling. He didn't bother looking at the roster of volunteers that lay on the passenger seat of his F150. Flame already knew several of the men on the list and also knew they would have a blast kicking TPD's ass in flag football.

He drove deeper into the park, scanning the open fields that surrounded the pavilions. Flame noticed a group of men standing under one of the shelters and parked his truck to admire the view. It took a moment for his eyes which were focused on the toned bodies, to register the men were geared for flag football. His eye acknowledged what he was seeing before his brain registered what he was looking at.

Shit. It's the TPD practicing for the fundraiser.

Flame knew he should leave and not get caught spying on the opposing team. He had ethics but did not put his truck in gear. He was too focused on the athletic bodies that were taking up the football positions in the open field. Flame did not even realize his focus had narrowed to the sandy haired man who counted off the snap of the ball.

Son of a bitch.

Flame would recognize Tigger Flint through the thickest smoke a building could spit out around him. He watched as his rival ran the cops through plays that Flame remembered from high school. It had been a long time since Flame had seen Tigger in anything but a police uniform or his plethora of suits he wore now that he was Detective.

He stared at the man's legs, muscles tensed and braced as he fell back to balance himself before sending the pass downfield. Calves and thigh muscles looked like they belonged on a moving marble statue as Flame watched Tigger fall back into the pocket again and again.

Flame's observation of his nemesis did not stop at the man's legs. No, it traveled all the way up the rest of his rival's body. Strong back muscles flexed under the pale blue tee shirt his long time enemy wore every time the man cocked his bicep back to throw the football. This was not the kid he had tackled repeatedly back in high school.

The cramping hardness of his cock became painful enough to snap Flame out of his lust filled haze.

What. The. Fuck.

Flame gave his head a shake as if the movement would cause his aching cock to return to normalcy. The fact that he was hard over watching Tigger fucking Flint, the asshole, pissed him off.

It's just a reaction to a hot body, Flame rationalized. *There is no way in hell I am attracted to that jerkoff.*

Focusing his gaze to the other TPD players, he palmed his erection and willed it to go away. After watching the TPD's flag football team for another thirty minutes, Flame pulled his truck out of the parking spot. As he dropped the Ford in drive, he found his eyes resting on the toned body of Tigger Flint once more. He jerked his gaze away, instantly pissed off again, and pressed down on the accelerator harder than intended. Flame couldn't escape Lettuce Lake Park fast enough as images of his lifelong rival's body refused to leave his mind causing his anger to grow.

CHAPTER 3

A ringing phone pulled Tig out of sleep and he reached for his pants on the floor. There was no need for him to check the caller ID. Only one person would be calling him so early on a Sunday.

"Yeah," Tig's sleep graveled voice answered while he sat up in the bed.

"Morning sunshine!" Pat sounded a little too chipper as Tig headed to the bathroom to take his morning leak.

"We have a break?" Tig asked hopefully as he began to piss.

"Do you have to do that while I am on the phone?" Pat groused. "I really don't need to hear you piss."

"Hey, you're the one who woke me, remember?"

"I swear you do it on purpose." Tig ignored his partner's comment even though it made him grin.

"It's Sunday. Tell me there has been a break in the case and you're not calling me this early to invite me to dinner." Tig gave himself a few shakes and started back toward the bedroom.

He stopped in the doorway to look at the sprawled form of the snoring man on the bed. Toned shoulders and back muscles were spread above the thin sheet that covered a firm, tight ass and strong thighs. The sight of his hook-up from the night before stirred his cock. He ignored the temptation to fuck the man one more time before he left.

"Mary was going to have me call you later with the dinner invite. So, yeah, there's been a break. I'll pick you up in fifteen." Pat informed him as Tig began to get dressed.

Tig's hook-up from the night before – John? Josh? Jordan?... whatever - slept like the dead. The guy didn't even twitch while Tig dressed and continued to talk to his partner. They had fun the night before, after he picked the guy up at Bradley's. But that was all it was. Fun. The guy knew it and so did Tig, which suited him just fine, so he didn't feel guilty about bailing without waking the guy.

Finally dressed, Tig did not spare the bedroom, or the guy, another glance as he stuffed his wallet, badge billfold, and handcuffs into the back of his slacks. He really could use a shower if he was heading to the office but was far too impatient to get the details on the break in the case they had been working on for months. The mouthwash, deodorant, and cologne in the car would just have to suffice.

"I'm not at my place. I'll meet you at the station," Tig grudgingly admitted and waited for Pat to razz him about the fact. He didn't have to wait long.

"'Bout time you picked up some tail." Tig heard the grin in Pat's voice. "Thought you were becoming a monk. So, they smoking hot or is this the perfect excuse to chew your arm off and get the hell out of Dodge?"

Tig gave the buff man he'd fucked like there was no tomorrow, another glance. Definitely no need to chew his arm off to escape. As far as Pat knew, Tig wasn't interested in getting involved in a relationship, let alone settling down. And he wasn't.

"I'll meet you there." Tig repeated.

"After you hit it again?" Pat chuckled and when Tig didn't reply, he continued. "Just need to know if I am supposed to cover your ass with the Lt. Unless of course you are gnawing your arm off as we speak. Not hearing any chewing though."

"I'll see you in forty five."

Tig hung up on his partner and pulled his gaze away from his hook-up. The guy hadn't moved at all while he was on the phone. All the better because Tig hated the empty 'let's do this again sometime' shit that ninety percent of his one night stands said as way of goodbye. Tig locked the guy's door on his way out and was at the station thirty minutes later.

"We've identified one of Cortez's houses," Patty O'Brian's voice reached Tig before he even turned the corner into the bullpen. "He hasn't been sighted there yet but several of his lackeys have been seen coming and going. Looks like they are working out of there."

Tig took his seat at his desk across from Pat's and looked at his partner. "Awesome. When do we move?"

"Lt. is holding a task force meeting in an hour. We move out after that."

Tig nodded as he pulled out several files to review on the Cortez case before the scheduled meeting. It wasn't like he didn't know the contents forward and backward but it still didn't hurt to look them over once more.

The team filed into the conference room and Tig took an empty seat next to Stanson. Lieutenant Daniels walked in and took his place at the head of the table, dropping down a thick case file.

"An apartment complex on 34th was torched last night. Our CI, Gullis, said that Cortez had an apartment there and it was one of his labs."

They all knew the confidential informant, Travis Gullis, had been feeding them intel on Cortez in exchange for immunity when they finally nailed Alverez Cortez's ass. Tig had no love for the deals the D.A.'s were willing to make with the snitches but was intelligent enough to know they were vital to the process of nailing the bigger, main players. The only way to get the meth off the streets was to take out the cooks. Going after the small time dealers was a waste of time.

"Did the lab cause the fire?" Stanson wanted to know.

"The arson investigator hasn't filed his report yet but that is the assumption we are working with," their lieutenant informed them. "We are gathering statements from the residents but chances are they won't give us anything useful since they are all too afraid of Cortez."

"That leaves us where? Gullis gave us another location, right?" Wallace asked.

"Yes. He said there is a house on Slight that Cortez was cooking out of. He also gave us a timeline for when Cortez is expected to pick up his product. If it wasn't for that timeline, we would be moving out today."

This was a huge break in the case. Tig wasn't sure how Gullis obtained the intel since he hadn't offered much of significance up to this point. Tig's fingers itched. They always did when he knew an impending raid was going to happen. He ran his thumbs across the tips to scratch the itch while keeping his hands in his lap. Every cop had their tell when it came to anticipating a raid. Tig looked around the room at his teammates and was not surprised to see Wallace drumming his fingers impatiently on the table, Stanson curling her ponytail around two fingers, or O'Brian caressing the badge clipped to his belt like he was stroking his wife.

"So when do we move in?" Tig asked with the same anticipation the rest of the team had to raid the meth lab.

"Gullis said Cortez is doing the pick up on Thursday. We will move in around ten Thursday night when he should be there." The lieutenant wrapped up the meeting after going over the tactical play for Thursday.

Tig exited the conference room with the rest of the team and could practically feel the eagerness for the raid vibrating around the team. They all stopped by his desk and he knew they were waiting for him to speak. Even though he and O'Brian shared the same rank and his partner had been on the force longer, somehow he had become the unofficial leader of their little vice squad.

"Practice tomorrow at the field," Tig told his co-workers and was rewarded with big smiles that spread their lips. They all loved the tactical practice with paintballs they used to enhance their technique. "I'll contact Miller so his boys can pretend to be Cortez and we can do the same for his team. Go home and enjoy the rest of your Sunday." Tig grinned.

O'Brian spoke and broke Tig out of his planning for the raid in four days. "Guns & Hoses for a beer before we head to the house?"

Tig finished the notes he was jotting down on the file in front of him before lifting his head. "Sure." They had time since it wasn't even three o'clock yet.

"Mary is making pot roast tonight,"

"Sounds good," Tig smiled as his mouth watered. He loved Mary's pot roast.

Tig and O'Brian walked into Guns & Hoses and surveyed the Sunday afternoon crowd. The place wasn't crowded at such an early hour but there were still several off duty cops and firemen getting their drink on. Actually, Guns & Hoses always had customers regardless of the time of day or night. The bar shut down at three a.m. for an hour to clean and reopened as a bottle club until eleven a.m. when they could switch back to a regular bar. As they made their way to the bar, Tig nodded hello to several of the cops he recognized before plopping his ass onto the cushioned stool.

"Guinness and a Bud Light for my light weight friend," O'Brian ordered for them.

"Sure thing, sweety," Shelley replied, giving them both a bright smile. "But calling him," she nodded at Tig, "a light weight might be dangerous to your health."

Tig chuckled at their barmaid as Pat countered. "Anyone who drinks that watered down shit is a light weight. Don't let his size fool you."

Shelley just laughed as she fetched their beers. She was a retired county medic and was used to the sarcastic banter of cops and firemen and rarely was put off by anything they said. It's what made her an excellent barmaid. In fact, all of the staff at Guns & Hoses were either retired firemen or cops and outstanding at their new profession.

As Tig watched Shelley pull O'Brian's draft from the tap, he thought she looked too young to be retired, with her blond hair that framed her face and her blue eyes that shone too bright for anyone who had witnessed the horrors most EMS workers endured.

"Size matters, Patty," Shelley countered with a sexy grin and wink when she set their drinks in front of them. "And if anyone tells you different, they are lying through their teeth." Pat grunted at her come back and Tig chuckled as she sauntered off to serve another customer.

"You going to see your piece of ass again?" Pat asked casually as he took his first sup of beer.

Yeah, he's fishing. "No time to date," Tig replied honestly.

"There's always time for the right one."

"Well, I'm not looking for Mrs. Right." *Isn't that the truth! Not looking for Mr. Right either,* Tig thought but kept his mouth shut. "My system works just fine thank you very much."

Pat just shook his head as Tig took a swig from his bottle of Bud. "Hit and runs are an accident waiting to happen."

Tig grinned wryly. "I play safe, daddy." *Yep, no chance of an accident happening with the men he preferred.* "Don't we have more important things to discuss than my sex life?" Tig grumbled and was saved from Pat's reply when Wallace joined them at the bar and Pat started talking about the case.

The first thing Flame saw when he walked into Guns & Hoses was Tigger Flint. The bar was the only place they ever crossed paths and that suited Flame just fine. He had other bars he went to in St. Pete but knew he would never run into the man or his co-workers there. It was just as well too because the last thing he needed was that asshole to find out he was gay. Flame wasn't really in the closet but he didn't advertise his orientation either.

He only spared a passing glance to the man and other cops at the bar as they made their way to a table. Their asses had barely gotten comfortable when Shelley called out to them.

"The usual, guys?"

"Yeah," Brostowski replied and moments later a pitcher of Bud Light and two frosted mugs were placed before them on the table.

Both men watched Shelley return to the bar and in the process, Tigger ended up in Flame's line of sight. The man was dressed more for a club than for Guns and Hoses where most of the cops and firemen tended to show up in their work clothes. Tig wore black dress shoes that were in better condition than the man's normal work shoes, black dress pants with a well-defined crease, and a sharp burgundy button down shirt that was currently tight across the man's broad shoulders. Flame knew he only noticed because of his body's fucked up reaction to the man while he played football the day before.

Must be heading to the club tonight, Flame thought and couldn't help but wonder what clubs would be doing anything on a Sunday night. Quick on that thought, he wondered why he cared at all where the man was going.

"She's so fuckin' hot." Brostowski broke into his unwanted thoughts about Tigger Flint and shifted his focus back to Shelley.

"She's single. Ask her out." Flame suggested with a grin, looking at his fellow firefighter.

"Like she would say yes to a good old Polish boy like me," Brostowski laughed. The man was constantly trying to play down his intelligence with the Polish references but Flame knew better, it was just a defense mechanism.

"What's the worst that could happen? She says no?"

"No. The worst that could happen would be she laughs in my face."

"So what?"

"*So*, I don't need my fragile ego bruised, that's what."

Flame looked his friend over. Brostowski was attractive with his blond hair and blue eyes. He was fit, firefighter fit, and Flame knew he wouldn't kick the man out of his bed if the man swung that way.

"Won't know unless you ask," Flame continued. "Maybe I should ask for you." The grin he shot Brostowski was full of mischief.

"Don't you fucking dare!" Brostowski's voice was loud and caused several heads to turn their way.

Flame just laughed at the look of panic on his friend's face and took another drink of his beer.

"Don't you fuckin' dare!"

Tig turned toward the voice that cut through the relative silence of the Sunday afternoon crowd. That was when he noticed that asshat Flame with his cohort. He took in the appearance of both men with a glance. They looked like they had just come from the gym…or football practice.

"Shit," Tig muttered and turned his attention back to Brostowski and Wallace.

"Just ignore them, man," Pat told him. "I don't know why you have such a problem with him but I know it's more than department rivalry."

It wasn't the first time that his partner had inquired what his problem was with Thomas Flame. It wasn't the first time he was going to ignore the inquiry, either. There was no way he was going to try and explain his history with Flame. No way would he come off sounding like a pansy ass about the shit that happened when they were younger.

"Not going there so drop it, Pat."

His partner just wouldn't let up. "What? He steal a pick up from you?"

Doubt that would ever happen, Tig thought as he wished Pat would just shut up about Flame.

"He fuck your sister?" Wallace joined the conversation.

"Whatever history you two have, you need to bury the hatchet. This hatred," Pat waved his hand between Tig and Flame, "It's gonna eat you alive."

"What time is dinner?" Tig pointedly looked at his watch to change the subject. He was grateful they allowed him to change the topic and didn't press the issue of his hatred for Flame further.

Pat checked his own watch. "About now," Pat said before he pulled out his phone to call his wife to let her know they were on their way.

"Hitting the head first. Meet you at your place." Tig stood and said his goodbye to Wallace as Pat got up to head toward the door.

"Yep," Pat took the last swallow of his beer. "See you there."

Tig pushed through the door to the men's room and knew he had the worst fucking luck on the planet. Twelve people in the whole damned bar including Pat, Wallace, and Shelley. And he, just happened to have to take a piss at the same time as Flame.

Jesus Christ. It was bad enough ignoring the bastard when they were in the same establishment but now he had to ignore him while he took a leak too. *Why the hell did they keep running into each other recently? Maybe I just need to pay more attention to where he is before I take a piss.* Running into the asshole in the men's room twice in as many weeks was bullshit.

Tig stepped up to the urinal next to Flame and not for the first time ignored how similar they were. They were practically the same height, Flame only an inch or two taller, and the same body type, both muscular and toned. Tig knew that Flame's job kept him in shape, unlike his own. If Tig wanted to maintain his physique, he had to hit the gym regularly. By the way his nemesis was dressed, it looked like he had just come from the gym as well. He hated that he was even noticing.

Why the hell do I even care?

Flame glanced over his shoulder, like he always did, when the men's room door opened. He briefly took in the frown on Tig's face and his sharp dressed form before cursing at himself under his breath for even noticing. As the man he despised stepped up next to him, he cursed himself again as the images of seeing the dickhead playing football the day before flooded his mind.

Flame finished his business at the urinal and turned to wash his hands at the sink. He stared at Tig in the mirror as he rinsed his hands under the cold water. His eyes were drawn to the man's wide stance that caused his dress pants to mold to his ass perfectly. It wasn't until Tig shook and began to tuck himself that Flame realized where his eyes were lingering.

Son of a bitch. Flame gave himself a mental shake while he turned off the water and he pulled towels from the dispenser. Like his ass was on fire, he bolted out the door without a backward glance or comment thrown at the man he had hated since the day the guy moved in across from his house nineteen years ago.

Tig finished at the urinal and heard the bathroom door close before he even turned around to head to the sink. He had been totally prepared for another verbal go-round with Flame when he entered the restroom. He was beyond surprised when the man kept his trap shut.

Miracles never cease.

Tig finished washing his hands and dismissed Flame from his thoughts in favor of thinking of Mary's delicious pot roast.

CHAPTER 4

THE week of the raid on Cortez's meth lab moved as slow as a snail across sand acting as if every grain was a speed bump. The tactical practice on Monday and Wednesday with Miller's S.W.A.T. team went smooth as silk and they were as ready as they were ever going to be to bust the drug dealing asshole. Of course, something could always go wrong and Murphy's Law almost always guaranteed something would. However, there was nothing they could do to plan for the unpredictable.

Gullis gave them more information late Wednesday afternoon. There would be at least four people in the house; three cooks and a dealer, before Cortez showed his ugly mug for the pickup of his product. They would all go down for manufacturing, possession, intent to distribute, and anything else they could slap the bastards with to make sure their asses rotted in jail for a very long time. There were sure to be weapons charges and knowing Cortez's crew, resisting arrest as well.

Tig rode in the S.W.A.T. truck with the rest of his team. The anticipation to close this case, get the dirt bag off the streets was a tangible thing as they all checked their vests and weapons one last time. The S.W.A.T. truck parked on the street in front of the house that sat directly behind Cortez's lab. The team poured out of the back and they were assaulted by the stench of acetone. The signature smell of the meth lab burned their noses and almost made the eyes water.

Gonna smell like this shit for days, Tig frowned. It was the only thing he hated about raiding these labs. His clothes and body needed to be washed several times before the stink subsided.

The team waited for the prearranged signal from Gullis that Cortez was on site. When their CI finally contacted them, it was not with the news they were expecting. Cortez changed his schedule at the last minute and would not be picking up the product as originally planned. Too much planning and effort had gone into the raid for them to cancel and even if they couldn't get Cortez, at least they could put a dent in his production.

Tig's squad and the S.W.A.T. team moved out, jogging silently along each side of the house that abutted the back of the meth lab. Half of Miller's team continued around to the front of the house while Tig, O'Brian, and the remaining S.W.A.T. members positioned themselves to breach the back door. Guns drawn, held pointed at the ground, Tig nodded to Miller. Miller in turn nodded to his teammate who held the battering ram that would bust open the back door and allow them entry. The man pulled the battering ram back and was just letting the heavy metal's momentum swing it forward when Murphy's Law bit them all in the ass. The ram never made contact with the door when the explosion occurred.

Tig witnessed it all in slow motion like the cosmos wanted to make sure he didn't miss a damned thing. The door in front of them blew outward, slamming the S.W.A.T. team member and sending the man flying through the air to land several yards away in the back yard under the door. At the same time, three windows at the back of the house shattered, sending shards of glass to pelt the team like some kind of fucked up sideways rain.

The glass barely preceded the flames and concussion of the blast that sent them all flying backwards into the yard.

Blinking several times, Tig rolled onto his side and fought to catch the breath that was knocked out of him. His face felt like it had been attacked by millions of bees as he looked back at Cortez's house. There would be no busting of drug dealers today. Hell, chances were there wouldn't even be bodies to recover.

Tig tried to stand and only made it half way before his ass planted back down to the ground. He looked first at his fellow cops before sparing another glance at the house. They all looked like he felt. Shaken. Cuts covered their faces and hands just like they did on him but otherwise they seemed okay. Even the S.W.A.T. team member who took the door in the chest appeared to be more rattled than injured.

As the distant sounds of sirens reached Tig's ears, he turned his gaze back to the house. There wouldn't be any evidence left to collect after the raging fire was extinguished. Their raid was a bust and not in the way they had planned.

At ten o'clock, tones blasted through the station. It was their nineteenth call of the shift and Flame knew that the chaos was due to the full moon. Things always went bat shit crazy around the full moon. Most people thought it was a myth. Flame knew better and the statistics didn't lie.

As the numeric code for the call blasted over the speakers in the station, Flame forced his tired ass into his bunker gear again. The way this shift was going, he was wondering why he even bothered to take the gear off every time they returned to the station. He was climbing into the engine with the rest of his co-workers when the speaker droned out a repeat of the call code and the address.

Explosion, he thought. *We don't get many of those before the 4th. Must be a gas station.* At that thought, his mental map of the address kicked in and he realized it was in a residential area. And not a very good one at that.

Propane then, Flame thought and was thankful it wouldn't be a taxing fire to put out. That thanks went right out the window when dispatch gave them updated information before they reached the scene.

Two alarm house fire. Flame knew that this could still be propane related even though Tampa did not offer natural gas to its residents.

The billowing smoke of the burning house came into view before the flames that were hungrily eating the structure. As the engine came to a stop and Flame and the others poured out, he was surprised at the number of police already on the scene. Usually one or two cops would arrive to handle crowd control but the parking lot of police cars and uniformed cops standing around before him made him wonder if it was a cop's house on fire.

Shitty neighborhood for a cop; even on their salary. Poor bastard.

There was no saving the house from the fiery beast that was consuming the residence. All they could do was make sure the flames didn't jump and spread to the surrounding homes.

"Anyone inside?" Flame asked a uniformed cop that stood nearby.

"Dunno," the cop replied. "Ask S.W.A.T."

Ask S.W.A.T.? Flame thought as the cop nodded in the direction where a group of cops stood together.

It was then that he noticed that the cops were dressed in tactical gear. They all looked like shit. Dirty and covered in cuts that were likely the result of glass or splinters from the wood frame house. The Captain was busy directing the lines to be pulled so Flame approached the cops. This wasn't a propane explosion if S.W.A.T. was here and if they were going to kill this beast, they needed to know what they were dealing with. He stopped in front of the group of cops before he spoke.

"This a bomb?"

Tig had watched the fireman approach a few members of the raid team as he and O'Brian came up behind the man. Full bunker gear and a helmet made the man just another civil servant whose goal was to save lives. Until he spoke. The voice that reached Tig's ears left no doubt that the firefighter in front of him was Flame. Tig should have guessed based on the man's size but then again, there were at least two other firefighters that were just as built.

"Meth lab," Tig answered to Flame's back and the man turned toward him.

Holy mother of God. Tig's breath caught at the sight of his rival in his turn-out gear. After all the years they worked their respective jobs, they hardly ever crossed paths in the field. How that was possible, Tig didn't know. Hell, years of being in the same city together and never crossing paths made the few times it happened in the last month seem extreme. As much as

Tig hated the man before him, he knew this image of Flame in his bunker gear was being burned into his brain.

Shit. Who knew he had a thing for tall, muscular, bunker geared men. Certainty not him.

Flame turned toward Tig's voice as the man answered his question. Funny how he could recognize that voice anywhere considering how much he despised the man. He looked like shit; shiny bits of glass glittered and sparkled under in flashing red lights of the engine where they were embedded in his tactical vest and pants. His face had several cuts, a few which looked like they still had glass in them, and it was obvious that the medics had not seen to the man yet.

"You look like shit," Flame said without thought.

"Fuck you, asshole." Tig couldn't believe the dickhead was going to start shit with him on a scene.

Tig's reply sapped all concern that Flame wasn't even aware he felt for the man, away. He tried to tell himself it was professional concern for a fellow civil servant but if that was the case, he would have mentioned the guy see a medic.

"Not happening, dickhead," Flame retorted. "See the medic," he started to walk in the direction of the Captain before he turned back to look over his shoulder at Tig. "Then again, don't. That look might actually be an improvement."

Tig watched Flame walk away to do his job and he cursed under his breath. He wasn't sure if he was cursing the man's words or the way his eyes followed the way Flame's body moved under the bunker gear he wore. Either way, he had no plans to see the medic until Flame was engaged with the fire, regardless of how bad his face stung from the cuts.

"C'mon," O'Brian grabbed his arm and it was then that Tig realized he was still staring after Flame's retreating body. "Medic then home."

Tig just nodded and allowed his partner to pull him along to the back of the ambulance where the medics were seeing to the rest of the injured S.W.A.T. team.

Tig felt tired as shit when he finally made it into the station around eleven on Friday morning. When his phone went off at two o'clock to remind him of the football league meeting he had to attend as the police liaison, he wasn't feeling any more energized.

"Heading to meet with the Brothers and Sisters rep," Tig informed O'Brian. "We hear from Gullis yet?"

"No," Pat frowned as he replied.

"He set us up." Tig stated without a trace of doubt in his voice.

"Maybe. He did give us the heads up about Cortez not doing the pickup though," Pat pointed out. "Maybe the explosion was meant for him."

"Maybe," Tig conceded. "I'm outty. See you tomorrow for practice."

"See ya."

Thirty five minutes later, Tig pulled into the parking lot of the Big Brothers and Sisters. He asked for Paul Brandson at the reception desk and was led to a conference room. He had just dropped his tired ass into one of the chairs when a very tall, very attractive, black man entered.

"Detective Flint?" the man stuck out his hand and Tig stood to shake it over the table. "I'm Paul."

"Tig, please."

The shake lingered and Tig tried not to read anything into it too much. As he sat back down, he looked the man over. Paul Brandson was shorter than him by an inch or two and not nearly as toned as the men Tig usually went for but that didn't mean the man was skin and bones by any stretch. No, he was built like a basketball player. His dark green polo was tucked into his black slacks and fit snug across his chest. All of this Tig took in at a glance even as he reminded himself that just because the shake lingered did not mean the man was gay.

Paul took his seat just as the door to the conference room opened. Tig was not surprised when Flame walked into the room. He knew the guy wouldn't pass up the opportunity to play again even if it *was* only flag football. However, his childhood nemesis did not hide his surprise fast enough at seeing Tig sitting at the table. The flash of surprise and the look on Flame's face as the result caused Tig to smirk.

"Paul Brandson," their host introduced himself to Flame and stuck out his hand to shake.

Flame whipped his gaze away from Tigger and focused on the good looking man who held out his hand.

"Thomas Flame." Flame took the man's hand and grinned when he noticed the gleam in the man's eyes. "My friends call me Flame."

"Flame. An appropriate name for a firefighter." Paul smiled and when he indicated that Flame should take a seat, Flame's gay-dar pinged loud and clear.

Maybe after the fundraiser game. Flame entertained the idea of the man writhing beneath him for a moment before he replied.

"They say fight fire with fire," Flame replied with a smile of his own and purposely did not look at Tig.

Tig grunted at Flame's reply. Like he hadn't heard the asshole stroke his own ego enough back in high school. If he didn't know any better, he would think his rival was flirting with their rep by the playful tone in his voice.

Yeah, right. Not likely.

If Flame were the least bit gay, Tig was sure their paths would have crossed in the bars down in Ybor instead of just at Guns and Hoses.

"This is Detective Flint."

Tig interrupted Paul, "Thomas Flame. Yeah, we've met before."

Paul looked between him and Flame and Tig schooled his face to reveal nothing but neutrality. No reason to drag the man into their personal war shit.

"Okay then," Paul cleared his throat and took his seat. Tig knew his abrupt interruption had put the man off his game. "We would like to have three games on back to back weekends. Best two out of three to determine the winner. Tickets will be ten dollars and split between all three of our charities. Same with the proceeds from the concession sales."

"The TPD has decided to give their third to you," Tig informed Paul.

"TFR has done the same," Flame added.

"That's very gracious of both departments," Paul replied with a smile and if nothing else confirmed the man was gay, it was the way he said those words.

Unbeknownst to both Tig and Flame, they both had the same thought at Paul's tone and words. Neither man displayed their knowledge of the man's obvious gayness or acted upon it.

"We would like to schedule the first game in two weeks so that the last game will fall three weeks later on 4th of July weekend. We are planning to incorporate a field trip for the kids down to Channelside for the fireworks after the game. Would that be agreeable to the departments?"

"TFR is at your disposal as far as the game schedule is concerned," Flame replied before Tig could open his mouth. His Captain had already approved his shifts off to play in the charity games.

"That will work for TPD as well."

"Perfect." Paul smiled at them both and looked at least five years younger. "Well, gentlemen, let's schedule the first game in two weeks." Paul typed on his tablet, where he had been making notes, before he stood.

Flame and Tig followed suit. Paul escorted them to the door and after Flame shook his hand, Tig handed the man his business card.

"Please call if there is anything else the TPD can do to help." Tig stuck out his hand and Paul once more seemed to hold the handshake for a moment longer than necessary before letting go.

"I'll email you both the time and field information next week." Paul smiled at them both again. "Have a good weekend."

"You too," Flame replied.

Tig gave Paul a nod and followed Flame out of the building. The moment they stepped out into the heat of the Florida sun, Flame spoke.

"Just have to 'one-up,' don't you?"

"What the fuck are you talking about?" Tig was not sure why he was even replying.

"'Please call...' Nothing like being a suck up," Flame sneered. "Not like it will do your ass any good. We are still gonna kick your ass on the field."

Tig was tired, too fucking exhausted to verbally spar with the asshole. "Whatever. It's called being polite." Tig unlocked the door on his Camaro.

Flame frowned at Tig's response. It wasn't like the man not to have some sort of smart-assed insult to throw back at him. As he passed in front of Tig's car on the way to his F150 that was parked on the other side, he really looked at the man. Tig looked like shit and it wasn't just because his face still looked like it had been attacked by a weed eater. The cuts on his face were still healing and for a moment, Flame was tempted to ask the man if he was okay. He had enough brushes with death himself to know they could rattle you for a few days afterward. Where his concern for the man he had always hated came from, he didn't know, but it was the second time in as many days that the feeling had snuck up on him.

Tig glanced across the roof of his car and caught Flame frowning at him while standing in the door of his truck. *Jesus Christ.*

"I don't have time for your shit, asshole," Tig grumbled and dropped his ass into the bucket seat of his car and slammed the door.

Flame cursed as Tig drove off and forced himself not to give the dickhead another glance before he took his own ass home.

CHAPTER 5

TIG was *still* tired, and in a shit mood because of his exhaustion. It had been a long week. Felt even longer after the explosion two days before. They had not heard from Gullis since he had informed them that Cortez wasn't making the pickup. If the explosion was meant to kill the snitch, it failed miserably. They were fortunate that his team and S.W.A.T. only sustained minor injuries.

Not like the fucks who were cooking the shit that poisoned the streets.

If the explosion was planned to take TPD out, it failed epically. If it was just the result of the tweekers fucking up, well, they paid for it with their lives. No way to know what caused the explosion until the arson investigator's report was filed and a copy landed on Tig's desk.

Grabbing the flag football gear from the backseat of his Camaro, Tig climbed out of his car and tried to push the thoughts of the case out of his mind. As he walked to the pavilion next to the field they chose for practice at Lettuce Lake Park, his mind shifted to his meeting for the charity games the day before. He no longer had any doubt that the representative from the Big Brothers and Sisters, Paul, was flirting with him. He replayed those handshakes and was sure of it. If it hadn't been for the presence of that asshole Flame, Tig may have explored the flirtation. Paul was a good looking man. Not as built as Tig, or Flame for that matter, but not too shabby for his age. Tig estimated that he was in his late thirties to early forties. It wouldn't be the first time Tig had hooked up with a man close to or more than ten years his senior.

Maybe after this charity shit.

No sooner had the thought crossed his mind did Tig nix the idea. He never hooked up with anyone associated with his job. It was better, safer, for everyone that way and he sure as hell wasn't looking for a relationship. Add to that, the dickhead Flame also knew the guy. Definitely a 'no go' zone.

Fucking Flame.

Of course that asshat would be the liaison for the Tampa Fire Rescue team. If the guy was anything like he had been in high school, then he had a hard on for anything that had to do with football. Just the thought of having to deal with the prick on the field again made him frown.

"What crawled up your ass and died?" O'Brian's voice broke through Tig's thoughts about his rival.

"Just thinking about the games we're going to play against TFR," Tig forced his frown into a more neutral expression.

"Oh shit," O'Brian shot him a concerned look. "Flame is playing on the TFR team, isn't he?"

"He's the liaison," Tig replied and fought the frown that attempted to return to his face while he dropped the flag football gear on the picnic table.

"Fuck, Tig. We don't need a brawl in the middle of a charity event."

"There won't be a brawl," Tig reassured his partner and hoped he could keep his word.

"Then why did you look like you wanted to skin something alive before you slit its throat to put it out of its misery?"

"It's just a game," Tig repeated and continued when Pat's doubtful frown remained focused on him. "For charity," Tig emphasized. "I'll be professional."

Pat snorted. "Yeah, until Flame says or does something to get under your skin then you will go all Rocky Balboa over his ass."

Tig grunted, because he knew his partner was right. Pat and he had been partners long enough that the man had to step in more than once when he and Flame were about to come to blows. It couldn't be helped. Tig and Flame were oil and water. A collision of hate and violence just waiting to explode anytime they were in proximity of one another.

"Let's just practice," Tig closed the subject of his hate for Flame when the other volunteers for the TPD flag football team approached the pavilion and grabbed their belts and flags.

Flame walked down 7th Avenue in Ybor City and made his way to the night club Shadows. It had been a long time, years in fact, since he had strolled down these streets. Ten years, at least, since he went club hopping in Tampa's party district and the clubs he passed were not the hip-hop or grunge bars from his past. Now, Ybor was nicknamed 'Gay-bor' and for good reason. Almost every bar on 7th catered to the gay community in Tampa.

Rainbow colors announced to anyone with half a brain that they were gay friendly. As Flame passed a bar named Bradley's, he let his eyes roam over the drag queen posters that decorated the windows of the club. All of the queens were stunningly beautiful posing in their glamor shot pictures. It had been years since he had seen a drag show.

Might have to come back and check it out another night.

As he approached the corner of 7th and 15th where Shadows was located, he made his way toward the line that was snaking its way around the corner. Flame pulled his cell from his pocket as he stood outside the door of the club. Through the door the club-goers shuffled, Flame could see a large black man who he could only assume was security.

I'm here, Flame texted.

BRT, Flames phone vibrated a second later.

Flame smiled as he spotted his friend pushing against the tide of patrons trying to enter Shadows.

"Hey man. Glad you could make it."

"Been awhile, Nick," Flame replied as they shook hands. "Thanks for the invite." Flame pulled his friend into a brotherly hug. "What's the occasion?"

"Let's talk inside. I need to keep an eye on things."

"Sure." Flame studied Nick as he followed him, bypassing the line into Shadows.

Flames eyes never left the back of his friend as Nick cleared a path for them through the Saturday night partiers. Nick had been one of his guest trainers when he was in the military and after running into each other, literally, down at Channelside one night, their friendship blossomed. They hadn't hung out much but the few times they had met for a beer, or three, they had bonded.

The club soon distracted him from his friend. Flame looked around the club as he followed Nick toward a VIP area. The whole place was shrouded in darkness. No, not darkness, shadows. The only light breaking through the darkness came from over the bar and the laser strobes bouncing off the glittered dance floor.

This place certainly lives up to its name, Flame admitted as he eyed the sheer curtains that dropped from the ceiling to conceal tables and chairs scattered around the dance floor. The deep base of Jason Derulo's *Talk Dirty to Me* thrummed through the floor and off the walls. Flame felt every beat as Nick led him to one of the alcoves in a red roped off VIP section.

Nick slid onto one side of the wrap around bench and removed the 'reserved' card from the table as Flame planted his ass across from his friend. Before Flame even had the chance to get comfortable, a small framed waitress with long black hair and a sultry smile appeared to take their order.

"Usual Nick?" the waitress asked, sexy smile still in place.

"Yeah, Sin, and whatever my buddy here wants."

"Bud Light bottle works for me," Flame returned the smile the waitress aimed at him.

"Sure thing, honey," the waitress shot him a wink before turning on her very high, four inch heels and somehow made her way back toward the bar to fetch their order.

Flame was watching her go when Nick spoke. "Don't get any ideas, bud. She's taken by a big ass dude who makes me look like a midget." Nick laughed when Flame looked back at him.

Nick wasn't small by any means. His friend was only a few inches shorter than he and slightly more muscular. If the waitress' boyfriend was larger than his friend, then the guy had to be huge.

"No worries there. Not my type, remember?" Flame grinned. "So, how have you been?" Flame inquired as they waited for their beers.

"Doin' good," Nick replied with a smile and Flame thought his old instructor looked happy. "How 'bout you? It's been awhile since we've hung out. Found Mister 'right' yet?"

Flame chuckled. The night he had run into Nick outside a genealogy business in Channelside, Flame had been wrapped around his date. His very *male* date. The impromptu run in effectively outted him to his former military acquaintance. At the time, Nick didn't seem too bothered by the fact that Flame and his date were hanging all over one another. His friend just seemed to take the whole encounter in stride. Thankfully, Nick finding out he was gay didn't change the dynamic of their friendship and for that Flame was grateful.

"With my schedule? Who you kidding?" Flame continued to grin. "Why? You volunteering?" Flame joked. Sort of.

Nick was just the type that Flame went for when he was on the prowl for a hook-up. His friend was tall and muscular; no fear of hurting the masculinity that sat across from him. But as attractive as Flame thought Nick was, he would never make a move on his friend. Straight guys weren't his thing.

"Sorry, I'm taken," Nick laughed.

"Here you go boys," their petite waitress set two bottles of Bud Light on the table before them.

"Thanks Sin," Nick grinned.

"Sure thing. Flag me down when you're ready for round two."

"Will do," Nick replied as the sexy nymph moved away into the crowd to serve the poison of choice to the next customer. Both men watched the small waitress weave her way into the crowd before Nick spoke again. "Actually," Nick picked up their conversation where they left off. "That's why I asked you out."

Flame took a sip of his beer. He knew there was no way in hell that his buddy was talking about his volunteering comment so he waited for Nick to continue.

"I'm getting married."

"Congrats man!" Flame raised his bottle and clinked it against Nick's.

"Do I get to meet the lucky bride before the big day? Wait. I am invited to the wedding, right?" Flame asked through his smile of happiness for his friend.

"Well," Nick paused and focused his gaze on Flame as he took another swig of his beer. "You could meet the *groom* before the wedding. We are heading to New York soon but I wanted to invite you to the reception we are having here."

Flame knew the look of shock was clear on his face but he could do nothing to school his features.

Nick is gay? No fucking way! No wonder he didn't freak down at Channelside.

"So, you'll come to the reception, right?" Nick asked as he laughed at the look on his friend's face.

"Fuck," Flame exclaimed as he pushed thoughts of his friend, the friend he previously thought straight, with another guy from his mind.

"Is that a yes?" Nick continued to laugh as he watched Flame adjust to the information about his sexual preference.

Flame knew it wasn't just his utterance of shock that made his friend laugh at him. He could only imagine what his shocked face looked like.

"Yeah," Flame finally answered and took a drink of his beer as he tried to adapt to the new view of his friend.

He would never have guessed that Nick was into men. The man screamed 'straight.' Then again, no one ever guessed he was gay either. But before he could inquire about his friend's love life, a loud, shrieking noise overrode the thump of the hip-hop that flooded the club.

Tig sat at the bar and nursed his beer. He knew he should be home in bed after the hellacious week he'd had, but he was beyond the point of exhaustion where sleep would claim him. The flag football practice earlier this afternoon had revived him enough to tempt him into hitting the bar.

Bradley's was just as full as it was last Saturday when he sat on the same stool. There were several weekend regulars that he had no interest in and plenty of other new faces to catch his eye. A good fuck or at least a blow job was exactly what he needed to relax him enough for a solid night of sleep. A good night's sleep was just what he needed to recharge his battery.

Tig never had to physically look for a hook-up. Still, that did not mean he didn't glance at his Grindr app to see what potential was nearby. A glance at the app showed several potential candidates for what he needed and Tig looked up from his phone to locate their physical forms. He could never trust the pictures attached to the profiles on Grindr. He wanted to see the men in the flesh before he decided on his choice of entertainment.

Tig glanced down to his phone again at the profile of a buff bottom before his gaze raised and locked on the same man across the bar. The profile picture looked much hotter than the man in the flesh but that was usually the case. It wouldn't matter. They all looked the same when he was looking down at the top or back of their head. Hell, his own picture did not show anything more than his pierced cock.

He stared at the man for a few more moments before sending his message through the app for a quickie. He blindly hit the send button as he stared at the man who he hoped he would soon find some sort of release. The instant the man across the bar received Tig's Grindr message was obvious when the guy looked up from his phone and scanned the bar. Their eyes met for a second before Tig's phone vibrated.

I'll be in the bathroom, Buff-boy replied.

Perfect, Tig thought and grinned as he watched his Grindr hook-up move away from his friend's at the bar.

The moment the guy walked toward the restroom, Tig killed his beer and pushed himself off the bar stool that was causing his ass to go numb. The door to the men's room had not even finished closing after Tig's hook-up entered before Tig pushed it open again. The tall, built hunk of male flesh entered the handicap stall and Tig followed on his heels. Tig latched the door behind him and his hook-up was already seated on the john, fully dressed, and licking his lips. No words were needed to be exchanged. No names. They both knew what this was about.

Tig stepped between the man's spread legs and unbuckled his belt as hook-up boy ran his hands over Tig's slack cover thighs. Tig freed his hard dick and appreciated the look of hunger on the other man's face as much as he appreciated the pink tongue that licked the plump lips that were soon to be wrapped around his cock.

"Condom?" Tig asked as he held the base of his cock, pushing down on the shaft so that it was pointing at the man's face.

"No."

Tig didn't sweat the man's recklessness at giving him head without protection. He only asked out of courtesy. He knew *he* wouldn't be getting off in the guy's mouth. He also knew that the likelihood of getting HIV from getting a blow job or swallowing a load was next to nil so he wasn't worried about the man's nonchalance at sucking him off without protection. Still, he would play it safe.

With the last step to close the distance between them, Tig brought his cock to the man's lips. He sucked in a hissing breath when the hot, wet, suction surrounded him. One hand remained on the base of Tig's cock while the other rested on the other man's shoulder as he rocked his hips into the bobbing head at his crotch.

Tig allowed his mind to wander into fantasy as his body succumbed to the sensations of pleasure the mouth around his cock was providing. Strong hands dug into the back of his thighs, under his ass, and urged him to thrust harder into the willing throat of the man he was face fucking. Tig, the gentleman that he was, complied and thrust harder, deeper, through the lips that wrapped around him.

The tingling at the base of his spine registered nanoseconds before Tig felt his balls scrunch up tight against his body. The warning of his impending orgasm was something he was so familiar with feeling he barely had time to pull out and point his twitching cock at the floor. The last tremors and shuddering jerks of his hips, had not even subsided before a loud blaring noise shattered his orgasmic high.

"What the fuck?" The muscular hunk, who had just gotten him off, exclaimed and shot to his feet. "Is that the fire alarm?"

Tig was still busy resetting his mind but his subconscious brain knew that the loud noise that was killing his post orgasmic bliss was indeed the club's fire alarm.

"Yes," Tig replied calmly as he stepped back to allow his cocksucker more room to stand between them while he tucked himself back into his slacks.

The man bolted from the restroom, not surprisingly, and Tig followed at a more relaxed pace. The club was what he expected. Panicked chaos. Mostly men, and some women, scrambled toward the two exits of the bar.

There was no 'don't run, stay calm' shit and Tig did not even attempt to implement such an evacuation plan. Instead he stood clear of the herd that was flooding the entrance in order to escape the fire alarm. The pounding of the DJ's club beats were over ridden by the incessant high pitched noise of the fire alarm. Bartenders and security tried to keep everyone moving out of the club in an orderly manner.

Tig did not smell any smoke as the bar cleared out but that didn't mean the place wasn't actually on fire. He did a sweep of the inside of the club before he made his way to the hoard of humanity at the front door. He waited until the three bartenders and two security guards were in line to exit the club before he fell in step behind them.

CHAPTER 6

FLAME followed Nick's lead when the club's fire alarm screeched, ruining everyone's Saturday night. He helped usher patrons out of the door and was relieved when he heard the distant sound of sirens. Somewhere in the chaos of the fleeing Saturday night crowd, he'd lost Nick. But the location of his friend was the furthest thing from his mind.

He concentrated on the building in which Shadows was situated. Next to Shadows was the bar called Bradley's and next to that a pizzeria, but it was not the ground floor businesses that concerned Flame. No, it was the residential floors above where he directed his attention. He did not see any smoke or flames but knew that if any of those apartments triggered the fire alarms in the businesses below, the place could turned into a bonfire any minute. The crowd bumped into and around his solid form as he searched for the first tell-tale signs of the fire's point of origin. The beast would show itself. All he had to do was wait.

There.

On the third floor, the barely discernable hint of smoke leaked out of a window. Had Flame not been searching for the smoke, he would have never seen it.

Fuck.

The fireman in him itched to battle the beast of flame that he knew was only growing stronger by the moment. But there wasn't shit he could do about it, even if he were on call. All he could do was ensure that the crowd was out of the way of the engine when it arrived. So that's what he did, even though he hated crowd control.

Tig was still stuck trying to get out the door of Bradley's but even though everyone in front of him was trying to do the same, he found himself stuck in a human traffic jam. He wasn't panicked, wasn't concerned he would be trapped and turned into a crispy critter or anything so trite.

There was no smoke leaking into the empty space behind him into his favorite gay bar. No sight of flames, yet, that would prompt him to high tail it out of there in a panic like the rest of the crowd. No, there was just the hoard of bodies before him that were preventing him from reaching the safety of 7th Avenue. All he could do is shuffle forward as the mass of humanity moved out into the warm night.

The crowd in front of Shadows began to thin as they made their way across the street. The same couldn't be said for the bar next door. Flame frowned at the recessed entrance and human dam of the bar he had walked by earlier. The patrons of Bradley's seemed to be at a standstill and from where Flame stood, they didn't seem to be in any rush to move, to clear away from the building that was on fire. Several sure steps later, Flame was urging people away from the door so that those still inside could get out.

"Move across the street," Flame told the mass of people. "Just keep moving. Clear the way. Keep going. Tampa Fire Rescue is on the way," Flame's voice remained calm. "Across the street, that's it."

Tig heard Flame's voice before he searched for the man outside the door and he groaned at his shitty luck. He continued to shuffle behind the mass of people that had been partying in Bradley's. He frantically looked for an escape route that did not involve crossing Thomas Flame's line of sight. Unfortunately for Tig, he was shit outta luck because Flame stood directly on the other side of the threshold that was funneling everyone away from the potential fire.

Shit.

Tig knew there was no way that the asshole wouldn't see him as he exited Bradley's. It wasn't as if he was in the closet, even though no one at work knew he was gay, but he sure as fuck didn't want to give the man he had hated for most of his life any more ammunition for their personal war.

Mother fucker, Tig cursed under his breath when Flame's large form finally appeared ushering people away from the door. It could not be avoided. The asshole would see him leaving a known gay bar and there wasn't shit he could do about it. So, he did the only thing he could. He followed the person in front of him which put him right in the dickhead's line of sight.

Flames eyes remained focused through the door of the club in an attempt to see how thick the crowd remained inside. It looked to be thinning. That's when he saw Tigger Flint. Shock at seeing the man exiting a gay bar did not even begin to describe the feeling that overcame him. There was no schooling his features. No hiding his surprise at seeing the detective.

Maybe he is working, Flame thought even though he knew the man rarely worked weekends.

That thought shattered when he took in his rival's clothes. Tig was dressed for a night out on the town. His button down dark cobalt shirt was unbuttoned more than would be acceptable for work and his sleeves were rolled halfway up his toned forearms.

When their eyes met, Flame saw Tig tense and for once he didn't have the urge to mouth off at the man. Instead, Flame forced the shocked expression off his face.

Tig looked back over his shoulder. He knew it was a futile attempt to delay Flame from saying something to him. He braced himself for whatever shit might come out of the asshole's mouth while staring daggers at the man. Shock and surprise were clear on Flame's face before his look became more neutral. The sneer or look of disgust that Tig had expected never appeared.

"Anyone left inside?" Flame forced his voice to remain professional as Tig crossed the threshold of Bradley's.

Tig followed Flame's lead to ignore the white elephant that stood between them in front of the gay bar but still resented that the man thought he would leave anyone inside before exiting the building.

"I did a sweep. I'm the last," Tig replied and continued walking away.

Flame reached out and grabbed Tig's arm to stop him. "Restrooms too, right?"

Tig stopped and narrowed his gaze on Flame. He tried not to read into Flame's question. There was no way Flame would know what went on in the restrooms of gay bars. The firefighter was just being thorough because he knew people panicked and thought bathrooms were safe in a fire.

"I was the last to leave the men's and cleared the ladies before playing human traffic cop. So yeah, there's no one hiding in there." Tig pulled his arm free of Flame's grip and turned his back to walk away. He did not see Flame's raised brow at his revelation.

Tig did not let his surprise at Flame's lack of smart-assed gay comments show on his face as he made his way across the street.

Maybe he's just too focused on the fire. The digs are sure to come later. Probably when the dickhead has an audience.

Flame jogged a few steps and fell into step next to Tig as he crossed 7th Avenue and ignored the aggressive, annoyed look the cop shot him.

"Thanks for clearing the bar," Flame said when they reached the curb in front of the Honey Pot. From the corner of his eye, he saw that Tig's expression did not change before he began to push his way through the crowd toward 15th Street. Flame reached out and stopped Tig again.

"Could use help with crowd control until the units arrive on scene."

Tig looked back at Flame and tried to read the guy. Flame was never, ever, nice to him. Never. They had hated each other for far too long to be the slightest bit kind to one another. Tig looked away from Flame, at the bars that lined 7th Avenue. The majority of the bars that lined the street were gay bars.

Could Flame actually be gay? Tig looked at Flame and scrutinized him. *If he was, I would have seen him down here before.*

Still, Tig let his eyes roam over how Flame was dressed. Much like himself, he was dressed in clothes appropriate for hitting the Saturday night club scene. The burgundy polo he wore did nothing to hide his muscular chest, hard nipples, and paint roller abs. The polo was tucked into black stone washed jeans that only accented his trim waist and well-developed thighs. Tig could admit to himself that if he didn't know what an asshole Thomas Flame was, he would be Tig's type. Just the type Tig would try to pick up and fuck senseless.

Flame remained quiet as he watched Tig quickly give him the once over from head to toe and willed his body not to respond. The last thing he needed was to let Tigger Flint see how turned on he was becoming by the man's appraisal. Still, Flame could not stop the smirk that transformed his normally angry glare, whenever his path crossed Tig's, into something softer. Cocky. Sexy.

Tig glanced at Flame's face again and by the guy's expression knew that Flame didn't miss his head to toe observation.

Great. More fodder for the asshole to taunt me with later. Tig turned his head back to the clubs that lined the street.

Next to Bradley's was a straight bar called Shadows. Tig had never been in the club but knew that must be where Flame was spending his Saturday night before the fire alarms sounded.

When Tig remained quiet, Flame suddenly realized that the guy didn't want to stick around, didn't want to run into anyone else that he worked with or knew. But Flame really could use the help with the crowd control as the sirens in the distance continued to grow louder. They needed to get the partiers down the street to make room for the fire trucks.

"You came out of Shadows, right?" Flame said and hoped the cop would get the message that he wouldn't out him to their colleagues.

Tig's head whipped around to stare at Flame. The cop in him wanted to help clear the scene so the fire department could focus on the job of extinguishing the fire. But, he couldn't figure out why Flame would give him the option to lie about which bar he had been visiting.

"Yeah, Shadows," Tig agreed and watched Flame's lips morph into a smile that Tig was damned sure he had never witnessed aimed in his direction over all the years he had known the man.

Tig accepted the temporary truce because he knew it was only because Flame wanted his help with the crowd. Getting the crowd away from the building that now had flames shooting out of several windows was a higher priority than their personal hatred for one another.

"I'll take this end." Tig walked away, toward 15th Street and took his badge from his back pocket before asking everyone to move up the block.

Flame only watched Tig for a moment, grateful his rival's cop side won out, before he started ushering the crowd in the other direction.

By Wednesday, they still had not heard from Gullis and were starting to believe their CI was either dead or had fled town to avoid Cortez. All thoughts of Flame's strange behavior on Saturday were the furthest thing from Tig's mind as he had remained focused on the case. That was until he walked into Guns & Hoses.

Flame and a few of his firefighter friends were sitting at a table and for the briefest moment, Tig considered turning on his heel and leaving his after work haunt. He was already in a foul mood and the last thing he wanted or needed to end his shit day was a run in with the asshole about his sexual preference.

I have beer at home, Tig reminded himself and was about to leave when Shelley called out to him.

"Bud Light Tig?"

No escape now, Tig thought as he saw Flame turn his head toward where he was standing just inside the door.

Shit.

"Sure," Tig forced himself to smile at Shelley as he made his way to a stool at the bar.

Flame turned his head toward the door when he heard Shelley say Tig's name. He wasn't surprised to see the cop dressed in his typical suit for work.

Huge difference from Saturday, Flame thought. *Would never know how built he is, covered up by that suit.*

Flame's mental image of Tig in his club clothes abruptly shifted to his memory of the cop wearing shorts and a TPD tee shirt for flag football practice. His body responded from the image of Tig on Saturday night and from the guy a few weeks ago at Lettuce Lake Park. It really didn't matter, both looks were hot as hell. He was just glad the table hid the tightening of his jeans.

Fuck!

Flame forced his mind and gaze to return to his co-workers and willed his cock to go down. It was about an hour later when he noticed Tig stand and head to the men's room. The temptation to follow the cop that he had never gotten along with was strong. He tried to ignore the urge to follow the man. Told himself it was a very bad idea to follow him into the men's room. However, his resolve to remain at the table with his co-workers did not win out over his body's desire.

"Gotta piss. Be right back," Flame told his friends. He heard them order another pitcher of beer as he walked away and knew it was going to be one of 'those' nights.

Tig was washing his hands when the bathroom door opened. Flame stepped in and proceeded to lean against the door, effectively blocking Tig's exit.

Great. Just what I don't fucking need. Tig continued to mentally curse Shelley for spotting him before he could leave the bar without being seen.

"What the fuck do you want?" Tig went on the offensive. If he was going to be cornered and forced into a verbal battle with the asshole, he might as well metaphorically come out swinging. "Come to gloat? Give me shit about seeing me in Ybor on Saturday?"

Flame stared at Tig and understood the man's anger even if busting the guy's balls was the furthest thing from his mind. No, verbal sparring wasn't why he followed his rival into the bathroom. He wanted, no, needed, to confirm his assumption that his longtime nemesis was indeed gay. He could no longer dismiss his attraction for the man and pushed away from the door to take a step closer to Tig. He wasn't surprised when the cop held his ground. Tig never backed down from a fight in all the years they had known one another. Especially if that fight was with him.

"So, you're gay." Flame made his words a statement; not a question as he held his breath and waited for the answer.

Tig stepped toward Flame when the asshole brought up his sexuality and never noticed how quietly the man said the words. Still, Flame's words pissed him off. He had no desire to deal with the bullshit from some of his colleagues or friends at Guns & Hoses.

"Get the hell out of my way, asshole."

Flame didn't budge as Tig ignored his comment and moved closer to him. Instead, he held his ground and smirked because the lack of denial was answer enough as Tig got in his face.

How had I never noticed how hot his anger could be? Shit. Flame felt his body starting to respond but his eyes never left Tig's angry gaze. *If he looks down...* Flame didn't finish the thought because he was torn between wanting Tig to see his arousal and keeping his sudden attraction to the man hidden.

"No answer." Flame continued to bait his lifelong rival. "Guess that means 'yes.'" Flame raised an inquiring brow and waited to see what Tig would do about his taunting.

"Get the fuck out of my way, dickhead," Tig growled and refused to acknowledge Flame's accusation. "Move or I will move you."

"Try it," Flame dared Tig to touch him. "You're a scrambler, not a tackler." Flame taunted again knowing his words would remind Tig of all the times he slammed him into the ground during football practice in high school. "Answer me."

Every word that slipped through Flame's lips just added fuel to the fire of fury that coursed through Tig. He pushed out a hand to shove by Flame as he stepped to the side to move passed the asshat. Flame responded by bringing both hands up to shove Tig's chest, forcing him further back into the bathroom.

The shove was all it took for Tig to see red. They were long overdue for a good throw down. Tig launched forward and grabbed one of Flame's wrists, pulling it out to the side, as he shoved his body into Flame's, spinning the man around. The arm he held was yanked roughly behind Flame's back while Tig used his body to slam Flame's chest into the bathroom door. Before Flame could react to the aggressive assault, Tig had one cuff on the wrist he held and was pulling the asshole's other hand down to meet the first at the center of his lower back.

Flame may be good at tackling on the field but Tig had more than enough experience at restraining suspects and even though Flame matched him in size and strength, he had no problem over powering the dickhead.

Flame did not resist Tig's rough manhandling as he felt the handcuffs cinch tightly on his wrists. No. He did not resist or fight back. He was too busy trying not to cum in his jeans because of the pressure Tig applied against his balls with his knee and his ass as the cop's body leaned into him.

Holy fuck, this is hot! Flame knew this was one more memory of the man he had always hated that would haunt his thoughts.

"Still no answer," Flame goaded Tig over his shoulder. "You getting off on this Tigger?" *'Cause I sure as hell am.*

"Shut your fucking mouth, Flame." Tig pulled Flame back by his cuffed wrists before slamming his toned body into the door again. "Or I'll walk you out of this bar in cuffs even if I can't charge you for harassing me."

"Umph," Flame grunted as his body made rough, solid contact with the door again and said with surety, "No you won't." Flame searched out Tig's eyes over his shoulder but the cop's face was out of view. "You do and you're as good as outted." Flame knew his threat was a lie but Tig didn't know that he would keep his mouth shut. He understood Tig's desire to keep his bedroom activities hidden from his co-workers because he did the same.

"Resorting to blackmail?" Tig growled against the back of Flame's neck. He gave no thought to how close he was to Flame or the scent of the man that was filling his nose. "I could arrest you for that alone."

"Yeah and out yourself in the process," Flame chuckled. "This cop foreplay?" He couldn't resist taunting Tig again.

Son of a bitch! Tig's anger climbed a notch higher but this time it wasn't directed toward Flame. This time it was directed inward because he let his tempter get the upper hand. Now he was in a compromising position with the last man on Earth he even wanted to be near and he wasn't sure how to get out of this unscathed.

"Just keep your fucking mouth shut, Flame, or I'll turn the tables and let everyone know you were really at the Honey Pot instead of Shadows," Tig growled again and reached for his keys to release Flame's wrists from the cuffs.

"Like anyone would believe you." Flame shot Tig a cocky grin after he turned around and began to rub the red marks the cuffs left behind on his wrists. Tig was still in his personal space, close enough that a slight movement would allow Flame to pull their bodies flush against one another. Instead, he kept rubbing his wrists because he couldn't trust himself to do just that.

Tig stepped back as he realized how close he still stood to Flame. His eyes never left Flame's and he expected some sort of retaliation for his rough treatment of the man. When none came, he spoke.

"Move."

Flame stepped aside and Tig did not let his guard down as he left the men's room. He stopped briefly by his seat at the bar to leave money for his beers before he bee-lined for the exit. It was not until he climbed into his car that two thoughts seemed to occur to him simultaneously: Flame never resisted his pseudo arrest and his cock was now rock hard. He had no idea what the first meant and he didn't even want to think about the second.

Fuck!

CHAPTER 7

THE field at Hillsborough High School, where the first charity flag football game was being held, looked like any other high school football field. The only exceptions were the cones that had been moved to represent the new end zones. The grass was still new enough to look green even during the third week of June and metal bleachers were moved closer to the field for the attendees to get a better view of the game. The hot dog and soda vendor concession stands sat at each end of the bleachers. The only thing missing was a beer vendor but that would never happen on school grounds. Let alone at a fundraiser for an organization that helped needy kids.

Aside from raising money through ticket and concession sales, TPD and TFR donated tee shirts. Cardboard boxes were placed around the bleachers for clothes and toy donations. By the time both teams took the field, the boxes were at least half full.

Flame and the rest of Tampa Fire Rescue claimed the bench they were assigned on the sidelines. He purposely did not look at the Tampa Police Department's team. Or more accurately, he did not look at Tigger Flint. His thoughts had been full of the cop that he used to hate since their encounter in Guns & Hoses. Flame had lost count of how many times he jerked off to the memory of the handcuffs restraining him while Tig's body pressed him into the bathroom door. If he allowed his thoughts to wander to the man, or their last encounter, he knew his jock would become more than uncomfortable.

Tig handed out the Velcro belts and two blue flags to each of the men who volunteered to represent TPD for the charity game. The game was scheduled to start at one o'clock. He understood the logic of scheduling the game so late in the day. It would give the cops and fireman who worked third shift the chance to get some sleep before the game. But, playing any kind of sport during the hottest time of day in June was sure to be brutal on everyone's hydration. Cops, fireman, and spectators alike. Round orange coolers of Gatorade, three in total, sat at the end of each team's bench and on a table between them. Two other coolers, full of ice water and hand towels, sat behind the team benches. Dehydration was always a concern when sports were played in Florida and that was the primary reason why a few EMT's were standing by at the edge of the field.

At exactly one o'clock, the referee blew his whistle and Tig jogged onto the field. He purposely ignored Flame who jogged by his side.

"Alright gentleman," the ref began as Flame and Tig stood opposite one of another. "This is *flag* football for *charity*. Pushing and shoving is fine in order to grab the flags but I don't want to see any purposeful tackling. Remember, you boys aren't wearing any pads so I don't want to see any unnecessary roughness that could cause injury."

The ref, who was easily twenty years their senior, gave them both a look that said he meant business about any thoughts they may have had of tackling during a flag football game. Tig doubted the man's warning would mean anything to the asshole that stood across from him on the field. All, Tig could do was tell his guys to behave and try to keep out of Flame's reach.

"This is for charity and the first of three games. Let's have fun putting on a good game and not give the EMT's any work today. Am I clear?"

"Yeah," Tig replied at the same time Flame said, "yep."

"Okay," The ref continued as he pulled a coin from his pocket. "Let's get the flip out of the way and get this game started."

"I'll take head," Flame said with a grin when the coin flipped up into the air. His gaze never left's Tig's face to see if the guy caught the purposeful drop of the 's.'

Tig tried not to growl at Flame's innuendo about his sexuality while he avoided the dickhead's gaze. The coin landed between their feet on the grass. Heads up. TFR declined the ball which made Tig frown at Flame. Only an idiot would pass on having first possession of the ball and Tig knew that Flame was no idiot. He also knew that by Flame giving TPD the ball, it would put him and Flame on the field together first.

"Grab your teams," the ref ordered and both men made their way to the sideline.

Tig almost thought that Flame was going to keep his trap shut. Almost. Of course, he couldn't be that lucky.

"I'm gonna grind your ass Tigger," Flame warned as they approached their teams. "Don't care what the ref said. Your ass is gonna be mine."

Tig knew Flame was just giving him shit about being gay and trying to fuck with his head before the game by making innuendos. His brain knew but his body didn't seem to care and the tightening in his jock just pissed him off more.

Hell, I don't even like the asshole, Tig reminded his body while trying not to think about how his body reacted to Flame in his turnout gear after the raid explosion or after their encounter in Guns & Hoses.

"Fuck you," Tig growled without looking at Flame.

Flame chuckled, "You wish."

Before Tig could reply, they reached the sideline where their teams waited to play.

The first three quarters of the game went smoothly. Both teams remained on their best behavior. There was rough pushing and shoving, along with body checks, but no actual tackles. Tig was genuinely surprised. Several times, Flame got close enough to put his ass on the turf before he released the football to fly down the field. Flame was just trying to psych him out and knowing that allowed him to relax as he dropped back into the pocket and looked down the field again. Even relaxed though, Tig always kept an eye on Flame. The last two charges, Flame had only grabbed his flag instead of tackling him but he still didn't trust the son of a bitch.

Three minutes were left in the fourth quarter. The teams were tied up at twenty-one and TPD was in a shit place on the field even though they had possession of the ball. The sixth yard line. If Flame was going to actually tackle his ass it would be when he dropped back into the pocket, placing him in the TPD 'end zone,' for this last play.

The ball was hiked and Tig dropped back into the pocket without thought. Just like he predicted, Flame tore around the end of the TPD defenders and forced Tig to scramble if he wanted to avoid his rival. A quick glance at Flame barreling toward him was all he needed to know the man wasn't aiming to grab a blue flag on his hip. Tig side-stepped to the right and kept his eyes downfield, looking for someone, anyone, he could off load the ball to. It would not stop the Mack truck that was Flame from hitting him but at least he wouldn't be sacked in the 'end zone.'

"Fuck!" Tig cursed a moment before the wall of firm, toned muscular body of Thomas Flame slammed into him and brought him to the ground. Hard.

Flame had impatiently waited the whole game to take Tig's ass down. If he had tackled the man too early, the ref would have benched him but with only a few minutes left in the game, and the bonus of TPD being in their own backfield, his patience paid off. He easily spun off the defender that was *supposed* to block him from Tig and saw the moment Tig realized he was coming for his ass. The guy could still scramble even after all of these years. But even though Tig was side-stepping out of the pocket, there was nothing he could do to avoid the hit that Flame was about to land.

Flame's arms wrapped around Tig's chest, under the quarterback's arms, around his body and his momentum slammed them into the ground. The lack of pads made the hit hurt Flame almost as much as Tig, regardless of the cop cushioning their impact with the ground.

"Omph!" It was the only sound Tig could make as the wind was knocked out of him. The ball in his hand came loose and Tig couldn't even move in an attempt to recover the fumble.

"Omph," Flame echoed Tig at the same time the noise escaped the man's lips.

Flame saw the ball come loose and knew he should be moving to recover the fumble but after thinking about nothing else all week except how Tig would feel beneath him, his body didn't even attempt to move off Tig. Flame's hands were trapped between Tig's back and the ground, effectively forcing him to remain on top of the man. Not that he was planning to move away. His knee was digging into the grass between Tig's spread legs while his groin pressed into the cop's hip. A slight movement of his leg would press it into Tig's groin or a shift of his hips would grind his jock covered cock into the man beneath him.

Tig forced himself to breathe as he realized that Flame was not hustling to recover the fumbled football. He watched the ball bounce away from them and several members of both teams tried to reclaim it. TFR finally picked up the ball and ran toward the other end of the field with TPD hot on their heels. All of the game action was shifted away from where Flame still pinned him to the turf.

When Tig finally forced himself to look at his rival, he braced himself for the verbal assault that was sure to come. But when he looked into Flame's blue eyes, it wasn't animosity that returned his gaze.

What the fuck? Tig wasn't sure what to make of the look Flame was leveling on him. He wasn't sure what to make of the steady pressure Flame's body was still exerting on his own, either. However, he didn't read anything into the man's strange behavior before he went on the offensive again.

"Get the fuck off me."

"Told you I'd grind your ass into the turf," Flame replied and there was no doubt in Tig's mind about feeling Flame press into him when the man purposely ground his groin into his hip.

"Getting off on fucking with me now that you know I am gay?" Tig sneered. "Get. The. Fuck. Off." Tig brought his hands up to Flame's chest with the intention of shoving the man away.

"Maybe."

Flame's reply not only stopped Tig's movement, leaving his palms to rest against Flame's hard, pebbled, *pierced?*, nipples that he could feel through the sweat soaked tee shirt, but also made his eyes go wide.

"What are you going to do about it if I am?"

For a moment, Tig thought Flame was serious and remained frozen like a deer in the headlights of an oncoming truck. That moment thawed at the sound of Flame's laugh.

Flame knew he fucked up the moment he laughed at Tig's shocked expression; he just couldn't help the noise from escaping him. He knew his lifelong rival would not be open to his advances. Hell, if someone had told him a few weeks ago that he would be trying to get into Tigger Flint's pants, he would have declared them insane. But somehow, ever since he had seen the guy practicing for the football league, his body was interested. His mind got on board with the idea after seeing Tig leave Bradley's last weekend and both were on the same page after their rough encounter in the bathroom at Guns & Hoses.

The whistle blowing and cheers from the side line broke Flame out of his thoughts at the same time Tig gave his chest a rough shove. Hard. Flame rolled to the side of Tig because he had no choice to do otherwise.

"Fuck you, asshole." Tig did not spare Flame a glance as he pushed himself off the ground. He resisted the urge to kick the dickhead or adjust his jock, as well, as he made his way off the field.

"Maybe."

Tig heard Flame call out and refused to think about the chance that the asshole was serious.

The smell of smoke saturated Flame's skin and he loved it. Up until the three alarm fire, the shift had been dead. There had only been one medical call to distract Flame from his thoughts of Tig. He knew the man still hated him with a passion but he was determined to turn that passion into something they would both enjoy in bed. Flame was sure that Tig had been checking him out when they ran into one another in Ybor. The fact that they didn't end up brawling at the charity game had to mean something too.

That has to be a good sign, right?

Most of the gay bars Flame frequented were in St. Pete since he lived on that side of the bay. Hell, if Guns & Hoses wasn't just over the bridge on the Tampa side of the bay, he likely wouldn't have frequented the place. But it was and that was where most of his co-workers and friends liked to hang out. The thought to check out the gay bars in Tampa never crossed Flame's mind. He knew of them but they were just too far from his place to bother visiting to find a hook-up. After seeing Tig in Ybor, his opinion changed.

Since his shift was far from over, he couldn't leave the smoke he loved to wear like cologne on his body. The guys just wouldn't tolerate it so he grabbed his toiletries and headed for the showers. He washed by habit as his mind continued to think about Tigger Flint. The memory of the sack at the end of the charity game was enough to make him hard. He had no reservations about beating off in the station's shower so he soaped his hand before dropping it to his throbbing erection.

In his mind, he replayed the feel of Tig beneath him but imagined they were both naked. Skin on hard skin. It wasn't the first time he explored this fantasy and he was sure it wouldn't be the last. The mental vision of them grinding together, covering each other in massive amounts of sweat as they chased their pleasure, sent Flame over the edge. One last stroke, pointing his cock toward the drain and he stifled the moan that threatened to echo in the shower stall.

Flame dried and dressed in a clean work jumper. His mind was still on how he could get Tig naked so he could do wicked things to the cop's buff body. He wondered if Bradley's was Tig's regular Saturday night haunt. Since he was scheduled off for the charity game on Saturday, he would just have to find out.

Tig and the rest of the TPD guys were determined to win the second game against TFR. Last week's game was close and if it hadn't been for Flame's sack causing Tig to fumble, TFR would not have recovered the ball to score the game winning touchdown. Three games were scheduled regardless of whether the TPD tied up the standings but it was a matter of departmental pride that they won today.

Tig stood before the Gatorade cooler drinking to pre-hydrate before the game when Flame stepped up behind him. He purposely stepped close, into Tig's personal space, after checking that no one was paying them any attention.

"Ready to be under me again?" Flame flirted but knew that Tig would assume his words were a taunt.

Tig looked over his shoulder when he heard Flame's voice and almost startled at how close the man was standing to his back. He was so close that Tig imagined that he could feel the body heat rolling off of the firefighter. He was not in the mood for Flame's gay innuendo taunts and decided that two could play this fucked up little game that his rival initiated. Most straight men were uncomfortable as hell when another guy flirted with them and maybe, just maybe, Tig could unnerve Flame enough to shut him up.

"You have to catch me first," Tig forced himself to give Flame his sexiest grin. "And even if you do, you couldn't handle me beneath you."

Tig crumbled the paper cup he had been drinking from, causally threw it away, and purposely brushed Flame's arm when he moved back to the TPD bench. He knew the touch would unnerve the straight fuck more than his words.

"Oh, I could handle you, alright... and then some."

When Flame's quiet reply reached Tig's ears, it took everything he had in him not to turn around and stare in shock. *What. The. Fuck?*

Flame knew his flirty reply was spoken low enough that only Tig would hear. He was amused when Tig kept walking as if he hadn't heard.

Too bad I can't sack that tight ass before the fourth quarter without the ref kicking me to the bench. Flame grinned at his thought and planned to get Tig under him again.

The ref blew his whistle to call Flame and Tig onto the field for the coin toss. Once more, TFR won the toss and passed the first possession over to TPD. Flame smirked and shot Tig a wink when Tig frowned at him.

There is no way he is flirting with me. The asshole is just trying to throw me off my game. Regardless of what Tig told himself, he couldn't deny the sexiness of Flame's smirk and wink when they were shot his way. Tig gave himself a mental shake and tried to push Flame's words and actions from his mind so he could concentrate on the game.

CHAPTER 8

AGAIN, the game was close but TPD was up by a touchdown. Since there were no field goals in flag football, every touchdown was worth seven points. Twenty-one, fourteen.

Flame was impatient to sack Tig again but he could tell the man kept his guard up. Several times he rushed Tig and stole the flag from his hip, forcing TPD to lose ground. Now, it was finally time to do more than grasp the blue plastic that fluttered in the wind with every movement Tig made.

Tig knew that Flame would sack him soon. Shit, he knew the guy had a few chances to sack him already. Tig successfully scrambled away from Flame several times but he just *knew* a hit was coming. He felt it in his bones. The whole game, Flame's flirty words bounced around in his mind, even though he knew the guy didn't mean them. Still, the words were enough to make him keep his guard up.

The hit came when there were eight minutes left in the quarter. Flame's sack did not catch Tig off guard as much as it had the week before. Probably because he was sure the hit was coming. So, instead, when he saw Flame rush him, he gave up trying to complete the pass and tucked the ball into his belly.

Everything happened in slow motion for Flame after the snap. He pushed away from the TPD defender and barreled into the pocket with his target, Tig. The moment Tig tucked the ball, Flame knew the guy was bracing for the hit. Tig turned his back to Flame and tried to scramble out of the pocket to gain a few yards.

Flame didn't give a shit about the yards. All he cared about, all he focused on, was getting Tig's bulk under him again. He slammed into Tig's back, wrapping his arms around the man and causing them both to spin once before they hit the ground with loud grunts. The ball never came loose from Tig's grasp and Flame more than enjoyed the way Tig's body, especially his ass and hips, buckled to protect the pigskin under him.

Back to chest, Flame covered Tig and immediately felt his cock stiffen in his jock. He ignored the uncomfortable tightness his hard-on caused him in this position as he breathed in the sweaty scent of Tig.

"Seems I am handling you just fine."

Flame's whispered words against his ear and the hard press of the firefighter's body along the length of his body, had Tig growing hard.

Fucker! Tig thought and tried to buck Flame off of his back. His arms were trapped around the football that was still snuggly tucked into his stomach so the result of the movement was his ass grinding into Flame's groin.

Flame had to resist the urge to bite down on Tig's neck and grind his now painful cock against Tig's ass when the man pushed up into him. The moan that escaped his lips couldn't be helped but he didn't care if Tig heard him or not.

Tig thought he heard a muffled groan escape Flame but decided it was his imagination and before he could reply, Flame pushed off him, using his body for leverage.

Flame pushed to his feet and watched as Tig rolled onto his back and released the ball before accepting a hand to stand from one of his teammates.

The next four minutes of the game passed without giving Flame another opportunity to sack Tig. If he was going to get the man beneath him one more time today in order to feel that hard body again, he had better do it soon.

Tig was more than distracted by Flame's strange behavior. How he had managed to play any football after that full body contact, he didn't know. He enjoyed the feel of the man on top of him way too much. Straight or not, friend or foe, it didn't seem to matter at the moment. After that sack, Tig just wanted the game to be over and done with so he could get out of the fucking jock that was pushing his piercing into an extremely uncomfortable position.

Déjà vu made an appearance on the field. TPD was still winning by a touchdown when the last snap of the game put the football in Tig's hands.

Flame knew this was his last chance of the day to get Tig right back where he wanted him. Stretched out beneath him so he could enjoy the man's hard body, his strength, under him one more time before the game ended.

Somehow, Tig was not surprised when Flame made his move to sack him again. He had plenty of time to ditch the ball, attempt to make the pass to one of his fellow cops, but they didn't need the score to win. With a spur of the moment decision, Tig decided to take the hit to see if Flame's strange behavior would make another appearance.

The hit came and Tig braced for the impact with the ground. He purposely did not spin away, did not present his back, to absorb Flame's tackle. He wanted to look into the man's eyes to see if Flame was just fucking with his head about being gay.

Flame slammed into Tig again and they both hit the ground brutally; Tig harder than Flame since he was on the bottom. Tig's quarterback skills were still evident when he did not let go of the ball.

"You let me take you down on purpose," Flame accused Tig and grinned. "Like me on top, huh?"

Flame's face was so close to Tig's that it was hard for him to focus on the man. The fact that they were in the same intimate position as the week before when Flame caused him to fumble did not help Tig's focus one bit.

"Why are you fucking with me?" Tig asked before he realized he should have kept his trap shut.

"I haven't even begun to fuck you."

Tig felt Flame blatantly push into him after he replied and the man's choice of words did not escape his notice. But before Tig could even fathom a retort, Flame pushed off of his body again to stand and walked away without a backward glance.

Flame dressed with care as his mind remained on the football game earlier in the day, and his aggressive flirting with Tig. It was a gamble that the man thought he was serious in his interest. They had been rivals and hated one another for so long that he was sure Tig thought his advances were bullshit and some sort of twisted prank or something. Hell, even he would think so if their roles were reversed. He was surprised Tig hadn't already tried to beat the shit out of him for the stunts he pulled on the football field. He took a moment as he splashed on some Drakkar to consider what his reaction would be if the shoe were on the other foot. Yeah, there was no way he'd be receptive to Tig hitting on him if he didn't know the man was gay.

Well, that will change tonight if I have any luck at all.

Flame took one last glance in the mirror above his dresser and once more hoped that Bradley's was Tig's choice of gay bar on a Saturday night.

Tig was pleasantly amazed that Bradley's had opened after the fire a few floors above almost burned the joint down last Saturday night. The windows of the apartments above the bar still showed the remnants of the fire. Black soot stains surrounded the gaping holes that once held window glass but surprisingly none of the dirty run off from the water used to extinguish the flames marred the recessed entrance to Bradley's.

Tig nodded to the club's security employee who sat on a stool checking IDs outside the door before he made his way inside. He stood behind a small twinkish guy who occupied his favorite stool and order a beer. J.J., the bartender, gave him a nod of hello as he handed over the bottle of Bud Light.

Less than fifteen minutes later, the twink vacated Tig's stool of choice, which gave him the perfect view of the length of the bar, and Tig claimed his spot to observe the potential entertainment of the evening.

Flame only felt slightly uncomfortable when he stepped into Bradley's. It had nothing to do with the club being a gay bar. He had been to enough of them not to be nervous. No, it had everything to do with what his plan was where Tigger Flint was concerned. Flame scanned the crowded bar but did not see his reason for bringing himself over to this side of the bay on a Saturday night. After ordering his beer and politely declining a few advances from men he would likely hurt in bed, Flame decided to see if Tig was on Grindr.

It was on a whim that he even thought of the app. He wasn't surprised at the number of profiles that indicated men within a few feet of him in Bradley's. As he scanned the usernames, his own at the top of the list, he couldn't help but grin at some of them.

Periodically, he glanced up from his phone to match profile pix with the men present. The fifth profile down caught his eye and it wasn't because of the beautifully pierced cock that was in place of a face shot for the profile picture. No, it was the username that caught his eye: TPACUFFS. Tampa cuffs. If that wasn't Tig, he would eat the hose off the rig.

So, he's pierced. I would have never guessed, Flame thought and his mouth watered as he eyed the Prince Albert.

Twenty five feet away. Flame scanned the club again but the crowd was so thick that he couldn't locate the man he was hoping to encounter. It didn't matter. With a tap of his thumb on the screen, he typed his message.

Tig's phone lit up and vibrated next to his hand and with a swipe of the screen, he saw the Grindr icon on his task bar. He always kicked on the app when he was in Ybor and wasn't surprised when a potential hook-up notice alerted him. What did surprise him, or maybe shock was a better word, was the username and photo attached to the message.

The picture did not include a face shot but instead displayed pierced nipples surrounded by tribal ink framed by the red fireman suspenders. The picture ended just below the slightly opened bunker pants and just above the guy's crotch. A dark happy trail disappeared into the gear. The picture was mouthwatering but as hot as it was, Tig had to blink several times at the username: TPAFlame.

There was no way in hell that profile belonged to Thomas Flame. It had to be a coincidence. A stripper, maybe, or something. The firefighter picture could be one from online and since no arms were displayed, there was no proof that it was actually Flame. Tribal tats on a chest didn't mean they bled into the ones on Flame's arm. It wouldn't be the first time Tig had encountered a hot online picture being used as a profile picture on the app.

Tig talked himself into that reasoning as he scanned the bar. There was no sign that Thomas Flame was in Bradley's. Regardless of the app saying the hottie that sent him the message was only twenty five feet away. He looked over the men he could see and only acknowledged one or two who could qualify for the hot bod in the profile picture, if it was even a real guy and not some online model. Tig finally tore his gaze away from the crowd and read the message.

You have your cuffs?

The message was typical. He frequently had potential hook-ups refer to handcuffs because of his username. He loved using his cuffs in the bedroom which was why he had chosen the username and always carried them. There was no harm in replying to the message, since he was, after all, looking for a hook-up tonight.

Always. Don't leave home without them, Tig typed and hit send.

Flame smiled when he read Tig's reply. Seemed his rival had a kinky streak. As if the pierced cock staring back at him from the phone wasn't proof enough. He didn't hesitate to reply with a tee shirt quote he had once read.

Cuff me, fuck me?

Flame had played the Grindr game enough times to know the invitation he was issuing. He wasn't a fan of bottoming and as much as he would rather have Tig beneath him, he would go there if it meant he could get some naked skin on skin action with the cop.

If nothing else solidified the Grindr guy was not Flame, it was the reply that flashed on Tig's phone. Flame's aggressive innuendo's on the field, even if the man was only fucking with him, gave every indication the firefighter would be a top if he was even gay. Tig took another swig of his beer and thought about a reply. It did not take him long to come up with something that could verify if the picture on the profile was a real guy in the bar or not as opposed to some internet model picture.

Only if you wear your bunker gear. Most posers didn't know the firefighting gear was referred to as 'bunker' gear.

Flame raised a brow when he read Tig's reply. He had no idea the cop was turned by on his gear. As a firefighter, he kept his turnout gear in a locker at the station but he knew no one would question him if he took it home after a shift. Plenty of the guys did because their wives or girlfriends got turned on by fucking them while in their bunker gear. His reply was automatic.

It's at the station. I don't bring it clubbing. Flame sent the message before adding, *Next time, I'll throw it in my truck.*

Tig expected a reply along the lines of the one he received. It wasn't the first time he had encountered a role player on Grindr.

Soon he will ask to meet me in uniform. Too bad he would be disappointed by my suit, Tig thought to himself as he considered his reply. He was enjoying the unusual flirting on Grindr with the want-to-be firefighter but he wished he had more to go on than an internet profile picture. Not that he was superficial. All of his hook-ups looked the same while he was slamming into them from behind or looking down on their bobbing head.

You're pretty sure there will be a next time. There hasn't even been a 'this' time yet. Tig sent his message and was curious to see what the guy's reply would be.

Flame's lips quirked into a wryly grin. If there wasn't going to be a 'this' time, they wouldn't still be talking. For once he wasn't annoyed at the Grindr game.

Oh, there will be a 'this' time, Detective.

Tig read the reply from TPAFlame and his head whipped up to search the crowd again. There was no way anyone on Grindr could know he was really a cop, let alone a detective on the force. Most of his Grindr hook-ups just thought his reference to cuffs was kink related.

Shit. Could that really be Flame? Tig continued to search the crowd for Flame's familiar form. *Why would he fuck with me here?* Tig refused to believe in the possibility that he was *actually* bantering with Flame through Grindr. *What if it really is Flame? What if he isn't fucking with me? What if...?* The thought crept into his mind as he sat frozen on his stool.

Flame was afraid he had gone too far by bringing up Tig's detective status with the TPD. He was sure the guy had no idea that it was him he had been flirting with, even though his profile name and picture made his identity blatantly obvious. Flame was still cursing himself for the slip when his phone lit up and vibrated with Tig's reply.

Bathroom. Now.

Flame grinned, even though he was sure the invitation Tig extended wasn't of the sexual nature Flame had been aiming for.

CHAPTER 9

TIG pushed away from the bar and didn't even take his half full beer with him as he stormed to the men's room. As he pushed into the handicapped stall, he still held out hope that he wouldn't recognize the man he had invited to join him in the restroom. That hope shattered when the sound of the restroom door closed at the same time the stall door opened.

Son of a bitch! Tig thought before his mind went blank at seeing Thomas Flame step into the stall and slide the door latch closed behind him.

Flame leaned against the stall door and waited for the verbal, or physical, attack to come. He hid his uncertainty of how this encounter might play out behind his sexiest smile. Hands buried in the front pockets of his jeans, Flame continued to wait to see what reaction Tig would have to his presence.

Tig wasn't sure what he felt. Anger at Flame for fucking with him, annoyance that the man was even here in Bradley's, let alone in a bathroom stall with him, or arousal that Flame could actually be gay and serious with his flirting. None of the feelings or thoughts of their hatred for one another entered Tig's mind as he stood staring at Flame in shock.

Tig took in Flame's tight black jeans that left nothing to the imagination where his package was concerned. His very hard package. Tig forced his gaze away from Flame's junk and let his eyes roam over the pale blue polo he wore before meeting his steel blue-grey eyes. What he saw in Flame's gaze almost made him gasp. Heat, hunger, and lust that Tig knew the man couldn't fake, was not what he was expecting. Regardless of the hard on the man sported. He wasn't sure how to respond to the blatant invitation in Flame's steady gaze.

Flame remained silent and wondered which way Tig would go as the guy looked him over. This encounter could either end up in a verbal battle or an aggressive session that would get both of them off. He hoped for the latter but would understand if it ended in the former. While he waited for Tig's reaction to seeing it was him, he drank in the sight of the man dressed in his clubbing clothes. Tig looked just as sharp as he did the Saturday before when the whole block was threatened by the fire above the bar. Dark slacks molded his thighs beneath his tucked in navy button down shirt. His sleeves were casually rolled up his forearms again but the sleeves of his shirt weren't what caught Flame's eye. No, his gaze seemed magnetically drawn to the open buttons at Tig's throat that revealed the slightest dusting of chest hair. Seconds of staring at one another turned into minutes and Flame realized it would be up to him to break their silent standoff.

"Do you really have your cuffs on you, Detective?" Flame asked quietly but loud enough to be heard over the thumping music outside of the bathroom.

Flame's words seemed to shatter the momentary shock that had overcome Tig at seeing his lifelong rival standing before him in the stall.

"What the fuck, Flame? What are you doing here?"

Flame didn't hear any of the expected aggression in Tig's voice. The man's tone conveyed more confusion than anything else and Flame took that as a good sign.

"You avoided my question." Flame forced himself to remain leaning on the stall door even though he wanted to do nothing more than push Tig into the wall. Feel the man under him, pressed against him. Again.

Tig was still trying to reconcile that the man who was unashamedly looking for a hook up on Grindr was one and the same as the man who now stood before him. *Flame.*

"You're not gay," Tig said, on autopilot, while he continued to wrap his mind around the situation he now found himself in with Flame.

"Still avoiding the question," Flame smiled at Tig as the memory of the handcuffs cinching on his wrists flashed in his mind.

Tig gave himself a mental shake to jog his memory about what the hell Flame was talking about. *Cuffs. Handcuffs. Right.* The visual of slamming Flame against the bathroom door in Guns & Hoses came unbidden to his mind and he felt himself growing hard.

Fuck it. A hook up was a hook up and I'll call the son of a bitch's bluff. Tig's body made the decision for him as he reached behind his back and pulled out his handcuffs.

Flame's cock hardened more at the sight of the shiny, silver police issue cuffs, if that were even possible, that now dangled from Tig's fingers.

"You want these?" Tig asked and tried to keep the curiosity out of his voice. "Then get on your knees and put your hands behind your back."

As much as Flame wanted to feel the harsh sensation of the metal around his wrists again, he wasn't about to meekly kneel at Tig's feet so the man could cuff him.

"Make me," Flame pushed off the door and took the few steps that closed the distance between them.

Flame's bold steps into Tig's personal space and his pseudo aggression sent a jolt of lust straight to Tig's groin. If his lifelong adversary had docilely kneeled at his feet, Tig knew he would have lost all respect for the man. And he did respect Flame, even though he never liked him.

"You really want to go here?" Tig asked, but didn't give Flame a chance to reply. The moment he saw Flame's way too kissable, plump, lips begin to form a reply, he grabbed the man and spun him around.

Flame's reply died on his lips the moment Tig's hands landed on his bare forearms and spun him into the wall between the john and the sink. The cold metallic, cock-raising gabble of the handcuffs closing around his wrists registered loud in his ears even though his rational mind knew that Tig's body pressed so close to his own muted the metal on metal clicking noise.

Tig heard Flame suck in a breath and knew the reaction was because he was pressing him into the wall while securing the cuffs. No longer did Tig think he was calling Flame's bluff because there was no way in hell that his rival could be faking his reaction to Tig's semi-rough treatment. Flame didn't resist, didn't fight back, as Tig maneuvered him into the position he had held dozens of suspects in before. Only this time, Tig was aroused beyond measure. Cock aching, Tig pulled Flame away from the wall and planted his ass on the toilet in the same position that the nameless hunk from the week before occupied.

Flame loved every minute of Tig's manhandling and only regretted that he couldn't touch Tig's rock hard cock due to his hands being restrained behind him. But that was okay. He could deal with it because he knew where this was leading the moment Tig pushed his ass down to sit on the toilet. Flame couldn't even begin to recall the last time he was on the 'giving', instead of 'receiving', end of a blow job in a restroom but he really didn't care as Tig began to unbuckle his belt.

The look on Flame's face did not change as Tig freed himself from his slacks. He had thought for sure that he would call Flame's bluff the moment he began to undo his pants. That was not the case. In fact, it was so far from the case that Tig almost couldn't believe this whole encounter was really happening. He only stroked himself once before pointing his cock at Flame's lips.

"So, you really are pierced," Flame said and licked his lips.

Tig didn't even bother to comment before he pushed into Flame's mouth. The hot, wet, heat that surrounded him warred with the high that flooded through his body at the realization that the man he had hated his entire life was right now sucking his cock. The thought that Flame might bite him, never crossed his mind. In fact, all thought abandoned him as Flame's tongue swirled around his piercing.

Flame sucked on the open ring of Tig's Prince Albert, thrusting his tongue through the two balls that graced the metal ends. He teased the piercing and Tig's slit before he took him fully into his mouth. The man tasted like heaven and after Flame's initial desire to explore the Prince Albert passed, he opened his mouth wide to run his tongue over the thick veins that ran along the underside of Tig's hardness.

Any doubt that Tig had about Flame knowing what to do with a cock in his mouth disappeared when the man played with his piercing and put just enough pressure and suction on his cock to almost push him over the edge.

Fuck! He can suck cock!

Tig refrained from grasping Flame's head to thrust himself deeper because some fucked up sense of pride didn't want to let Flame know how undone the firefighter's mouth was making him. That didn't stop him from rocking his hips to feel more, though.

Fuck, this is a nice cock, Flame thought when Tig began to rock his hips to increase the sensation.

Flame adjusted his oral grasp to accommodate the movement. Tig was being much gentler than Flame had expected him to be and since his hands were cuffed behind his back, he couldn't spur the cop into the aggressive roughness that he desired. All he could do was pull off and spit out the beautiful cock that he wanted buried deep in his throat.

The groan that escaped Tig's mouth when Flame pulled off his cock could not be helped. There was no denying how much Flame was getting to him and that noise was all the confirmation either man needed to know the truth of the matter.

"This isn't my first rodeo, Tigger." Flame licked his wet and swollen lips as Tig's cock slapped back against his button down covered abs.

Tig looked down at the man he never in a million years would have expected to be sucking on his cock, and pushed his dick back toward Flame's mouth.

"Okay." Tig guided his throbbing erection back to Flame's lips with one hand while he brought the other up to grasp the hair at the nape of Flame's neck.

Flame opened for Tig's pierced hard-on and groaned against the prick in his mouth when he felt Tig's fingers fist to pull his hair and move his head closer to Tig's groin. He was determined to make his rival come undone and put every ounce of his oral skills into play. Just because he was usually on the receiving end of bathroom blow jobs did not mean he didn't enjoy giving head. In fact, sucking cock was one of his favorite things. Second only to being buried deep in a tight ass.

Fuck! Tig mentally cursed again as Flame's mouth caused sensation after delicious sensation to course through his body. He realized he had vocalized his thought when Flame groaned in agreement. The vibration of Flame's moan was almost his undoing and caused Tig to tighten his grip on the dark hair he held in his fist.

Tig's reaction to the noise he made encouraged Flame in his quest to make the man come undone. He ignored his own aching cock, as hard as it literally was, and hummed around the shaft of silky iron that continued to thrust into his mouth.

Shit, if only my hands were free, Flame cursed his sudden fetish for handcuffs. Still, the restricted movement of his hands did not stop him from moving his head.

Tig couldn't help but feel the moment he passed the back of Flame's mouth and entered the man's throat. The first thrust sent a jolt of euphoria through him. There weren't many who could take his eight and a half inches down their throat without gagging. Because of this, Tig tended to be more gentle than aggressive when lips were wrapped around his cock. But the first breech of Flame's throat without the expected gagging noise was an invitation that he could not ignore.

Flame felt the change in Tig when the man realized his throat was opened to being fucked. He still regretted having his hands cuffed but he could not deny that the restraints jacked up his arousal while Tig fucked his face. Flame, throat open, enjoyed the feeling of Tig's cock caressing his tonsils. Disappointingly, but not surprisingly, the feeling did not last long enough. Way before Flame was ready to end the blow job, Tig's hand tightened in the hair at the base of his skull and pulled his cock out of Flame's mouth. Flame felt the slight swelling of Tig's cock and the increase of pressure from the piercing against the walls of his throat moments before the pulsing sensation of Tig's cock disappeared from his mouth.

Tig's orgasm almost caught him by surprise. He barely had any warning. The typical spine tingling and the feeling of his balls drawing closer to his body was so slight, he almost didn't pull out of Flame's mouth fast enough. One moment he was enjoying the tight heated caress of Flame's throat and the next he was pointing his cock toward the floor between Flame's legs to unleash his release.

Flame panted and buried his disappointment that Tig pulled out of his mouth when Tig moved away from his lips. He knew from experience how sensitive Tig's cock must be but couldn't help but wonder if the piercing didn't make it worse. He also couldn't help but wonder why Tig didn't just cum down his throat.

Who would have thought he would be pierced? Not me, Flame thought as he watched Tig step back from him. *Shit, it's hot as fuck though.*

Flame couldn't stop his thoughts as he watched Tig tuck himself away. He couldn't stop thoughts of what the man's mouth would feel like around his brutally throbbing hard on, or thoughts of what being buried deep inside the man's ass would feel like or, surprisingly, what it would feel like to have that pierced cock buried deep inside of him.

Tig tucked himself back into his slacks and prayed Flame wouldn't see how unsteady on his feet he was as he buckled his belt after shoving his loose shirttails into his pants. Normally, this would be where the hook-up ended, wordlessly, and they each went their separate ways. Not only did the handcuffs prevent a clean escape from the encounter but the fact that Flame *was* the hook-up complicated matters.

Flame knew that if he didn't say something, anything, Tig would remove the cuffs and walk out of the bathroom without saying a word. It was what he himself had done every time to end a quickie in a bar bathroom, minus the cuffs. He couldn't afford to give Tig any time to think about their hook-up because if he did, he knew the man would bolt.

"Return the favor?" Flame gave Tig his sexist grin.

Flame's voice prompted Tig to move. He dug his keys from his pocket and stepped to the side of Flame's seated form to gain access to his cuffs. Tig forced himself to ignore Flame's crotch as he unlocked the cuffs and returned them to the back of his belt. He also forced himself not to look at Flame's face when he stepped to the door and slid the latch open. Without a backward glance at Flame, Tig stepped out of the stall and bathroom but not before Flame's parting words reached his retreating back.

"So not cool, Tigger," Flame called out before Tig left the bathroom.

Rubbing the red marks on his wrists, Flame stood and pulled his cell from the clip on his side. The Grindr app was still open but Tig was no longer online. That didn't matter, though. The man would get Flame's message the next time he logged into the app.

I'll put my gear in the truck for next time. Flame grinned to himself as he thought about fucking Tig while wearing nothing but his bunker pants.

The thought of fucking pulled his mind to the ache at his crotch and with another swipe of his thumb, he found someone to take care of it.

CHAPTER 10

A tip came in on the location of another meth lab. Whether it was one of Cortez's or not, did not matter. TPD and S.W.A.T. raided the fucker anyway. None of the junkies they busted confessed to working for Cortez. It seemed they were more afraid of the drug dealer than going to jail. Of course, a jail sentence wasn't an automatic death sentence so Tig was not surprised that none of the low life's they busted turned snitch. They still had not heard from Gullis and the case was suffering without the inside information the CI had been feeding them. There wasn't shit they could do about it either. It just was what it was.

All week long, Tig tried to immerse himself in work to banish the images of Flame's lips wrapped around his cock but there was just too much downtime to prevent the memory from assaulting him. It did not help that the memory was his new favorite jerk off flick, either. No matter how many times he started beating off to one visual, or porn, the vision of Flame cuffed and deep-throating him always ambushed him. There was no hiding from it. It was that image that sent him over the edge. Every. Fucking. Time.

"Earth to Flint," Pat snapped his fingers over the space between their desks.

"Yeah?"

"You've been zoning out all week. What's up, man?"

"Just thinking about the case." Tig lied.

III

"I'm calling bullshit on that, bud." Pat grinned. "If you don't want to tell, that's cool but don't lie to my face."

"Alright." Tig returned Pat's grin and did not elaborate further on what was distracting him.

"I see how it is." Pat stood and Tig laughed at the mock hurt expression his partner shot his way. "I'm just gonna have to get you buzzed so you will spill. C'mon." Pat slid into his suit jacket. "I hear booze calling our name."

No amount of alcohol was going to get Tig to tell Pat about his run in with Flame, let alone the best blow job of his life that the man provided.

"You can try, Irish. You can certainly try," Tig taunted and followed his partner from the station.

The after work hour's crowd in Guns & Hoses was thicker than normal for a Thursday. Tig soon discovered the why for it when he spotted balloons and a banner attached to one of the side walls.

'Happy Birthday Flame!' The banner read. The letters were various firefighter related items: hoses, ladders, and axes. The crowd around Flame and the tables that were pushed together on which his cake and gifts were placed was so thick that Tig did not see the man.

Regardless, the banner with the man's name on it made his heart rate spike and sent blood rushing southward to fill his cock. If he hadn't been with Pat, Tig would have turned on his heel and left even though his body was begging for a repeat of Flame's talented mouth. He had not even realized he was frowning while he stared at the firefighters until his partner spoke.

"Don't start any shit with the guy," Pat said as they took their seats at the bar. "He looks buzzed enough that you guys would end up trading blows and there are way more of them then there are of us."

Tig knew that Pat's reference to 'them' was the TFR and the 'us' was the TPD. The thought of trading punches with Flame never crossed his mind as he took a sip of the beer that Shelley had placed in front of him. No, punches weren't what he was thinking of trading with Flame. Tig shifted in his seat to try and get his suddenly hard cock into a more comfortable position. He didn't feel guilty, not really, about leaving the man hanging in Bradley's last weekend. He never reciprocated with his bathroom hook ups but those hook ups weren't Thomas Flame.

I'll keep my gear in my truck for next time.

Flame's parting Grindr message popped into Tig's mind. He couldn't help but wonder if the guy was serious. Not only about the bunker gear but about the 'next time.' After experiencing Flame's oral talents, Tig had no doubt about the man's sexual preference. There was no way in hell a straight guy or even a bi guy, for that matter, could suck a dick the way Flame had devoured his. *Never would have guessed he was gay. Fuck!*

"There you go again," Pat commented.

Tig glanced at his partner but Pat wasn't looking at him as he took a sip of his Guinness.

"You know you can talk to me about anything, right?" Pat finally turned his Irish green gaze on Tig. "I won't judge you about whatever has you so distracted."

For a moment, Tig thought Pat was referring to his sexual preference for guys and he wasn't sure how to reply. That moment was fleeting when Tig realized that there was no way in hell that his partner could know he was gay.

"Yeah, I know. I appreciate it but really, it's nothing." Tig took another swig of his beer before asking about Pat's wife, Mary, to change the subject. Thankfully, Pat rolled with it.

Flame lost count of how many shots he had as he raised another Kamikaze to his lips and tossed it back. He was well on his way to becoming sloppy drunk but not so far gone to realize it and knew he would pay hell in the morning for his indulgence.

It was on his way to take a piss that he spotted Tig at the bar with his partner. Even with the copious amount of booze flowing through his system, his cock still managed to stiffen at the sight of the cop. Flame did not avert his eyes when he met Tig's gaze but instead shot the man another sexy grin as he passed on his way to the restroom. He hoped the grin was inviting, not too stupidly drunk, and that Tig would follow him. A repeat performance for his birthday would be a great gift.

To Flame's disappointment, Tig did not enter the restroom behind him. He lingered as long as he could. So long in fact, that Brostowski came to check on him.

"Thought you fell in or I'd find you puking your ass off," Brostowski laughed and tossed an arm around Flame's shoulder to help him back to his party.

Tig had to resist the urge to follow Flame when the firefighter unleashed his sexy assed grin. It was a clear invitation. If Pat had not been with him, he doubted he would have been able to keep his ass planted on the bar stool. He watched as Brostowski steadied Flame while they returned to the man's party.

Oh well, for the best since his ass is so drunk.

Flame didn't spare him a glace and Tig wasn't sure if he was relieved or disappointed. As his peripheral vision followed Flame's progress back to his party, Tig remained in conversation with Pat. Several drinks later, Pat called it a night and Tig knew he should do the same. Flame's party was winding down, only a handful of his friends remained. Tig cursed himself when he found his eyes once more on the fireman.

Time to go, Tig decided and killed his beer while digging cash from his pocket and placing it on the bar to cover his tab. A quick trip to take a piss then he would take his sorry, horny, ass home.

Finally! Flame thought when he spied Tig heading toward the men's room.

He had stopped drinking after seeing the cop at the bar but was still comfortably buzzed enough to disregard how unhealthy his plan for Tig was if he wanted to remain in the closet with his coworkers.

"Gotta piss," Flame stood.

"You okay?" Brostowski asked when Flame swayed slightly when he stood. "Let's me help you."

"I'm good. I got it." *Shit!* He couldn't have his way with Tig if Brostowski tagged along to the john. "Really, I'm a big boy. I can take my ass to piss just fine." Flame hoped he didn't sound as suspicious to go to the restroom alone to his friends as he did to his own ears.

"Alight," Brostowski gave him a grin. "Piss then we are outty."

"Sounds good," Flame called over his shoulder as he forced himself to walk as sober as possible, in his current state, to the men's room

Tig was still standing at the urinal when Flame walked – more like stumbled – into the men's room. He *knew* the firefighter would follow him even though he gave no indication the man should do so.

It's exactly what you wanted, too, a small voice whispered in Tig's mind.

"What do you want?" Tig asked Flame over his shoulder while he continued to piss.

"Maybe I am thirsty?" Flame took a few unbalanced steps toward Tig now that he didn't have to put up the sobriety act to piss without an escort.

Tig didn't stop his brow from rising at Flame's words. "Into water sports, huh? I would have never guessed." Tig was just buzzed enough that his reply did not come out as aggressive as he had intended. In fact, he *was* actually curious if Flame was serious or not.

"I'm into a lot of things you would never guess." Flame closed the distance between them and pointedly looked down at Tig's pierced cock while the man aimed his golden stream into the white porcelain of the urinal. "I am sure you are too and I am used to working with water and hoses."

Tig watched as Flame's body tilted until he leaned against the wall between the urinals. The man's gaze was locked onto his cock and Tig had to suppress a groan from escaping his throat when Flame licked his lips.

Fuck, he's serious! Tig's flaccid cock began to grow hard and he gave it a few shakes.

"You're drunk," Tig replied and began tucking himself away.

"Not *that* drunk," Flame reached out and grabbed Tig's rapidly thickening prick. "Not too drunk to know I wouldn't mind a repeat of last weekend." Flame's eyes locked onto Tig's so the man would know he was serious. "And then some. You *do* owe me."

As much as it pained Tig to do it, he removed Flame's hand from his dick and zipped up his slacks before replying.

"I don't owe you shit, Flame." Tig turned his body to face the man. "You know how the game is played."

"I do," Flame replied and stepped close enough to put his hands on Tig's hips. "Doesn't mean I don't want a repeat." When Tig didn't step away or reply, Flame continued his persuasion. "You know you would enjoy it, Tig, and I have my gear in my truck." Flame winked.

Tig knew he was in trouble when Flame's wink along with the visual of the man splayed out in his bunker gear made his cock twitch in anticipation.

"You're drunk," Tig repeated, lamely, before adding. "You better not be driving."

"I'm not. Give me your phone." Flame grinned and knew he had the man hooked by the bulge he could see in Tig's pants.

Tig was relieved, more than he wanted to admit, that Flame wasn't planning to get behind the wheel of his big assed truck. He was also caught off guard by the request for his cell.

"What?"

"You're phone. You know that thing that allows you to talk to anyone anytime," Flame's surprisingly sober request had Tig unclipping his cell from his waist and handing the device over.

Flame's cock gave a happy twitch when Tig handed him his phone. It only took a moment to focus on the screen before he opened up the contacts and punched in his information. Name, number, and most importantly, address. He handed the phone back to Tig before he spoke again.

"You're just as hard as I am, Tig. Come to my place and do something about it."

"I don't even like you, Flame." Tig tried to put some bite into the words and failed when his mind ambushed him with visions of all the nasty things they could do to one another if they were alone, in private. "And you sure as fuck don't like me."

"Says you," Flame grinned and was just about to kiss Tig when the door to the bathroom opened.

"Yo, Flame!" Brostowski's voice preceded the man and was the only warning they received.

Tig stepped back and pushed Flame away from him, causing the firefighter to bump into the wall behind him.

"Shit," Brostowski's voice changed from happy-go-lucky to concern when he realized who was in the bathroom with Flame. "None of this bullshit tonight," he stepped between them and faced Tig. "It's his fucking birthday, give it a rest."

"Tell that to him," Tig turned toward the sink and began to wash his hands.

Brostowski grunted. "Let's go Flame. Time to get you home."

Tig glanced up to the mirror and saw Brostowski pulling Flame toward the door. Before both men stepped out of the bathroom, Tig locked his gaze on Flame's. The firefighter's eyes held the same lust filled, hungry look that he had witnessed in the handicapped stall of Bradley's before the man swallowed his cock in the best blow job of his life. Neither man said a word as the firefighters made their exit but there was no doubt in Tig's mind when the door closed behind them that Flame was serious about the invitation he had issued.

Tig leaned on the sink and stared at his reflection in the mirror while he battled with himself about accepting the invitation from the man he had always hated. The whole idea of going to Flame's was a bad one and had disaster written all over it. If he did take Flame up on his offer, then they would be crossing over the 'hook-up' line. Not that he hadn't ever had a hook-up at someone's place before, because he had, but never with someone after receiving head in a bathroom stall, and certainly never with someone who he knew and hated, his entire life. He just didn't do return visits.

The memory of Flame's throat constricting around his cock ambushed him again. It shattered his resistance to the offer.

Fuck!

Tig's body made the decision for him and he stormed out of the restroom. A quick glance in the direction of the tables where Flame's party had been held revealed the firefighters had cleared out.

"Night Tig."

"Night Shelley," Tig called back as his hand pulled his cell phone from the clip on his hip.

By the time he was behind the wheel of his Camaro, he had Flame's address pulled up. He stared at the contact information as if in a daze.

Am I really going to do this?

Yeah, I am.

With a press of his finger, the GPS was loading the map and directions to the house of the man he never imagined he would ever be visiting.

CHAPTER 11

BROSTOWSKI drove Flame home in his truck and hitched a ride back to his car with Jennings once Flame was securely settled inside his apartment. Flame only waited long enough to ensure that his fellow firefighters were gone before he went back out to his truck. It took only a moment to retrieve his bunker gear from the bed compartment where he kept his tools and take it inside.

He had no idea if Tig would take him up on his offer to come over but he wanted to be prepared if the guy did show up. Flame's earlier drunk had mellowed into a comfortable buzz. Still, he popped a few Tylenol and drank a bottle of water to hopefully head off the hang over that he was sure to have as a result of all the shots his buddies bought him. He tossed the empty water bottle into the trash and eyed up his bunker gear.

Fuck it, he thought as he moved toward his couch where he had dropped his turn out gear. *If he does show, I'll make sure he is tempted to come in.* Flame grinned and began to change.

Tig pulled into a parking space in front of the address his GPS had led him to. Even without the female voice informing 'you have arrived at your destination,'

Tig would have recognized Flame's jacked up, black, Ford F150 with the Tampa Fire Rescue decal splayed across the back window.

Am I really going to do this?

Tig sat in his car and stared at the apartment door before him. The outside light was on but that wasn't the only indication that Flame was still awake. Lights shone through the front window and every now and again, Tig thought he could detect a shadow of movement.

His cock throbbed between his legs and begged him to either take Flame up on his offer or jerk off in the car to gain some much needed relief. Before he could talk himself out of knocking on Flame's door or remind himself what a really, *really* bad idea this was, he killed his engine and stepped out. The sound of his closing car door sounded loud in the warm Florida night. *Yeah, he was really going to do it.*

Tig exhaled to steady his unbidden bout of nerves as he knocked on Flame's door. Nothing could have prepared him for the sight that greeted him when the door pulled open. His mouth went dry at the sight of Flame.

Holy fuck!

Flame couldn't help but grin like an excited kid on Christmas morning when the knock on his door sounded. That grin morphed into a wide smile at the look on Tig's face and the gasp that escaped the man's lips.

Tig blinked several times when Flame answered his door wearing nothing but his bunker pants and red suspenders. His dry mouth disappeared as he fought the urge to drool. If he had any plan to say something to his rival when he answered the door, it had abandoned him. All he could do was stare at the image of the Grindr profile picture he was presented with the week before.

Only this time he had an up close and personal live version.

"Still have your cuffs Detective?" Flame teased and stepped back to allow room for Tig to enter his apartment.

He was amused at the cop's reaction to him in his bunker gear. It wasn't as if Tig had never seen a fireman dressed out before. They had been on a scene before so Flame knew that was not the case. Tig's reaction to the gear was because *he* was wearing it.

Damn if that isn't an ego stroke. Flame's cock twitched against the button fly of his work pants.

It took a moment for Tig's brain to register Flame's words and movement that invited him inside. Tig did not reply before stepping passed Flame to enter the apartment. Flame's apartment was well furnished. A leather couch and chair were arranged across from a large flat screen TV that sat in an impressive black and chrome entertainment center. The music from the stereo distracted Tig from looking around the rest of the space.

I walk in the spot, yeah, this is what I see, okay,
Everybody stops and they staring at me,
I got a passion in my pants and
I ain't afraid to show it, show it, show it,
I'm sexy and I know it.

Tig turned around to find Flame leaning against his apartment door like he had in the stall at Bradley's. LMFAO still filled the air and Tig couldn't help but think that the song fit Flame to a T as he stood with his thumbs tucked into where the red suspenders met the soot stained yellow of his bunker pants.

"So do you?" Flame prompted Tig to get a response from the man. Not that the way Tig was visually fucking him wasn't response enough.

"Always." Tig allowed a small smile to grace his lips.

However, he wasn't sure he wanted to cuff Flame again even though he was turned on by restraining his hook-ups in such a manner. No. He wanted to feel Flame's hands on him this time.

"The question is," Tig pinned Flame with his gaze. "Do you really want me to cuff your ass again? Because if you do…" Tig let his insinuation speak for itself. He still did not think Flame was a bottom, even a closeted bottom.

Flame pushed off his front door and moved toward Tig, who stood in the middle of his living room. The song on the radio changed and damn if it wasn't fucking too appropriate. Flame could not resist singing along with the song as he moved closer to Tig. He was still buzzed enough to enjoy teasing Tig by singing softly to Jason Derulo.

> *Tonight, take me to the other side*
> *Sparks fly like the Fourth of July*
> *Just take me to the other side*
> *I see that sexy look in your eyes*
> *And I know, we ain't friends anymore*
> *If we walk down this road*
> *We'll be lovers for sho'*
> *So tonight kiss me like it's do or die*
> *And take me to the other side*

Tig almost adjusted his rock hard cock when Flame started singing to the radio and approached him.

The man knew he was sexy as fuck and Tig wouldn't argue with the fact.

This could be perfect
But we won't know unless we try, try
I know you're nervous
So just sit back and let me drive

Flame continued to sing and knew he was turning Tig on. He also realized that Tig was waiting for a reply to his question when he stopped within touching distance.

"If you don't," Flame responded to Tig's innuendo about what would happen if the cop cuffed him again. "I'll bury myself so deep in you that you won't remember why we hate each other so much."

Tig ass clenched at the thought of Flame riding him to orgasm. *So, he is a top. Or at least versatile.* Tig weighed his options on how to achieve the best orgasm he could get from this encounter; he seriously doubted there'd be another. He never took advantage of Flame's arousal when he left the guy hanging at Bradley's last weekend. Even though he had seen Flame's hard cock through his jeans when he was buried balls deep down the man's throat, he wanted to see that prick in the flesh. Flame began to sing to Pitbull on the radio and brought Tig out of his thoughts. It was as if the damned station was playing all the right songs to fit this fucked up hook-up.

This loving I'm giving
It's worth more than money
You need it, you want it
All over your body (hey)
I know that you want this
Wild, wild, love

Boldly, Tig reached out a hand and grasped the front of Flame's pants to pull him forward and close the distance between them.

"I think you have that backwards," Tig mumbled as he pulled Flame flush with his body.

"No, I don't." Flame smirked as he slid his hands under Tig's suit jacket to grip his waist.

The heat from Flame's naked chest rolled off the man in waves and was beginning to make Tig sweat. He wasn't sure where he wanted to start with the solid wall of flesh before him. Tig couldn't decide if he wanted to cuff Flame and suck on the hard cock that his fingers were brushing or if he wanted to let Flame ride his ass like there was no tomorrow. He had no delusions that this encounter would be gentle. One or both of them were sure to be sore in the morning.

Flame moved one hand to untuck Tig's dress shirt from his slacks while his other moved behind the cop's back and played with the handcuffs at his waist. Flame almost distracted himself with the feel of Tig's hard muscles under the palm of his hand. He never broke eye contact with Tig and resisted moaning at the hunger reflected in Tig's stunning green eyes.

Years of knowing the man and how many punch ups? How had I never noticed what color his eyes were? Flame did not know but he sure as hell noticed now.

A shiver raced down Tig's spine as Flame's hands traveled over his body. He did not care if the man felt the shudder or not. Flame licked his lips and the movement pulled Tig's gaze away from the sapphire blue eyes that were boring into him. The urge to ravish that mouth overcame Tig and he did not resist. His hand clenched into a fist, fingers digging into the rough, insulated material of the bunker gear, as his mouth crashed onto Flame's lips. The kiss was harsh. Aggressive. Full of lust and want.

When Tig's mouth clashed with his, Flame gave as good as he got. Teeth clinked together and a lip split. Whose, Flame didn't care while he fought with Tig for dominance of the kiss. His hand fisted Tig's dress shirt at the same time one of Tig's grasped the back of his head. The feeling of Tig's fist at his waist, short, sharp nails scratching below his navel, his knuckles brushing the head of his cock, had Flame growling into the kiss that was consuming him from the inside out.

The vibration from Flame, along with the tongue that was trying to reach his tonsils as they fought for control, shot straight to Tig's throbbing cock. Buttons popped off of his shirt and the sound of material ripping did nothing but hike Tig's lust to a new level. He fumbled with the buttons of Flame's bunker pants and was so turned on that he couldn't even be grateful that the hook and first button were already undone. Still, he fought to undo the pants that fit too tightly to get his hand inside.

Their kiss was sloppy in its aggressiveness. Mouths open as their tongues battled. In their hunger for one another, harsh breaths exchanged so they didn't even need to stop for air.

Hissss.

The sound was breathed into their mouths as naked chests touched. Who it escaped from, neither man knew. Neither man cared.

It barely registered in Tig's mind that his shirt was being pushed off his shoulders, taking his suit jacket with it. They stumbled, the result of gravity, causing their hungry kiss to break. Whether Flame stepped back or Tig pushed him, didn't matter as they fell onto the couch with Tig on top. Both men panted as emerald green eyes met breath taking blue.

Flame wasn't sure when, or how for that matter, he ended up with Tig's handcuffs in his hand. But as Tig lay atop of him, both of their legs hanging off the couch, he grinned at the man and raised his hand.

"Ever been cuffed, Detective?"

Tig glanced at the shiny metal of his cuffs as they dangled from two of Flame's fingers while his mind tried to come up with a witty reply. He failed.

"Wouldn't you rather have my hands on you?"

Tig grinned and shifted his weight onto one hand that braced against the back of the couch. When Flame groaned, Tig's grin slid into a smirk. He moved his other hand over Flame's tattooed shoulder, down his toned chest, before stopping over a pebbled, pierced, nipple. His eyes never left Flame's as he gave the pert bud a pinch before lowering his mouth to play with the black barbell.

Flame hissed when Tig's fingers pinched his nipple. That hiss turned into a moan when Tig's mouth latched onto him. His nipples had always been sensitive; more so after having them pierced. As his hand came up to grasp Tig's sandy blond hair to pull his head closer, he tuned into the latest song playing.

> *So do what u want, what u want with my body*
> *Do what u want, don't stop let's party*
> *Do what u want, what u want with my body*
> *Do what u want, what u want with my body*

Yes, please, Flame thought as Tig's warm, wet tongue swirled around his nipple and nibbled on his piercing, Flame couldn't agree more with Lady Gaga. Tig was relentless with his sucking and when Flame felt his teeth graze roughly on his hyper sensitive nipple, he had to fight the tightening in his balls that forewarned his impending orgasm. The handcuffs were dropped and forgotten as Flame brought his other hand to Tig's waist and pulled him closer and gain the friction his cock craved.

Tig consumed Flame's nipple like he had consumed the man's mouth. He could taste the bitterness of Flame's salty sweat as it beaded around the hard bud in his mouth and it made his cock twitch. Flame made another wanton noise when Tig bit and tugged on the barbell with his teeth. The noise and the bite of pain from Flame pulling his hair made his cock leak even more. The feeling of his pending orgasm along with the distant thought of cumming in his pants like a teenager made Tig pull away. The movement settled him on his knees between Flame's spread thighs.

Flame was enjoying the feel of Tig abusing his nipple and grinding down into him when he felt Tig's head press back into his hand. He did not prevent Tig from moving away. In fact, when Tig knelt between his knees, he liked the view and the implication of the position even better.

Tig's eyes roamed up from Flame's erection, the mushroom head glistening through the open buttons of his bunker pants, to his chest. Beads of sweat covered the smooth, almost hairless plane of muscle as Tig looked from the swollen nipple he had abandoned to the other that was begging for the same attention. Tig's hands moved over the coarse material of Flame's bunker pants of their own accord until they rested like a picture frame surrounding the porno portrait of Flame's cock.

Flame continued to catch his breath while he watched Tig's eyes practically eat him alive. The feel of the man's hands on his legs, resting in his groin so close to his aching cock, had him on the verge of begging the cop to touch him, taste him. Flame shifted his gaze from Tig's face to the rest of his body. A navy blue tie with small white stripes hung loosely around Tig's neck and against his bare chest but it wasn't the tie that Flame focused on. It was the tattoo that started just above his right pec and traveled down his chest to curve around his ribs. The black ink, lines both thin and thick, was a multitude of geometric shapes and swirls that disappeared into his slacks. Tig's gun was still in its holster on his hip and the vision of the man fucking him while wearing the weapon bombarded his mind and made his dick jump painfully.

Tig watched Flame's eyes follow his ink and saw the moment the man's gaze settled on his service piece at his hip. His hands felt, more than his peripheral vision saw, Flame's cock twitch.

Cop kink. Tig tightened his grip on the junction between Flame's thighs and hips where his hands rested. *No worse than my fireman kink.*

A noise escaped Flame's throat and Tig wasn't sure if it was a moan, groan, or growl. Regardless, the sound was sexy as fuck. He fought the tingle at the base of his spine when he spoke.

"Turns you on don't it?" Flame's eyes snapped back up to Tig's face. "Me being armed." Flame licked his lips and tried to pull Tig forward to grind against him again. "Want me to fuck you while wearing my piece? Maybe handcuff you first before burying myself balls deep in your tight ass?" Just the visual his words created was almost too much for Tig to withstand but before he could release Flame's weeping cock, Flame bolted off the couch.

Tig's words and the image they created in Flame's mind caused him to react. He had never been so turned on when he shot forward, catching Tig off guard, and knocked the man backwards onto the floor. His hands fumbled with Tig's belt while he sat astride the cop. He could feel Tig opening his bunker pants and when Tig's hand wrapped around his throbbing hardness, he could not stop his hips from thrusting into the firm fist that gripped him.

Tig grunted when his back hit the carpeted floor. Flame attacked his belt, his pants, and Tig was right there with him in his hunger. Flame's mouth crashed down onto his at the same moment Tig felt the man's calloused fingers pull him free of his slacks.

The kiss was just as hard, just as aggressive, brutal and rough, as the first time their mouths collided but it wasn't the kiss that almost short circuited Tig's mind. No. It was the feel of the silk covered hardness that pressed against his aching cock. Even fisting each other's cocks, Tig felt enough of the hot iron-like cock that pressed harshly into his own.

Flame moaned into Tig's mouth at the same time Tig groaned into his when their cocks touched through their fisted grips. Between Tig's strong grasp, hips pushing up, and Flame's own thrusting down, Flame knew he wasn't going to last. As he sucked on Tig's tongue that invaded his mouth, he didn't care.

Holy fuck! Was all Tig had time to think as his toes curled inside the dress shoes he wore for work and his back arched up into Flame's chest. The orgasm that slammed into him came out of nowhere and he came so hard, he saw stars as he shouted his release into Flame's open mouth.

The slight tensing of Tig did not even register in Flame's mind. The cop's back arching off the floor into him did. Flame shot his load into and over Tig's fist before he even realized he was cumming. His hips jerked erratically down into Tig's that were just as sporadically thrusting up into him. Flame broke the kiss as sparks of glitter filled his vision while the most mind blowing orgasm he may ever have had wracked his body.

Tig opened his eyes, eyes he never realized he had closed, and tried to catch his breath. Flame sagged on top of him, his dark haired head buried in Tig's neck, just as out of breath. As Tig floated back down from his intense orgasmic high, he tried not to think about how good Flame's almost dead weight felt on top of him. Or how good the man's rough hand still felt on his semi-deflated cock.

Shit.

Flame fought to catch his breath as he inhaled the warm air between Tig's neck and the floor. The cop smelled terrific and he panted in his scent. Tig still gripped him and he knew if he just rocked his hips slightly, his cock would be ready for round two. Tig's cock in his hand suggested that he wouldn't need much time to recover either.

But would he even want a round two? Flame couldn't help but wonder. *Shit, I hope so.*

Tig felt Flame's head move against his neck seconds before he felt the man's lips. The kiss on his throbbing, racing, jugular was gentle and only lasted a moment before Tig felt Flame's tongue run up his neck toward his ear. As distractingly good Flame's tongue was on his sweaty skin, Tig's mind tuned into the song that filled the air around them.

You and I go hard at each other like we're going to war

You and I go rough, we keep throwing things and slamming the door

You and I get so damn dysfunctional, we start keeping score

You and I get sick, yeah I know that we can't do this no more

Tig forced himself to stop listening to Maroon 5. The words were hitting too close to home and were like a splash of ice water that reminded him of *exactly* who the man that felt so good, so right, on him was.

Flame felt Tig tense right before he felt his cock released. He lifted his head and was greeted by a frown on Tig's face. The look was one he had seen many times, usually directed his way. Tig's eyes were focused somewhere over his shoulder and he waited for the man to speak.

Try to tell you no but my body keeps on telling you yes

Try to tell you stop but your lipstick got me so out of breath

I'll be waking up in the morning probably hating myself

And I'll be waking up feeling satisfied but guilty as hell

When Tig finally looked at him, Flame smiled. When Tig's frown deepened, one of his own made an appearance. Tig pushed against his chest and Flame allowed himself to be removed from the hard body beneath him. His eyes never left Tig as he sat back on his haunches on his living room floor and watched the cop sit up.

Tig pushed Flame off of him and immediately felt the loss of the other man. The man he was supposed to hate. When he sat up, he could feel his and Flame's cum running down his chest and over his abs to pool in his pubes and around his dick. He didn't look at Flame when he stood and pulled his dress shirt free of where it was tangled in his suit jacket. He used the shirt to wipe himself down and tried not to analyze the insanity of what he had just done with a man he didn't even like. His shirt was ruined so he balled it up and dropped it on Flame's end table before shrugging into his suit jacket.

This is like any other hook-up. Get dressed, collect your shit, and get the hell out. Tig told himself while still not looking at Flame.

Flame watched Tig as he put himself back together. It was clear there would be no round two. *How many times had I done the same? Grabbed my shit and got the hell out of Dodge?* Flame sighed and stood. *Now I know how it feels.*

"Leaving so soon?" Flame asked before he thought better of opening his mouth.

"This doesn't change anything, Flame." Tig still didn't look at Flame. "You know how the game is played. We both got what we wanted."

Yeah, I do, Flame thought as he stared at Tig's broad shoulders and back. He watched as Tig made his way to the door and left without a backwards glance.

"Time to change up the game, Tigger." Flame said to the empty room and picked up Tig's balled up, ruined dress shirt. He bent to turn off his lamp and the glint of metal on his couch caught his eye. He grinned as he picked up Tig's handcuffs. *There will be a round two.* His smile was still on his face when he climbed into bed.

CHAPTER 12

ALL day Friday, Tig was useless. His mind kept replaying the night before when he was splayed under Flame. Thomas Flame. The man he had despised since sixth grade. The man whose body made him rock fucking hard with just a thought. How he could crave a repeat of the man's touch and want more while still hating the guy? He didn't know.

But do I really still hate him? Tig tried not to think of what options there were if hatred wasn't what he felt for Thomas Flame.

He could admit to the lust the man stirred in him. Could admit to how hot their hook-up had been. Could even admit his desire to lick every line of the tribal ink that decorated the man's body and that his cock hardened to the point of pain at the thought of a repeat. But that was just his body's reaction to Flame's physique being exactly what turned his crank. Still, Tig's emotions where Flame was concerned felt like they had been dumped into a blender that was set on puree.

"Flint," Pat's voice broke Tig out of his musing about Flame.

"Yeah?"

"You're zoning out again, man." Pat looked at him with concern and Tig felt guilty at seeing his partner worry about him.

"Sorry." Tig grinned and hoped Pat didn't press him on his distraction. "What's up?"

"Lt. sent another email. Two different tips have given us the address of another lab. One of the tips even mentioned Cortez's name."

"Gullis?" Tig asked, hoping that their CI had resurfaced.

"No idea. The tips were from different people. The male could be Gullis but if it was, I would think he would have given us more than just the location."

"You're probably right." Tig ran a hand through his hair. It was getting long again and he was overdue for a cut. "Sucks that he's disappeared."

Pat grunted in agreement.

"Detective Flint?"

Tig glanced in the direction of the voice that called him. It came from another vice cop, one who Tig thought worked the prostitution angle. The cop looked like a sixteen year old kid with his black eyeliner, thin band tee shirt, and ratty, ripped jeans.

"Yeah?" Tig replied and racked his brain for the guy's name. *Rich? Rick? Dick?* He really needed to make a point to know all the vice squad officer's names even if they did work different angles of vice.

"My Sergeant wanted me to bring this to your attention," the cop pulled a baggy of pale pink powder out of the front pocket of his skin tight jeans as he approached Tig's desk. "We were approached by one of the petty dealers last night. Gave me and JoJo a free sample of his 'new and improved, kick ass go fast.' He said this shit is better than speed, crack, and coke combined."

Tig took the bag of powder from the younger cop and held it up to his desk lamp. The pale pink crystals glittered like tiny prisms when the light penetrated the tiny zip lock bag. He had never seen anything like it. It didn't look like smack. It was too white, even with the pink tinge, to be heroin and PCP hadn't made the rounds on the streets since before he joined the force.

"Don't know if it's related to any case you guys are working but as much shit that is offered to me and JoJo, we ain't never seen anything pink before."

"What did he call it?" Tig asked for the street name.

"Dumbo," the cop laughed.

Tig chuckled along with him. Anyone stupid enough to do this shit was dumb so the name was appropriate even if the vision of a flying elephant wasn't.

"Thanks, Officer?"

"Kendry." The cop smiled. "But I prefer Rick."

"Thanks for bringing this up, Rick," Tig said as he waved the baggie. "I'll get it to the lab so we can see what is what. If you can discover a source of production without compromising yourself, that would help but don't do anything that would blow your cover. I'll get our drug undercovers on this regardless."

"Yeah. If the opportunity arises, I'll find out but your drug guys are better at finding out that shit than we are."

Tig returned the cop's grin before the man walked away. He couldn't help but notice the strategically placed tears in the cop's jeans that ensured the johns knew he was commando. Tig tore his gaze away from the undercover cop's ass when Pat loudly cleared his throat.

"He's gay, you know," Pat informed him and Tig tensed.

Shit! Tig wasn't sure what to say that wouldn't raise more questions than were already in Pat's eyes so he winged it.

"Okay," Tig schooled his features into something that he hoped Pat would buy as him not caring one way or the other. "I don't care what he does behind closed doors." Tig purposely did not look at his partner and instead studied the gram bag of pink powder he held. "Gonna take this to the boys at the lab and see what they can tell us."

Pat didn't reply as Tig stood but Tig could feel his partner's eyes on his back as he walked away. When he returned from the lab, Pat was gone and Tig tried not to think about why his partner felt the urge to point out that Officer Rick Kendry was gay.

Saturday, July fourth, found Flame full of anticipation as he approached the high school football field where the last charity game for the Big Brothers and Big Sisters was being held. Even as his eyes scanned the TPD team for Tig, he laughed, joked, and talked shit with the rest of the firefighters while they made their way to their bench on the sidelines.

Thoughts of the man had invaded his mind to the point that the word distraction didn't even begin to describe what was going on in his head. He and Tigger Flint had never gotten along and had such a deep mutual hatred for one another that Flame was more than surprised that his feelings for the cop had done a complete one-eighty. But that surprise did not last for long. No, instead, Flame embraced his new feelings for the man he had always despised. He had always embraced his emotions full out. Be they anger, hatred, friendship, or love. It was all or nothing, one hundred percent in, balls to the wall, when it came to how he felt about something or someone. Not that he felt love for Tigger Flint. No, not love but definitely lust. The hatred, hatred that he couldn't even explain, was gone; drowned out by lust, want, and desire to feel the man against him again.

Tig felt Flame's eyes on him before he even spotted the man among the TFR team as they moved to their bench. Tig ignored the feeling of being watched while he talked to his fellow cops. He reminded them that they were tied up with TFR and would have plenty of ball busting opportunities if they kicked Tampa Fire Rescue's ass on the field today. He also reminded them that this last game was for charity.

Tig was able to avoid Flame's gaze until the ref called them onto the field for the coin toss. It wasn't that he was embarrassed or ashamed of hooking up with the guy two nights ago. No, he was more concerned that he wouldn't be able to hide his desire for a repeat, for something more. Like being buried balls deep in the firefighter's tight ass.

Flame stepped up to the ref and stood across from Tig. The man was tense and wouldn't meet his gaze. He couldn't understand why the cop wouldn't look at him but knew he wanted to see those emerald eyes devouring his body again. He also knew that if Tig wouldn't look at him willingly, then he'd just have to force the man to do so.

The coin was tossed in the air and Tig spoke before it landed. "Head."

Flame raised his brow at Tig's Freudian slip as the coin landed on the turf tails side up. He couldn't help but chuckle and didn't know if it was because of Tig's slip or because he had won the toss.

"You want the ball or are you giving it up again?" The ref asked and Flame saw suspicion and curiosity in the man's gaze.

"We'll take it," Flame grinned and finally got to see Tig's green eyes when the man's head snapped up. "We have a game to win after all." He shot a wink at Tig before the ref handed him the ball.

"Let's have a good clean game," the ref said before blowing his whistle again.

Tig tried to put Flame's grin out of his mind as he made his way back to the sidelines. Three games in a row TFR won the toss and Flame gave over possession of the ball every time except today. He wasn't sure what to make of the change as TPD's defense and TFR's offense took the field.

I'm reading too much into it. He didn't look pissed about the other night and if he is? So what. I don't care. It was just a hook-up like any other.

Tig told himself and tried to believe the lie he was selling. He did care and that pissed him off because he knew he shouldn't give a shit about Thomas Flame's feelings. The only thing he should care about was getting his rocks off on that hard, sexy assed, body again.

Fuck! Tig gave himself a mental shake. *I shouldn't even care about that. He's nothing but a hook-up.*

A hook-up you repeated and want to repeat again, a tiny voice in his mind whispered.

The reminder did nothing to banish the memory of Flame on top of him, grinding into him while he emptied his cock on Tig's chest and abs. It did nothing to diminish his hunger for a repeat, either. All it did was make his cock thicken to the point that his jock felt like it was about to snap off his Prince Albert.

Flame forced himself not to look at the TPD bench where Tig sat. He forced himself to watch his offensive guys move the football closer to the TPD goal line. They scored and Flame cheered with the rest of his department. It was TPD's ball and Flame took the field with the rest of the guys from TFR who were playing defense.

The minute the football touched Tig's hands and he dropped back into the pocket, his eyes locked on Flame. Flame gasped when they made eye contact. The look was brief, only lasted a second or three, but there was something in Tig's eyes that made his body react. His semi-hard cock, just from seeing Tig, became a full on hard on in his jock. There was no time to become uncomfortable, no time to adjust himself and get around the TPD defender to reach Tig before the man let the ball fly.

Tig's eyes scanned down field before they shifted back to check on Flame. He knew Flame would sack him the minute an opening presented itself. First quarter or not. Their eyes locked again and Tig only had a moment to be grateful for Archer's block before he let the ball fly. Kennedy caught the ball and Flame never made it into the pocket. Tig wasn't sure if he was relieved or disappointed that Flame's body never crashed into him. Though, the ache in his throbbing cock let him know just how disappointed his body was that there was no contact.

The teams reset the line and TPD moved the ball, eventually scoring, without giving Flame the opportunity to put his hands on Tig. In fact, the man never even got close enough to grab one of the blue plastic flags that dangled from his hips. TFR took possession of the ball as they started the second quarter. The July heat was brutal and several of the men from both teams had removed their tee shirts, much to the delight of the crowd gathered to support the Brothers and Sisters.

Flame gave no thought when he removed his sweat soaked TFR tee shirt. Several cat calls came from the stands as his tattooed chest and back made an appearance but Flame didn't spare a glance at his sudden fan base. He did, however, look to see if his naked flesh caused any reaction in Tigger.

Tig had been covertly watching Flame so he did not miss the moment when the man's hands gripped the hem of his tee shirt and proceeded to raise it, almost teasingly, before it was totally removed and discarded on the bench. The sight of Flame's naked, sweat covered, tattooed chest made Tig's mouth go dry like it had the night the man greeted him in his open apartment door. If his cock could have grown any harder, it would have. Tig willed his eyes to look away but they seemed to have a mind of their own and wanted nothing more than to visually drink the man in, visually fuck the man silly.

Oh, now there is a reaction. Flame watched as Tig licked his lips while staring pointedly at Flame's naked chest. The cop wore the same hungry gaze as he had when in Flame's apartment. The urge to tackle the cop, have Tig under him again, was so strong that Flame caught himself stepping toward the TPD bench. Third quarter or not and the threat of being benched be damned. Flame had to feel Tig's hard body under him again. The ref's whistle blowing to indicate the change of possession was like the bell at a horse track that set them free to run and Flame was a horse biting at the bit.

Tig stood behind his center and was about to call for the snap when he glanced at Flame. There was no mistaking the sexual hunger that he saw in the man's eyes. That hunger was all Tig needed to see to know that Flame's body would soon be on top of him by way of another sack. His cock gave an eager twitch again and he gave Flame a grin that he knew dared the man to make it happen.

Flame recognized the look in Tig's eyes as the cop stepped up to the line. It matched his own. Arousal, hunger, and he knew that Tig knew he was coming for him. Knew that Tig wanted him to come for him. Almost in more than one way.

"Blue, red, hut!" The ball was in Tig's hands and he dropped back into the pocket again.

The ball snapped and Flame seemed to move by rote. His eyes never left Tig's as he pushed then spun away from the TPD defender. There was plenty of time for Tig to complete the pass, even as Flame rushed him, and he did. Ball in hand or not, Flame plowed into Tig and brought the man down.

"Omph!" Tig exhaled when he hit the ground. Even though he'd braced for the hit, he couldn't stop the sound from escaping his lips.

Flame felt, enjoyed, reveled in, every inch of Tigger Flint's body beneath him. He didn't want to move as they lay pressed together, sweat mingling, on the ground as a result of his tackle. No, he wanted to move. Wanted to grind his hard on, that was painfully trapped in his jock, into the man beneath him. Instead, he forced his body to remain still while he inhaled deeply the scent of Tig. Flame's face was pressed against Tig's neck and gave him the perfect opportunity to taste the man again.

Tig told his body to push Flame off of him but his body wasn't listening. The hot, moist breath that panted from Flame's lips brought images of their hook-up two nights ago to the forefront of Tig's mind. Like he needed anything to help remind him. It took all of his restraint not to push up into Flame as the man's heavy breathing filled his ears.

"Come over tonight," Flame whispered before caving to his desire to lick the sweat that ran down Tig's neck.

Tig heard Flame's request clearly before the ref's whistle reminded them both that they were playing a flag football game. For charity. He had no chance to reply before the heat of Flame's bulk was gone and Pat was standing over him.

"You alright?" Pat stuck out his hand to help Tig up and Tig took it.

No, I'm not.

"Yeah," Tig gave his partner a grin.

"That asshole fucking with you again?"

Yeah, in all the right ways. Tig was glad he was wearing a cup, even if the jock was causing his hard dick to cramp like a mother fucker and his piercing to snag uncomfortably.

"No more than usual." Tig brushed the grass off his ass as they made their way back to the line for the next play.

"Well, just ignore his ass. Don't let him get to you." Pat advised as he slapped Tig's back and jogged over to his position on the line.

Ignore his ass? Yeah right. He's already gotten to me. The thought crossed Tig's mind as he called for the next snap. He handed the ball off to Pat who ran wide and made a few yards. Flame never even made it into the pocket but Tig held no delusions that the man wasn't gunning for him, didn't want to press his hot as fuck body on top of him again. When Tig's cock twitched happily, if a bit painfully, again in his jock at the thought, Tig found himself grinning in agreement with his prick about how good it would feel.

The ball changed possession several times and it was the close of the fourth quarter before Flame had another chance to feel Tig's body beneath him.

CHAPTER 13

THE ball snapped, making a loud smacking noise against Tig's sweaty palms. Flame watched as Tig took three steps back into the pocket and let the ball fly while making no attempt to scramble out of the way to avoid the incoming sack.

"Grrr." The noise escaped Tig's throat when Flame plowed into him and they both hit the ground. Hard.

The growl from Tig caused Flame's body to react before he remembered that they were in the middle of a charity flag football game. His hips pushed down into Tig and he could have sworn the man thrust up into him at the same time.

"My place. Eight o'clock," Flame practically ordered on a growl of hot breath next to Tig's ear. "I have something that belongs to you."

Tig's first thought about Flame's comment was that Flame was referring to his dick, especially since there was no denying the extra pressure being applied to his groin. Then he remembered leaving his cuffs behind two nights ago. Tig turned his head at Flame's words. The firefighter pulled back and his lips were close enough that Tig could lick them. The temptation to do just that and much, *much* more to the man's talented mouth was strong, but unlike Flame, Tig remembered where they were.

Flame grinned down at Tig when another groan quietly escaped Tig and he licked his lips. Tig's pupils were huge with desire and even as the man pushed him away, Flame knew he would be seeing Tigger Flint later.

The game ended with Tampa Fire Rescue winning by one touchdown; the only interception Tig threw was the last play of the game. Bragging rights and jibes were already flying at the Tampa Police Department.

"Fucking assholes," Pat mumbled as they walked to the sidelines.

"We'd do the same." Tig grabbed one of the ice cold towels from the cooler and didn't see the glance Pat shot him as he wrung out the excess water over his head. The cold water felt fantastic and he covered his face with the towel to cool off.

"Heading to Guns & Hoses for the fireworks tonight after the barbeque?"

Tig wiped his face as he removed the towel and wrapped it around his neck. He had been so absorbed with thoughts of meeting Flame later that he had totally forgotten about the barbeque the Brothers and Sisters were throwing for the departments after the game.

"Dunno. Depends on how I feel after sweating my ass off all day." Tig grinned and rotated his waist to stretch out the muscles in his lower back.

"You okay? That ass hit you pretty hard," Pat asked before gulping down a full cup of Gatorade. "Wouldn't be surprised if that dickhead was trying to hurt you with how much the two of you hate each other."

Don't think 'hate' is the right word anymore, but fuck if I know what is.

"Nah, he didn't hurt me." *Unless the pain my piercing is causing from my hard-on being crammed into this damned jock counts.* Tig took a long drink from his own cup. "Think I am just dehydrated. Lack of fluids and shit making me ache."

Both men refilled their cups before heading toward the opposite end of the field where the barbeque was already in full swing.

"You really nailed his ass," Brostowski joked and gave Flame a slap on his bare sweaty back.

Flame looked in Tig's direction. *I wish.* "Yeah, he's a slippery son of a bitch but I took him down when I could."

And if I am lucky, I'll take him down tonight in all the right ways.

"Surprised the ref didn't bench you. Good thing the game was over after that last hit." Brostowski grinned. "Looks like you might have hit him too hard. You see him stretching his back out?"

Fuck! The last thing Flame wanted to was *actually* hurt Tig; unless it was in a good way.

"He'll get over it," Flame grunted to hide his concern.

He wanted to check on Tig, make sure the man wasn't really injured. There was no way to do so without raising questions from both of their co-workers. Everyone knew of their ongoing feud and if he suddenly became concerned it was sure to raise more than one eyebrow. He was kicking himself for not getting Tig's number. If he had it, he could at least send a text.

"Hot dog, hamburger, or both?" A teenaged girl asked and brought Flame's attention back to the food line where he and Brostowski now stood.

"Both" they said in unison and smiled. The girl blushed when she handed them their plates.

As they moved down the food line filling their plates, Flame's thoughts returned to Tig and how he could go about checking on the man. The only way to do so was to be an asshole and that risked the man not coming to his place later. *Shit.*

Tig and Pat were eating from their plates on the high school bleachers when Pat grunted and spoke. "I knew it was too good to be true."

Tig looked up and saw Flame and Brostowski approaching. Flame was still bare chested, the beads and rivulets of sweat decorating his toned pecs and abs. *Fuck if the man wasn't sex on a stick.* Tig remembered exactly what that sweat tasted like and took a drink of his Gatorade to prevent licking his lips.

"We're still at a charity event. Don't let that asshole goad you into anything," Pat advised.

Too late, Tig thought as the firemen came to stand before them.

"Looking a little stiff there, *Tigger*," Flame said with a sneer and hated himself for it. "Hate for you not to be able to get your freak on for the holiday."

Tig was used to hearing the tone Flame used to taunt him. The words, however, weren't nearly as nasty as he knew they could be. Tig gave him a smirk in return. He was *stiff* alright, but it wasn't just his back that had a kink in it. Tig also read into Flame's comment about getting his freak on later.

Shit, he thinks he hurt me.

Tig wasn't sure of what to make of Flame's concern but he allowed none of his confusion over the man's behavior to change the glower he gave the man.

"Like any chick would want to get freaky with an asshole like him," Brostowski goaded with a snicker. Sometimes it seemed like Brostowski enjoyed their feud more than they did.

"Like you give a shit, dickhead," Tig growled. "As for getting freaky," Tig shifted his gaze to Brostowski. "You can ask your sister tomorrow."

Tig hated bringing up the fireman's sister because he genuinely liked the woman. But he knew Brostowski was over protective of his baby sister and the insult would touch a nerve. When Brostowski dropped his half empty plate and stepped toward them, Tig wasn't surprised.

Pat was on his feet, intercepting Flame's co-worker before Tig even had a chance to set down his plate. Brostowski shoved Pat, who shoved him back in return, while Tig set his plate aside and stood. His gaze never left Flame's and even though he still scowled at him, concern shone clear in the man's stunning blue eyes.

"What the fuck is wrong with you asshats?" Pat gripped Brostowski's sweat soaked tee shirt and got in his face. "Charity. Event. Ring any bells?"

Flame grabbed Brostowski's arm and tugged him out of Pat's grasp. "Let's go, man. Marissa wouldn't even give a pencil dick like him the time of day." Flame dangerously shot Tig a wink. "Leave it."

"Don't even fucking speak about my sister again, *Tigger*, or you'll be lucky to be able to talk at all without teeth."

Tig snorted at the threat from the smaller fireman but held back from any retort as he watched Flame haul his buddy away.

"What?" Tig asked when Pat shot a glare at him. "I was just sitting here. You're the one who went all guard dog."

Both men sat back down and resumed eating when Pat spoke. "Yeah and if I didn't, you guys would have been beating the shit out of each other for the entertainment of all these kids." Pat sighed. "You know how he is about his sister."

"Well, she did get the looks of that family," Tig reminded his partner with a straight face.

"Yeah, she did," Pat agreed and they both laughed. "One of the hottest cops on the force, too. Bet her career choice really pissed off the men in her family."

"Probably more than being a lesbian did, that's for sure," Tig chuckled and thought of all the men that were instantly heartbroken when they learned that Officer Marissa Brostowski preferred women to men.

Both men talked sports while they finished their meal and looked over the crowd that turned out to support the charity. Tig's eyes tracked Flame through the throng and there were just enough people that he did not fear his partner noticing.

Flame felt Tig's eyes on him long after he stopped Brostowski from rearranging his lover's face.

Lover? Two hook-ups and now I am thinking of him as a lover? What the hell? Flame was still analyzing this new twist to how he viewed Tig when Brostowski interrupted his thoughts.

"See you tonight at Guns & Hoses for the fireworks," Brostowski slapped him on the back. "Bring a date or you'll be stuck with me."

Flame laughed and a moment later Brostowski joined him. He gave no thought to his friend's words or the pause before his buddy laughed. It wasn't until he became aware of Brostowski's hand still lingering on his bare back that the situation turned weird, turned uncomfortable.

"Will do, man. See you later." Flame stepped away from his friend's touch and made a bee-line for his truck.

Once inside his truck, A/C blowing on high to cool him and the truck down, confusion set in. He had known John Brostowski for the last six years. They had become best friends from the moment they met at the station. The man wasn't gay and bragged about the chicks he banged all the time. They had been way beyond shit faced together on more occasions than Flame could count so he knew his friend sure as fuck wasn't gay.

So what the hell was with the innuendo and the touchy feely shit?

If they were drunk, Flame would rack the whole encounter up to alcohol but there wasn't a drop to be consumed all day. If Brostowski *were* gay, Flame would take the comment, the touch as an invitation for a hook-up. But he wasn't. Flame's gay-dar didn't ping at all where his best friend was concerned.

"I'm reading too much into it. The heat is fucking with me," Flame spoke aloud to his empty truck while he put it in gear.

Brostowski's words and behavior were still on his mind when he pulled into his parking spot in front of his apartment. He let himself inside and, out of habit, turned on the stereo while his thoughts turned to whether Tig would show up or not.

> *I want your love and*
> *I want your revenge*
> *You and me could write a bad romance*
> *(Oh-oh-oh-oh-oooh!)*
> *I want your love and*
> *All your lovers revenge*
> *You and me could write a bad romance*

Damn if Lady Gaga didn't have Tig and him pegged. This was a bad romance alright and the fall out was sure to be a bitch. Personally, physically, and with both of their jobs and friends. But fuck if Flame cared as he thought about getting Tig under him again.

Tig watched Flame and Brostowski make their way to the parking lot. Shortly after, once he was sure Flame had plenty of time to leave, he said his own goodbyes. He still wasn't sure what to make of Flame's concern over potentially injuring him during the last play of the game. Finally, he racked it up to the guy just being worried about if they were still going to hook-up later.

His back was tight and hurt but not enough to pass up Flame's invitation. It wasn't a good idea to become fuck buddies with Flame. Hell, it wasn't a good idea to go to the man's house the first time but that didn't stop him.

Just the memory of Flame grinding down on top of him made him hunger for what it would feel like when they fucked. Tig rarely bottomed but he couldn't deny how his ass clenched at the thought of what Flame would feel like buried deep inside of him while that hard body slammed into him over and over again. He couldn't deny how his cock twitched and throbbed at the thought of doing the same to Flame, either.

By the time Tig arrived home, his cock was beyond painful and it had nothing to do with the way his piercing was snagged in the material that lined the cup of his jock. Clothes were dropped haphazardly on the floor as Tig made his way to the shower. His hand was already gripping the steel hardness that rubbed against his navel when he stepped under the tepid spray of the shower.

Barely any time or thought was given to the bar of soap he flipped over and over through his hand before he brought his suds-covered palm to wrap around his erection. The first stroke caused a moan of relief that he made no attempt to stifle, to echo off the sandstone tiles that surrounded him.

Tig placed his other hand, fingers splayed, against the cool tile while he let memories of Flame's hard cock, pressing and sliding against his, flood his memories. With his eyes closed, he could see them, feel them, both on Flame's carpeted floor. Rubbing, stroking, grinding. Two hard bodies, not fighting for once, but instead collaborating in coordination to reach the orgasmic high they both desperately craved.

The memory abruptly shifted to when he face fucked Flame in the bathroom of Bradley's. Flame cuffed and helpless while Tig pushed his cock into his rival's mouth. His hand tightened around his cock to match the remembered suction of Flame's mouth and his strokes became quick and jerky. The vision of Flame's lips stretched around his cock as he thrust deep and the memory of the moment he slipped into the man's throat, along with the even tighter grip he applied to his leaking cock, sent him over the edge. He never saw his cum splatter the tiles that he faced. He saw nothing but glittery sparkles behind his closed eyes when his shaking legs finally gave out and he slid down to the floor.

Tig did not know how long he sat on the tiles of the shower floor, limp dick still cupped in the palm of his hand, as he came back to earth from his orgasm. What he did know was that the water turned cold and he was totally screwed if the memory of being with Flame could rock his world just from jacking off.

Fuck!

Chapter 14

THE whole ride to Flame's apartment, Tig kept reminding himself of what a bad idea this was for them to become fuck buddies. Aside from the fact that they had always hated each other, neither of them was out at work. Even though Tig was a detective with vice, they crossed paths enough on the job that someone was bound to notice their change of behavior toward one another. Not to mention they frequently crossed paths in Guns & Hoses.

However, no amount of rationalization made Tig turn his Camaro around and head to Guns & Hoses to watch the fireworks with Pat and Mary instead. No, the fireworks he wanted to experience were behind the apartment door he now stood before.

Flame had just lowered his beer from his lips when a knock sounded on his door. 8:03. There was only one person that he was expecting and he couldn't stop the smile that spread his lips. That smile widened when he opened the door and saw Tigger Flint standing on his welcome mat.

Tig wasn't wearing what Flame thought of as club clothes nor was he dressed in a suit that he normally wore for work. Instead, Flame was gazing upon a whole different look from any he had seen the detective wear before. Stone washed jeans, just like the ones Flame usually wore; fit Tig like a glove and a dark green polo that did nothing to hide his muscular chest.

Fuck, the man is hot!

Tig watched as Flame looked him over from head to toe while he did the same to Flame. The firefighter wore black denim jeans that appeared well worn and comfortable. His red tank top had the same worn look and did nothing to hide the tribal tattoos that disappeared under the material or the barbells that pierced his nipples. Flame licked his lips and Tig felt himself grow hard at the sight. He couldn't resist smirking at the man.

"As much as I am enjoying the eye fucking, you gonna invite me in and offer me one of those?" Tig nodded to the beer in Flame's hand even as he wondered about the civil words that escaped his lips.

"Sure." Flame snapped himself out of the fantasy he was having about ripping Tig's clothes off right there on his doorstep. "C'mon in." Flame turned, adjusted his suddenly hard prick, and made his way toward the kitchen to grab another beer for himself and Tig.

Tig entered Flame's apartment and closed the door behind him. The radio was filling the living room with music and for once wasn't playing a song that was parroting his thoughts. Without the distraction of Flame half naked in his bunker gear, Tig was able to take in the rest of the place. A computer sat upon a desk along one wall and a large bookshelf which was crammed past capacity with paperbacks, sat against another. Out of nowhere, the curiosity about what Flame enjoyed reading struck Tig but before he could indulge his curiosity, Flame returned and handed Tig a bottle of beer.

"Here," Flame handed Tig a bottle of Bud Light. "Sit down."

"Thanks." Tig took a swig of the cold amber liquid while glancing at the leather couch.

There was no need to recall what had happened on that couch the last time he had been here. The memories came to him without any conscious thought. Tig took another drink while he settled himself on the soft leather. Tension filled the air between them; uncertainty and sexual hunger in equal measures. The undercurrent of lust and want was there as well, like it was a fuse just waiting to be lit by a spark.

Flame sat on the arm of his leather chair and took a long pull from his beer. He was nervous, which was ridiculous. There was no doubt in his mind that he wanted Tigger Flint but this hook-up felt more like a date. The frantic need to get off was surprisingly gone even though they both knew that was why Tig was currently sitting on his couch. Instead, he was curious to learn more about the man he never liked until he found out he was gay.

"How's your back?" Flame asked out of genuine concern and to break the silence.

Tig was caught off guard by Flame's question. In fact, he was caught off guard by the man's behavior thus far. The last time he had walked through Flame's door, they were both hot and heavy to get off. Now, that heat was like a simmering rumble under a volcano that was just waiting to erupt.

"Sore." Tig grinned and took another drink of his beer. "You still hit like a Mack truck." *Why did I just admit that?*

Flame winced. "Sorry." Tig's eyes widened at the unexpected apology and Flame continued. "I forgot we weren't wearing pads for protection. Though, I can't say I am disappointed with the outcome."

Tig fought not to frown but when he didn't reply, Flame spoke again. "You're hard to catch. I won't lie though; I wanted to sack your ass every time, if only to have you under me again."

A small knowing smile crossed Tig's lips and he drank from his beer again. He knew he could not prevent his body's reaction to the visual Flame's words brought to mind and he did nothing to hide the tightening in his jeans.

"You're really okay though, right?"

The amount of concern in Flame's voice made Tig feel...something. He wasn't sure what but it definitely made him feel.

"Yeah. I'm just sore but that won't hamper our fun." Tig grinned. "Thanks for asking." *When did we become so civil to each other? This is weird.*

"Maybe I should check for myself just to be sure." Flame set his bottle on the end table next to the chair he was perched on and stood.

Tig raised an eyebrow as Flame approached where he was seated on the couch. The man was in no rush, was not aggressive, but the lust and hunger were clear in his penetrating blue gaze. This hook-up with Flame was so different from the others it made his head spin in confusion. He wasn't sure what to make of this caring, gentler Flame but his body didn't give a shit about the mental logistics of Flame's more mellow behavior. No. His body was totally on board with allowing Flame to verify he wasn't injured from the sack that the man had laid on him earlier in the day. If it meant getting naked and having Flame's calloused hands on his bare flesh again, his body was *all* for it.

"Really?" Tig managed to say when Flame came to stand between his spread knees.

"Yeah, really," Flame grinned down at Tig and could see the slight confusion that the cop had in regards to how this hook-up was playing out. "But not here."

Tig raised an inquiring brow as Flame took Tig's beer from his hand and set it aside before holding out his hand to help Tig rise from the couch. Flame never took men to his bedroom; rarely ever brought them home, but all day he could think of nothing else but having Tig's hard body spread across his bed.

Flame wasn't sure which one of them was more surprised when Tig took his hand and allowed himself to be led to the bedroom. Flame flicked the light switch on the wall and the lamp on his night table allowed Tig to see his bedroom.

The queen sized bed that looked too small to contain Flame's bulk, let alone both of them, was covered under a burgundy comforter. Three lone pillows rested against a metal frame headboard. The bed was not made, per say, but merely looked straightened enough that it did not look like Flame had just crawled out from under the sheets. Flame dropped Tig's hand when they entered the room. When he turned around Tig spoke.

"What are we doing, Flame?" Tig really wanted to know where the man's head was because his own was like a viper's nest of confusion.

Flame recognized the frown on Tig's face. He had seen that look directed his way more times than he could count over the course of their lives.

"I'm going to check your back," Flame grinned and stepped toward Tig who remained standing in the doorway to his bedroom. "Then, once you're naked and I am sure you are up for it," Flame brought his hands to Tig's belt and began unfastening the buckle so he could access the man's hard-on. "I am going to cover your naked body with mine and ride your ass like there is no tomorrow."

The reply Tig's mind supplied was swallowed by his sharp intake of breath when Flame's knuckles grazed the bare skin of his abs under his shirt. One hand lifted to Flame's waist while his other grasped the nape of the man's neck and pulled him into a harsh, hungry, kiss. It was the spark that rekindled the smoldering fire between them. Just like the first time their mouths connected, teeth clashed and a lip split as they fought each other for control of the kiss.

Flame knew his words would earn him a reaction from Tig but somehow the man attacking his mouth was not the reaction he had expected. Aggression sure. Arguing over who would top whom, definitely. But not this crazy blind lust, hunger, need, and want that Tig poured into the attack on his mouth.

Finally, Tig's jeans and boxers hit the floor. How, Flame had no idea but he really did not care as his hands traveled over Tig's naked flesh. Tig's polo was pushed up at the same time he felt his own tank top become bunched up in his armpits.

Flame's sharp intake of breath when Tig tugged on both barbells at his nipples made Tig grin and pull out of the kiss. He had already kicked out of his shoes and stepped out of the clothing pooled at his feet when he backed Flame toward the bed.

"Off," Flame growled while tugging on Tig's polo with his hands. Reluctantly, Tig removed his hands from

Flame's chest but not before pulling harshly on each piercing again.

The moment Tig's hands left his body, Flame stripped out of his tank top. His mouth slammed into Tig's once more before the cop's polo even hit the floor. Flame wrapped a hand around the velvet steel of Tig's cock that now pressed against his jean covered erection. Tig's hiss broke their kiss and Flame grinned while tightening his grip. He didn't stroke but instead just used his firm hold like a human cock ring while his other hand at Tig's waist prevented Tig from thrusting into his touch.

Flame's touch set him ablaze and Tig's head fell back on his shoulders as he tried to thrust into the calloused hand that held him. Through his half lidded gaze, he could see Flame's grin, the knowing smirk that he was denying Tig the friction he sought. Tig's hands rested on Flame's shoulders while he lowered his head and used his body to force Flame to fall back onto the bed. The moment he landed on the man, Tig latched his mouth around one nipple and bit down. Hard.

"Fuck!"

Flame brought his free hand to the back of Tig's head and grabbed a fist full of sandy hair. Simultaneously, he pulled Tig's hair while pushing the man's punishing mouth closer to his chest.

Tig did not mind the bite of pain caused by Flame pulling his hair. In fact, he barely noticed the pain at all because he was consumed by the noises the man was making. When Flame's hands left his waist and aching cock, he didn't know nor cared. He wasn't even aware that he now had freedom to move as he rutted against Flame's jean covered groin.

The sensations from Tig's mouth, his teeth, as he nipped and tugged on Flame's pierced flesh were radiating out from the point of contact like a lit fuse on a stick of dynamite. And that stick was his painfully, jeans encased, trapped cock. *Fuck, I have to taste!*

Tig wasn't sure what had just happened. One moment he was feasting on Flame's nipple piercing while grinding his leaking cock against the rough denim of Flame's jeans to get more delicious friction and the next, he was flipped over, face down, and Flame was straddling his ass.

Tig tensed. "What the fuck?" He cursed as he looked over his shoulder and bucked his hips to throw Flame off.

"Relax Tig," Flame leaned forward to press his bare chest to Tig's naked back and whispered as he fought to catch his breath.

"You are *not* going to fuck me." Tig growled, dropping his head to the mattress and knew he was lying to both himself and Flame.

We'll see, Flame thought as he slid his hands over Tig's biceps to his shoulders. "Just relax," Flame repeated while resting his forehead against the nape of Tig's sweaty neck and fought his urge to plunge deep into the ass he was straddling.

"I'm just going to check your back." Flame applied pressure to Tig's tense muscles but when the man still did not relax, he spoke again. "I'm still dressed." Flame pushed his denim covered hard-on against Tig's ass to prove his point. He thought he heard Tig groan but couldn't be sure. "Scoot up."

Tig knew he was in a vulnerable position but Flame's hands massaging his shoulders and the man's solid weight covering him felt fantastic. He moaned again into the mattress and hoped that Flame did not hear him when he moved up the bed. Tig had not even resettled on the bed when he felt Flame grind into him again. Denim that should feel rough, but was surprisingly soft, pressed against the outside of his thighs and rubbed on his naked ass cheeks.

Flame expected more of an argument from Tig and was amazed he didn't get one. Once more, Flame pressed his hands into the muscles of Tig's shoulders. The thin sheen of sweat that covered Tig's body along with the man's natural body oils were enough to allow Flame's fingers to dig deep into Tig's tense muscles. He rubbed his hands along Tig's spine, fingers spayed to feel as much as possible. Several times he returned to Tig's neck, shoulders, and arms as he followed the contours of the man's muscles.

Tig was in heaven. Pure fucking heaven. Tension was bleeding from him like a victim bled out from a fatal gunshot wound on a scene. So relaxed he became, that he forgot that the man who was skillfully relieving his tension was one he wasn't even supposed to like. So relaxed, that he forgot this was just supposed to be a hook-up to get off. In effect, his cock was no longer a throbbing painful mess while it was trapped against the bed. Surprisingly, his mind emptied as the stiffness in his body dissolved and he did not fight the sleepy feeling that overcame him.

Flame worked Tig's shoulders, back, ass, and thighs until he was sure the man felt like Jell-o. He freed his aching cock with a sigh of relief and Tig never noticed, even when his cock left a trail of sticky precum over his ass. Flame massaged his leakage into Tig's pale ass while he moved further back to continue down the man's toned legs.

Tig never felt Flame's hands rub down his thighs and remove his socks. He never felt their return trip or noticed that Flame no longer sat astride him. Tig was in a comfortably mellow, half sleep state.

Tig's ass pushed up into his hands and Flame was sure the cop wasn't even aware that he was making the movement. The movement broke the tether of restraint that Flame had been trying to maintain. His hands spread Tig's rock hard glutes and he lowered his head. He took one long swipe of his tongue from Tig's taint, across his tight pucker, and along his crease before he came to stop at the base of Tig's spine. Flame felt Tig's relaxation dissolve but did not give the man time to react before burying his face into Tig's ass once more.

Tig was wrenched from the mellowness that blanketed his mind and body when he felt the heat of Flame's warm, wet tongue on his ass. His cheeks were spread and Flame's tongue was in his hole before he even had the chance to protest. He raised his head and looked over his shoulder as the nerve endings around his pucker were overwhelmed with sensation. Anything he had planned to say or planned to do, evaporated with a loud moan as Flame's talented mouth ate his ass.

Flame's fingers gripped and spread the hard muscles of Tig's ass so he could taste more of the man. The tangy, musky, taste of Tig's ass coated his tongue, his lips, and he couldn't get enough. He pushed his face closer and plunged his tongue deeper to taste more.

Pushed up onto his knees, Tig pressed his ass onto Flame's face and he never even realized he had risen off the bed. All he knew was that he wanted to feel more. Top or not, he needed to feel more.

Flame's thumbs joined his tongue in Tig's ass. Both digits moved in tandem opposite his thrusting tongue to cause the most pleasure possible. Spit flowed freely over Tig's hole, down Flame's chin and over his wrists while wet, sloppy noises filled the air along with the almost inhuman sounds that escaped Tig's mouth.

Tig's fists clenched the burgundy comforter that he lay upon and he ground his forehead into the cotton sheets that had been exposed by his movement. Flame's scent wafting from the linens flooded through his synapses while he pushed back to feel more of Flame's torturous mouth.

Flame circled his index fingers around his thumbs and tongue that was currently penetrating Tig's tight hole. Tig's ass practically sucked in Flame's tongue and fingers as he continued to stab, lick, suck, and nibble the tender flesh surrounding his face. Flame's arms created a diamond of counter pressure against Tig's ass and thighs as the man pressed into him. Both men created a perfect balance of strength against one another.

Flame's forearms and biceps bulged taut against Tig's equally taut ass and thighs that pushed back against him. No thought was given to grasping Tig's cock that bobbed freely between his body and the bed. No thought was spared to his own leaking prick as Flame devoured Tig's ass one stab, suck, and nibble at a time.

Tig wanted more. Vaguely, he realized that Flame had fingers in his ass but they were not reaching the itch inside that craved to be scratched. *Want more. Need more.* The need to scratch that deep itch was so unbearable that his sounds of pleasure turned into words to voice his want.

"Oh… Fuck… More."

Tig felt Flame's hum of acknowledgement, the vibration making his cock twitch as he felt the man's fingers enter him. Those fingers were still not enough and even as he thrust back to feel more, they didn't reach the itch that desperately needed to be scratched.

"More." Tig pushed back to emphasize his demand. "Fuck!

CHAPTER 15

FLAME heard Tig's request and his cock throbbed in agreement. "How long?" Flame panted.

It took a moment for Flame's words to register but when they did, Tig replied, "Years." Tig pushed his ass back into Flame and lowered his head back down to the mattress.

So caught up was he in Tig's desperation that he gave no thought to condoms or lube. Flame went from face planting in Tig's ass to kneeling behind the man without further thought. The only thought he spared was to make sure he was lined up before he began to push forward.

"Ugggh," Tig moaned and tensed when Flame entered him. *Shit that hurts!* Tig screamed in his mind while Flame stilled. *And this is why I don't bottom.*

It took every bit of Flame's restraint to still when the crown of his weeping prick breeched Tig. His fingers dug into Tig's hips so hard that he was sure there would be bruises by the time they were finished. He didn't care. It was either bruise Tig's hips or tear up his ass. Flame knew that if he wanted a repeat of this tight channel that was throbbing around the head of his cock, and he did, then he had better make this good for Tig.

Relax, relax, relax, Tig mentally chanted as he panted through the initial burning pain. He knew it would get better but that didn't stop the cock up his ass from hurting like a bitch before then.

As Tig's body became accustomed to Flame's sizable dick, he was grateful for the man's stillness and surprised at his gentleness. Tig rocked his hips slightly, the universal sign to continue, and Flame inched in deeper.

Another hiss escaped Tig's lips and he froze. Flame froze with him and fought the tightening in his balls. He wasn't even fully sheathed in Tig and already about to explode.

"Fuck...you're tight," Flame gasped when Tig took another inch of him.

"Don't...fucking...remind...me," Tig panted through gritted teeth.

The vise grip sensation around Flame's cock had his toes curling, his calves and thighs taut, as he fought off his orgasm. All of the sudden, Tig's body relaxed around him and it felt like Flame's cock was being sucked into the man's tight heat. Fully seated, his balls resting against Tig's, Flame continued to fight his body's impulse to jackhammer into Tig.

"Okay?" Flame panted out, his breath in sync with Tig's. *Please say okay, please.*

Tig nodded and knew Flame would see the bobbing of his head. Still, he replied, "Just fucking move."

Flame did not need to be told twice. He eased back, the friction sending a shiver of pleasure through him, before he plunged back in. Tig grunted at the same time Flame groaned when Tig canted his hips to change the angle. The shift and Flame's next thrust had both men cursing.

"Shit."

"Fuuuck," Tig moaned when Flame finally scratched his itch. "Again," he urged Flame.

Flame was happy to oblige. Shifting his grasp on Tig's sweaty hips, thumbs digging into Tig's lower back while his fingers splayed into the man's perfect 'V', he let loose.

As promised, Flame rode Tig's ass like there was no tomorrow. He was sure he would have finger bruises decorating his body as a result. Hell, he wouldn't be surprised if his thighs ended up bruised as well from the way Flame pounded into him.

Sweat poured off both men, running in rivulets down their skin before being absorbed into the comforter at Tig's knees and forearms. Neither man noticed. Neither man cared. They spiraled higher and higher into ecstasy, both chasing their release.

Tig knew that the slightest touch on his leaking cock would set him off and he was right. He shifted all of his weight onto one forearm and reached down to grasp his cock. Two tugs and he was emptying his balls onto Flame's bedspread.

Flame felt Tig shift his weight but didn't break his brutal rhythm. The shift barely affected his angle of penetration. It was as if Tig's hips, that slammed harshly back into his thrusting, adjusted as well so the man could continue to have his spot nailed.

As much as Flame wanted to reach around and give Tig a hand, he didn't dare let go of the man's waist for fear that Tig's thrusts back into him would force him out of the tight glove that surrounded his cock. Tig's orgasm tightened that glove, like a second skin, and Flame knew he wouldn't survive the sensation. The constricting, pulsing, and clenching of Tig's ass sent

Flame over the edge. He had fought the tingle in his balls and at the base of his spine but that fight became a losing battle. The feelings spread over every inch of his skin and he came. Hard. Flame couldn't help but collapse onto Tig's sweaty back as he fought to catch his breath.

Tig felt Flame fill his ass right before the man's body covered his. He barely got his hand from beneath him when his other arm gave out and he slammed into the mattress with a grunt.

For several moments, both men panted, gasped, to catch their breath, almost in sync at first. By the time they had both come down from their orgasmic high, they were breathing in time with one another.

Flame softened and Tig felt him slide out before the man rolled off of him. That was when Tig felt the wetness between his thighs, seeping out of his ass, which should not have been there.

Fuck! Tig groaned.

Flame lay on his back and heard the sound Tig breathed out loudly. There was something about the way it came out that told Flame it had nothing to do with the man bottoming for the first time in years. The noise didn't register like one of pain either, even though Flame was sure Tig would be feeling him for days. He turned his head toward Tig and was greeted with an intense green gaze.

"What?" Flame had to ask since he could not read what the expression on Tig's face meant.

"No condom." Tig's voice was flat as he watched Flame's face for a reaction while the man's load continued to drip from his ass.

"Shit." Flame scrubbed his face with his hands. He had never, *ever*, had sex without a condom before and it explained why fucking Tig was so intense. "I'm clean."

Shit. Tig was relieved that Flame did not present a threat for HIV. *Fuck. I am always so careful. Son of a bitch!* Flame was still waiting for him to say the same thing. Waiting for Tig to tell him he was clean as well. Too bad he couldn't.

Tig's silence settled on Flame's chest like a ton of bricks. "You're not," Flame groaned and covered his face with his hands again.

It was his own fucking fault. He couldn't even blame Tig for them getting so carried away. *Shit.* Tig even told him that he didn't bottom. It didn't matter that the catcher was at higher risk than the pitcher to contract the disease. There was still a risk he could be infected.

"I'm not positive for HIV," Tig said quietly and waited for Flame's hands to drop before he continued. He met Flame's steel blue eyes and did not look away when he spoke. "I've got Hepatitis B."

Flame blinked as his mind shifted into EMT mode. Hep B could be contracted through semen, vaginal fluids, and blood. Kissing sweat, and sharing utensils or glasses were safe.

Tig held his breath while he waited for Flame's reply and watched the wheels turn in Flame's eyes. He never experienced the vomiting, jaundice, or liver inflammation that accompanied the disease and was screened every six months for liver cancer. But he still had the disease and could transmit it to others.

"I've been vaccinated," Flame reassured Tig when the man's expression did not change. "I can't catch it."

Tig released the breath he was holding but it did not relieve the tightness in his chest. He had always taken precautions and should have with Flame as well. Regardless if the man was vaccinated or not.

Flame could still sense Tig's tension. He rolled onto his side to face the cop and rested his hand of the nape of Tig's neck. Slight pressure pulled Tig's face toward him and he leaned in to place a soft kiss on his lips.

Tig did not return Flame's kiss but the man's persistence for him to open up sent another spark of desire through him. Finally, he yielded.

Flame pulled out of their kiss and gave Tig a wicked grin. Tig wasn't sure what to make of the grin but couldn't help but smile in return.

"At least you won't have to wear a condom next time." Flame waited for his words to sink in.

It took a moment for Flame's words to register and when they did, Tig couldn't help but ask, "Next time, huh?"

"Oh yeah." Flame nudged Tig to roll onto his side so that they faced one another.

"Thought you were a top?"

"Thought *you* were a top," Flame echoed with a smirk.

"I *am* a top."

Flame raised a brow. "Uh huh." Flame would swear Tig blushed but couldn't be sure since his face was mostly in shadow. "I'm versatile but usually top," Flame continued. "But it's been a while since I've bottomed. Actually, more than awhile." *Why did I just admit that?*

Because you want to feel him buried deep in your ass, a small voice in Flame's head replied.

Tig was surprised that Flame was willing to bottom for him and tried not to read too much into why the man was offering up his ass. He could see himself buried deep in Flame's hard body and would fuck him senseless if the guy gave him the chance. Tig couldn't think of anything to say to Flame's admission so he just leaned forward and kissed the man again. The kiss wasn't the frantic, full of want consumption of mouths that preceded the incredible sex they had just had. Instead it was gentle, almost heartfelt, in its softness. Not one that belonged in a hook-up scenario at all. Neither man seemed to notice.

Tig was sleepy, comfortable. Way too comfortable kissing Flame softly and being held in the man's strong arms when music from the living room floated into his sated mind.

I notice that you got it
You notice that I want it
You know that I can take it
To the next level, baby

Tig broke the kiss as Flame tilted his head back and broke the intimacy. Their eyes locked as Britney Spears continued to serenade them from the other room.

I can't take it, take it, take no more
Never felt like, felt like this before

Flame couldn't read Tig's expression when he leaned back but fuck if he didn't feel like singing those lyrics to the man. Instead he spoke, "stay the night."

It wasn't a question but Tig lied to himself and took Flame's words as such. He wanted to. Really wanted to and that is what snapped his mind back to reality. Had Flame not said the words, Tig was sure he would have continued to enjoy lying in Flame's arms until they both settled into a satisfied sleep. But Flame spoke and broke whatever fucked up spell they seemed to be under.

"I need to go." Tig pulled away, rolled onto his back, and tried to ignore the feeling of Flame's calloused hand as it dragged across his hip before coming to rest on the bed between them.

"Why?" Flame asked although he already knew the reason. Still he pressed on. "You don't work on Sunday's."

He's right but I need to go. It's a bad idea to stay here. This was just a hook-up. The thought felt like a lie and Tig pushed thoughts of how he had spent the night before with other hook-ups out of his mind.

"Doesn't matter. This is just a bad idea." Tig covered his eyes with his arm at the same time he sighed.

Flame could sense Tig's reluctance to leave even as the man spoke again.

"This is just a hook-up, Flame Nothing more."

"It could be," Flame whispered but knew that Tig heard him when the man grunted.

"What are we doing, Flame?" Tig repeated his question from earlier. "What do you want from me? Whatever it is, it's a bad idea."

Tig lowered his arm and turned his head. He stared into Flame's stunning blue eyes to make his point and knew it was a mistake. The light from the bedside lamp shone just right and Tig could see the flecks of grey that were weaved into various shades of the blue that made up Flame's eyes.

"Nothing more than you are willing to give." Tig raised a brow at Flame's words. "We've had a good time tonight. You can't say we didn't. If you just want to be fuck buddies," Flame paused and almost got lost in Tig's

beautiful green eyes. They were so close that he swore
there were flecks of gold and blue in their depths. "I'll
take that. But I want to see you again."

"Why? We don't even like each other."

"Don't we?" Flame countered. "You can say you
still hate me, Tig, but I won't believe you." Flame's tone
was serious. "And I sure as hell don't hate you anymore."

Tig knew that Flame spoke the truth. He didn't
hate the man who lay only inches from him and the
realization scared the shit out of him. Still, he didn't
know what his onetime rival wanted from him. If it was
more than just sex, Tig wasn't sure he was interested.

Liar. Tig knew it was a lie he told himself, he
didn't need that little voice in his head to tell him. *I need
to go,* Tig reminded himself as Flame's words enticed
him to stay.

With a resolve he did not feel, Tig voiced his
thought. "I need to go."

"Alright." Flame's tone sounded disappointed but
Tig tried to ignore it. He failed when Flame spoke again.
"Shower is through there," Flame nodded in the direction
of his bathroom. "If you want to clean up before you go."

Tig ignored Flame's look that said the man knew
he was fleeing the scene of whatever was happening
between them.

You are, that small voice reminded him. *Shut up!*
Tig replied to the nagging voice.

"Thanks."

Flame gave Tig a nod before the cop rolled
gracefully out of his bed and made his way to the
bathroom. Seconds later, he heard his shower turn on and
the distinctive sound in the change of falling water that
indicated someone was under the spray.

He rolled onto his back and stared at the ceiling while the scent of Tig's spunk surrounded him. Flame's hand dropped to the wet spot on his bed where Tig had come and he ran his fingers through the silky puddle that had yet to be absorbed into the comforter. He raised his hand and brought his cum covered fingers to his lips. Tig's scent was more sweet than pungent and when he licked his fingers, it was just as sweet.

It didn't concern him that Tig had Hep B but he was curious how the cop had contracted the virus. It was likely sex related since cops did usually have the same contagious disease hazards as EMT firefighters. Still, he would ask if the time ever became right to do so.

Tig stood under the hot spray of Flame's shower and wondered what the fuck he was doing. This was supposed to be a hook-up and it was but Tig had the nagging feeling that it was more.

It has to be because I bottomed after so many years of topping. That had to be the reason his feelings were so out of whack after having sex with someone. *Not just someone. Thomas Flame. The man you always hated. The man you let fuck you up the ass and has you craving more.*

Tig couldn't stop the groan that escaped his lips. He couldn't stop his ass from clenching at the memory or his dick from twitching back to life either. Tig was almost, *almost,* pissed off at his body's reaction and in retaliation; he turned the shower knob to blast himself with cold water.

Flame heard his shower shut off and sat on his bed, phone in hand, while he waited for Tig to emerge from his bathroom. He had already picked up Tig's clothes and laid them on the bed. He only bothered to throw on a pair of sweats out of consideration for Tig's desire to leave.

Tig exited Flame's bathroom with a towel wrapped around his waist. He only paused for a moment in surprise at seeing Flame dressed in Tampa Fire Rescue sweat pants. Flame gave him a smile that almost looked shy and that surprised him even more.

The silence between them became thick as Tig dressed. There was really nothing further for them to say. Each man had already made their wants known and all that was left for them to do was part ways like any other hook-up encounter required.

Once Tig was redressed, Flame followed the cop to his front door. He wanted to pull Tig into his arms again. Hold him. Kiss him goodnight. But Flame knew that wasn't how hook-ups worked.

Tig opened Flame's door and stepped outside. He was reminding himself, again, that this was just a hook-up. This was what he did when he left a satisfying fuck. He walked away. He didn't exchange numbers. Didn't make promises to see them again. He just walked away. Satisfied.

So, why don't I feel satisfied? Tig pushed the thought away at the same time Flame's voice reached him.

"I was serious about next time," Flame quietly called out and smiled when Tig's step faltered.

Tig didn't reply. He just climbed into his Camaro and took in Flame's sexy assed body one more time as the man stood in the doorway to his apartment. He put his car in reverse and turned on his radio before dropping the car in drive. He gave Flame one last look and pulled away to take his ass home where he belonged.

CHAPTER 16

SUPPRESSING a groan and a wince, Tig sat down at his desk on Monday morning. His ass had recuperated, for the most part, but between the flag football game and Flame's pounding, Tig's body was sore as fuck.

"You said that asshat didn't hurt you." Pat gave him a stare that was equal parts concern and pissed off.

Only in all the right ways.

"Just a little stiff still," *thinking of Flame will do that to me.* "and haven't been sleeping well." Pat grunted as Tig opened his email. "Lab results are in on that shit Kendry brought us last week."

"Yeah? They figure out why it's pink?"

"Yeah," Tig snorted a chuckle. "You're not gonna believe this shit. 'Dumbo' is a combination of meth, coke, vitamin B,"

"Typical cut if they aren't using baking powder or aspirin," Pat interrupted.

"And...wait for it," Tig continued and paused dramatically. "Allura Red AC, E129."

"What the hell is that?"

"Red food coloring!" Tig burst out laughing at the look of shock on Pat's face.

"So let me get this straight," Pat frowned. "Some asshole is selling speed balls in powder form and dying it pink with red food coloring?"

"Un huh. Seems that way."

"What the hell for?"

"Marketing?" Tig guessed. "Who the hell knows?"

"If this isn't Cortez trying to throw us off then you know what this means." Pat continued to frown.

"New kid on the block."

"Yeah." Pat's frown turned thoughtful before he picked up his phone and dialed. "Allister," Pat began to talk to the Sergeant in charge of the undercovers in their drug unit.

Tig was already composing a short note and forwarding the lab report to Allister. If anyone could find out if this new shit was tied to Cortez, then it was Allister's team. Tig had just hit send when Pat finished the call.

"He's gonna get with Kendry and put one of his undercovers out there with the John squad to start making buys."

"Smart plan."

"Detectives," Tig and Pat turned toward the rough voice that called out to them.

"Hey Newton. What's up?" Pat greeted the stout woman.

Homicide Detective Jolene Newton was short and stocky. Built like a brick shit house which was impressive for her age. Nineteen years on the force and she had no plans to retire anytime soon.

"We've got a John Doe that looks drug related and you asked to be notified if any came across our desk."

Tig and Pat shared a look as they stood in unison from their desks. "Gullis," both men said at the same time.

"He's in morgue three," Newton informed them. "If you get an ID, shoot me an email and I'll send you the case file we started on him."

"Will do," Pat confirmed.

"Thanks," Tig gave their fellow detective a smile.

"Let's see if it's our boy." Pat slapped Tig on the shoulder after they put on their suit jackets.

"If it is, at least we will know he didn't bolt," Tig commented and Pat grunted his agreement as they left the station.

Flame lay on the weight bench next to the engine and concentrated on his leg curls. He was still sore from his bedroom acrobatics with Tig. It had been a long, long, time since he had been able to totally let go in the bedroom. Every movement reminded him of his hook-up with the man on Saturday. Every twinge of his sore muscles brought to mind the image of being buried balls deep in the cop's hard as fuck body. His goal to relieve his soreness by working out wasn't helping because it allowed his mind to wander. He had already jerked off twice while on duty and, still, he was growing hard again,

The music in the bay wasn't helping either. Several songs played on the radio that reminded Flame of the first time Tig came to his apartment. The radio disguised the sound of Brostowski's approach so when the man spoke, Flame startled.

"You're working out kinda hard in this heat."

Flame had no idea how long his best friend had been watching him. He sat up, dropped his towel over his groin, and waited for John to bust his balls over his hard on. It would have been impossible to miss while he had been lying on his back. The PT shorts provided by the Tampa Fire Rescue weren't made to conceal a soft prick let alone a raging boner.

Flame swiped his forearm across his brow to wipe away the sweat before he looked at his friend. He was about to speak when the words froze in his throat. John wasn't looking at his face. Instead, his gaze rested on the towel that covered Flame's lap.

What the hell?

All shift, Flame had caught his best friend staring at him and those looks were beginning to make him uneasy. Especially since they brought to mind the strange, almost flirty, touch after the flag football game on Saturday.

Flame swung his leg over the bench, effectively turning his back to John, before he used the towel to dry his sweaty face.

"Just working out some kinks from Saturday." Flame willed his thoughts of how he received those kinks from his mind and gave his cock a painful squeeze to help his hard on disappear quicker.

"Didn't see you at the fireworks," Brostowski commented. "Didn't see you at Guns & Hoses either."

Flame knew his friend was fishing for information but he wasn't going to get any. "Game took more out of me than I thought." Flame stood, finally confident that his dick had settled down. "Took a nap and slept straight through."

"I expected to see you."

What the fuck is up with him?

"Sorry man. I just crashed." Flame hated lying to his best friend but there was no way in hell that he was going to tell him why he missed all the 4th of July festivities.

"So you just crashed?"

Flame heard the suspicion in his friend's voice but thankfully the tones of another call flooded the bay and saved Flame from lying again. However, as he donned his bunker gear, he couldn't help but wonder what the hell Brostowski's problem was and why it felt like his friend was giving him the third degree about blowing off the fireworks at Guns & Hoses.

Tig was frustrated when he walked into Guns & Hoses on Wednesday night. It was Pat's anniversary so Tig was flying solo for his after work drink. Which was fine by him because when he felt like this, he was shit company.

The body in the morgue on Monday had indeed been their CI Gullis and there was no doubt that he had not only been murdered, but tortured first. Homicide turned the file over to them since it was related to their case because there was really no sense in wasting Homicide's man hours on the CI's murder. They all knew who was responsible for the death regardless of who actually pushed the plunger on the syringe full of acid into the man's vein.

"Bud Light and a shot of Jameson," Tig ordered as he plopped his ass on the barstool he favored. It gave him the perfect view of the bar.

"Rough week Tig?" Shelley asked as she set his drinks down.

"Yeah." Tig took his shot then took a sip of his beer to chase it down.

"Hope it gets better for you." Shelley gave him a sympathetic smile and once more Tig was reminded why he loved this bar.

They had all worked the streets and understood that talking about the job wouldn't change shit and was the last thing any of them wanted to do when they were having a shit week.

Tig hated being in this fucked up mood. There was only one cure and it wouldn't be booze. He needed to fight or fuck. Tig couldn't help smirking at the thought. Usually, he'd hit one of his bars for a hook-up or hope that Flame made an appearance for a fight. Now, he could get either or both from the firefighter if he only thought to get the fucker's number.

Grindr, idiot.

Tig opened the app, which he never accessed while sitting in this bar, and scrolled to Flame's profile. Flame wasn't on and hadn't been for over a week. Somewhere in the back of his mind, Tig realized the man's last time on Grindr was when they hooked-up in Bradley's. Just thinking about Flame and his comment about being 'serious about next time,' had Tig cursing himself again for not getting the man's number.

Fuck!

"Another," Tig called out to Shelley and pushed the rocks glass toward the edge of the bar.

Flame pulled his truck into the parking lot of Guns & Hoses and grinned when he spotted the royal blue, '68 Camaro parked out front. All week he had wanted to text Tig but between work and Brostowski's weird, hovering, behavior he'd never gotten around to it. Thinking about his best friend made him glance in his rear view mirror. The man in question was right behind him as they pulled into the parking lot. If he was going to shoot off a text to Tig, now was the time to do it.

Come over tonight? I still want our next time. I know you do too ;)

Flame hit send and caught movement in his side mirror. Before Brostowski reached his driver's side door, Flame opened it and climbed out. His best friend gave him another one of those strange looks he had been receiving all week, the same strange looks that were seriously unnerving him.

"I need a beer," Flame said and turned away to enter the bar.

Tig had just swallowed his second shot when his phone dinged. He swiped his screen and hit his message icon. Flame's name appeared. He had no idea how the man got his number but he wasn't complaining. It was as if just thinking of the man miraculously summoned the text message. A tap of his thumb opened the text.

Come over tonight? I still want out next time. I know you do too ;)

Flame's timing couldn't have been better for Tig's mood. *Fuck it. I do want a next time.* All the trepidation Tig had felt when Flame had uttered the suggestion after their last hook-up was gone. He gave no thought about how fucking Flame was a bad idea. Nope. No thought at all. The only thoughts that flooded his mind were those of fucking Flame just as hard, if not harder, than the man had fucked him.

Yes. Tig replied and hit send before adding a second message. *Meet you at your place in twenty?*

Tig had just hit send again when the bar door opened and the man he wanted to fuck until they were both too numb to move walked in. Followed by his best friend.

Fuck.

Flame's phone vibrated on his hip once, twice, as he stepped into the bar. His gaze immediately scanned the bar and found Tig's. The smirk on the man's face made his cock take notice. That smirk turned to a frown when Tig's eyes caught sight of Brostowski and he shifted his gaze back to his beer. Flame's fingers itched to check Tig's reply but he knew that if he checked his phone, Brostowski would start badgering him about it. Flame hated texting and Brostowski knew it.

"Gotta piss. Get me a beer." Flame didn't wait for John's reply before he bee-lined toward the men's room.

Flame stepped into the stall, phone already in hand. He didn't want to chance his best friend's questions if Brostowski decided he had to take a leak as well. Tig's reply surprised him. He didn't expect the man to be so ready for their next time. Flame cursed himself for not texting Tig before agreeing to hang out with John tonight.

Need at least an hour here. :(Flame sent and after a second added, *then I am all yours ;)*

Flame waited impatiently for Tig's reply, hoping he would get one before he would need an excuse why it took him so long to piss.

An hour and your ass is mine. Tig's reply flashed across his screen and made Flame's asshole twitch.

All yours if you can handle it. Flame sent back teasingly and knew he couldn't wait any longer for another reply. He had just left the bathroom when his phone vibrated again.

Tig grinned at Flame's reply. Oh, he could handle it and would. *I can handle it and will. The question is, can you?*

Tig glanced at the table where Flame and his best friend sat. Flame's hand reached for his phone but he stopped himself. The movement caused Tig to smirk and type again.

Humm… no reply? Nervous about how my hard cock is going to tear up your ass?

Flame felt his phone vibrate again and shot a quick glance at Tig. The fucker was smug and it was clear the man realized he wasn't about to check his phone in front of John. Before he looked away, Tig was typing again.

I am going to own your ass… on your leather couch, your kitchen table, counters, shower… Everywhere in your apartment so that no matter where you look, where you are in your apartment, you will feel my cock buried so deep that your tonsils ache.

Tig wasn't sure what had come over him to send such text messages to Flame. He wasn't a sexting kind of guy. It wasn't the Jameson. Maybe it was, knowing that Flame wouldn't be able to read the messages until he ducked into the restroom again or until he got into his truck to leave.

You're gonna beg me to get off while I plow into your tight as fuck ass. Cause I know you're tight, aren't you Flame. And it's going to be my thick cock that loosens up your hole. Tig hit send and waited until he saw Flame react to the vibration on his hip before he typed his next text. *I've got my cuffs, Flame, and I am gonna use them. They turn you on, stroke your cop kink, don't they? You won't be able to touch your big cock to get off. Won't be able to cum until I let you and I know that's what you want. Isn't it?*

Tig took another swig of his beer and chuckled to himself. He was making himself hard as fuck over the smut he was feeding Flame through the text messages. But catching Flame fidgeting to resist checking his phone in front of his co-worker was so worth it.

No need to answer that. I already know what you want... need. And you will get it.

Tig sent the message and rose to play the juke box. He was enjoying teasing Flame way more than he should and it had improved his mood considerably. He searched through the songs and made his choices. Every one of which, except the first, would spark the memory of their hook-up.

Flame's phone vibrated again right before Tig passed behind him on his way to the juke box.

Oh, oh, oh, oh, oh, oh-oh-e-oh-oh-oh
I'll get him hot, show him what I've got

Oh, oh, oh, oh, oh, oh-oh-e-oh-oh-oh,
I'll get him hot, show him what I've got

Flame had to suppress a groan when Lady Gaga belted out through the bar. *That fucker.*

I wanna roll with him a hard pair we will be

A little gambling is fun when you're with me (I love it)

Russian Roulette is not the same without a gun

And baby when its love, if it's not rough it isn't fun, fun

Flame had no doubt it was going to be rough with Tig and he couldn't wait.

"You gonna answer that?" Brostowski's voice pulled Flame back from the images of Tig fucking him that started to flood him mind.

"It's not important." Flame focused on his friend and tried to be dismissive about the repeated noises that were drifting up to them from his hip.

"You sure?" John raised an inquiring brow. "Because your phone never blows up, dude."

Flame tried to tell himself that his friend's words and the look he was receiving were not those of suspicion, but they were and he knew it. His phone vibrated again and he ignored what he knew was another text message from Tig.

"It's just a hook-up probably wanting a repeat," Flame said dismissively as he could. The look on his best friend's face made him realize his poor choice of words.

"Oh yeah? Sexting? Share, share." John reached for Flame's phone and Flame barely prevented his friend from grabbing it from the clip on his hip.

"Chill man," Flame growled and knocked John's hand away.

There was no way in hell that Flame was even going to look at whatever messages Tig was sending him, let alone let his best friend see them. He had put Tig in his phone under just 'T' when the man was in his shower but he couldn't risk showing John whatever Tig was sending him. For all he knew, the cop was sending him pix of his pierced cock and there was no way he could explain those to his best friend without outing himself.

"If *she* is hot, don't let me keep you from getting some."

There was no mistaking Brostowski's emphasis on the word 'she' and Flame narrowed his gaze on his best friend. There was no way, absolutely no fucking way that John could know he was gay but the man's behavior over the last few days caused doubt to creep into Flame's mind.

Maybe I should just tell him. He doesn't seem pissed if he already knows.

No sooner did the thought cross Flame's mind then he dismissed it. The chance of losing his best friend and the potential fall out at work just wasn't worth stepping out of the closet.

"You're not." Flame took the last drink of his beer and ordered another to prove his point.

His phone vibrated on his hip again right before he caught movement out of the corner of his eye. Tig was heading to the restroom and Flame's body wanted to follow.

No. He'll be at my house when I get there. Flame tried to convince himself but in reality, for all he knew, the cop could be pissed because he had ignored the man's texts. *Fuck.*

Tig didn't spare him a glance as he left Guns & Hoses and Flame forced himself to wait another ten minutes before he excused himself to piss again. He didn't read through Tig's texts when he stepped into the restroom. He could do that once he was in his truck.

Leaving in 15. Flame sent to Tig and hoped that the cop was already enroute to his apartment.

Chapter 17

THE drive across Gandy Bridge was practically traffic free when Tig's phone finally dinged to inform him of a text message. He rarely checked his phone while driving but knowing the message was likely from Flame, he didn't resist. The message was short and to the point. It told him two things: One, Flame hadn't taken any time to read the smut he had teased the man with and two; he still wanted Tig to meet him at his place.

It only took Tig twenty minutes to get to Flame's apartment and his phone went off again as he pulled into the parking spot.

Promises, promises. Tig smirked and chuckled at Flame's reply to his list of smutty activities that he had teased the man with.

Not a promise, a guarantee. Tig waited for Flame to reply but didn't really expect the man to if he was driving.

When he saw the lights of Flame's truck pull into the apartment complex parking lot, Tig stepped out of his car.

Flame backed his truck into his normal spot but never took his eyes off the cop who blew up his phone with enticingly filthy text messages. He wasted no time hopping out of the cab and making his way toward where Tig leaned against the side of his Camaro. A click on his key fob over his shoulder locked his truck a moment before he stepped in front of Tig.

Tig watched Flame approach. Determination screamed from the man as he closed the distance between them. Tig couldn't stop the smug smile that he knew was on his face when he noticed Flame's arousal. He didn't stop Flame either when the man almost violently pressed against him and attacked his mouth.

Like every kiss they had ever shared, this one was harsh, hungry, rough, and messy. In mirror fashion, each man grasped the other at the nape of the neck while their hands clawed at the barrier of clothing that prevented them from feeling bare skin. No thought was given, and neither man cared, that they were molesting one another in the parking lot of the apartment complex.

Moans and groans accompanied growls, that did not even sound like they could come from a human throat, filled the air around them. They couldn't get close enough as their hips rubbed together and it was only when Tig felt Flame's hand press between their flushed body's to get to his belt, that he pulled the man's hair back, hard, to break the kiss.

"Inside. Now." Tig panted and Flame blinked while fighting to catch his breath.

Flame forced himself to step back and his hand instantly sought out Tig's that was clutching his waist. Thankfully, his keys were still in the hand he had tangled into Tig's hair. His cock was so hard that he was sure there would be no way in hell he would be able to retrieve them if they were in his pocket. He couldn't get Tig into his apartment fast enough, couldn't get the man naked to feel skin on skin, feel the cop buried deep inside of him, before he exploded in his jeans.

Flame practically broke down his door, like a S.W.A.T. team raid, as he dragged Tig over the threshold.

Tig wasn't complaining since he was just as desperate for the privacy they needed to resume devouring one another. However, his desperation did not consume him to the point of forgetting the promises he made to Flame in his text messages. He barely had the chance to kick Flame's door closed behind them before the man was on him again.

Hands tore at clothing. Tig was pushing up Flame's tee shirt; Flame clawing at Tig's dress shirt until the buttons popped and flew in every direction.

"Off." Tig panted into their frantic kiss.

Flame's shirt hadn't even hit the floor before the man's hands were on him again. But it was in that millisecond of distraction that Tig pulled his handcuffs from the back of his waist where they were shoved into his belt. The moment that Flame's hand grasped his belt, Tig slapped one of the metal bracelets on his wrist. Flame never noticed. Tig waited impatiently as the fevered kiss continued until Flame managed to unbuckle his belt and open his pants. The moment Tig felt Flame's calloused hand wrap around his hard as fuck cock, he acted.

Flame's world tilted. His mouth was devouring Tig's and his hands finally reached his goal inside the man's pants when he suddenly lost contact with both. He blinked and it took his lust fogged mind a moment to realize he was now pressed roughly against the wall next to his front door. Chest to wall. It took another moment for him to realize that Tig had cuffed his hands behind his back and he couldn't stop the groan that escaped his throat. He couldn't stop the moan that followed or his ass from pushing back when he felt Tig's body pressing into him before the cop kicked his feet wide to make him spread his legs.

Tig had never been turned on by placing a suspect in the arrest position. That might change after tonight. Even if he wasn't already rock hard from Flame's hunger, he would be now by the noises the man made from this simulated arrest. Tig felt Flame jut his ass back and rub against the thigh he placed between Flame's legs for leverage to keep the firefighter pinned against the wall. He took a minute to catch his breath, settle his racing heart, and will his throbbing cock not to trigger in his slacks like some horny teenager.

Tig wasn't sure what it was about Flame that put him on the edge of orgasm so quickly but it was something. A good or bad something, he wasn't sure but fuck if he didn't like it all the same.

"You read all my texts, Flame?' Tig breathed hotly into Flame's ear.

"Yeah," Flame replied with panted breath.

"I'm gonna do everything. Everything I put in those texts," Tig whispered and pressed into Flame. "And you're not going to cum until I let you."

Another wonderful noise escaped Flame. "Quit fucking teasing me," Flame groaned and bucked against Tig. The movement forced his cuffed hands closer to Tig's exposed cock. "Fuck me already."

Tig's cock twitched when Flame's hands brushed against him, or maybe it was from the almost begging tone of Flame's request, and he had to repress his own moan.

"Oh, I'm gonna fuck you."

Flame had no time to comment before he was pulled away from the wall, moved, and bent crudely over the back of his couch. Tig's hands made quick work of his jeans and the cool air in his apartment was caressing his ass before he could even appreciate his aching cock being freed.

Tig shoved one hand into his pocket to retrieve the lube packet he had the forethought to grab from his glove box while his other hand maintained steady pressure on the center of Flame's back. He stuck the packet of lube between his teeth and tore it open. Tig dribbled some on his cock and the rest in the crease of Flame's ass before he dropped the silver Lifestyles foil to the floor. He gave his cock a few strokes to spread the lube and gather some on his fingers before he ran his dick along Flame's crack, between his cheeks. The urge to just plow into Flame was almost unbearable but Tig held back. He wanted rough but didn't want to *actually* hurt Flame. He forced his fingers to trace along the length of his cock that was nudging Flame's balls so that he could loosen the tight hole he was about to tear into.

"Shit," Flame exclaimed when Tig inserted his finger.

Flame pushed back into Tig's touch hard enough to stagger the man and cause him to grasp the cuffs on Flame's wrists tightly.

"Just fuck me already!" Flame pushed back for emphasis causing Tig's finger to sink deeper.

"Bossy bottom." Tig pulled his finger free and moved his hips back just enough to slide his cock along Flame's taint.

Flame's moan of pleasure turned into a hiss of pain when Tig breeched him. He pushed back into the burn that was quickly morphing into pleasure. Between his awkward backward move due to being handcuffed and Tig's steady push forward, sensations assaulted Flame. He loved that Tig didn't pause, didn't stop to let him adjust to the thick penetration that was already causing his balls to draw up tight.

Not enough lube, Tig vaguely thought as he continued to grasp Flame's cuffed wrists with one hand and his bare hip with the other. But that thought and the raw friction on his cock did not stop him from pushing forward until he bottomed out in Flame's ass. The heat, the tightness that surrounded him was excruciatingly pleasurable. If Tig had any thought that Flame had lied about bottoming, it was gone now. The man was just too tight, fucking virgin tight, and he knew, just knew that this is what his ass must have felt like to Flame.

"Fuuuuuck," Flame uttered on an exhaled breath when he felt Tig's balls rest against his own. The cop was big. Felt fucking huge. At least as big as Flame and he could feel how wide he was stretched. He also felt how deeply Tig was buried in his gut.

"Yep."

Flame heard Tig grunt just before the heat of Tig's balls left his own. He had no time to brace for the impact of Tig's thrust. Not that he could with his hands cuffed behind his back and his body thrown over the back of his couch. All Flame could do was tense his legs, press his thighs into the leather couch, and rise up onto his toes to meet Tig's assault on his ass. And an assault it was.

Tig slammed into Flame brutally. He ignored the pain along his cock from the lack of enough lube as he plowed repeatedly into the tight hole under him. His hands moved to Flame's hips to dig in like Flame had done to him days ago while his gaze locked onto where they were connected. Every time his pale cock thrust into the darkened flesh around Flame's asshole then pulled back, surrounded by fresh pink skin, Tig knew he would never get enough of the sight. Had his body, his mind, not been so consumed with pleasure, the fleeting thought caused by the sight may have concerned him. As it was, he had no concerns at all except for fucking Flame senseless.

Flame's cock was trapped, pointing toward the floor behind his couch, and the minimal friction to its head was not enough to do shit for him but drive him insane. A sharp pull on his hips did nothing to help his throbbing cock gain the stimulation he desperately wanted. Needed. It did, however, cause Tig's cock to nail his prostate in the most deliciously painful way.

"Fuck...Fuck...Fuck..." Flame chanted on harsh exhales almost in time with every thrust as Tig nailed his spot.

The pressure was building. Ratcheting Flame higher but without the extra stimulation to his aching, throbbing, prick, there was no way in hell he was going to get off. He had a feeling that Tig fucking knew it too.

Sweat drenched Tig. It soaked into his ruined dress shirt and into his suit jacket. Into his slacks from his thighs and Flame's when they met harshly with every thrust but Tig didn't care. He was past the brink, he was there. Tig pushed deep into Flame the moment he felt the first wave of cum erupt from his cock. No jerky hip movements to stimulate his orgasm along. He didn't need them while he pushed his groin flush with the hard as steel muscles of Flame's ass. Head tilted back, eyes closed, and with a loud moan, Tig rode out every twitch of his cock while he poured himself into Flame.

Another rough slam hit Flame's body and stopped before he felt Tig's release. The cock pulsing deep within him, flooding his gut with warmth sent a shudder through

Flame. His own prick begged for the touch that would send him over the edge but before he could voice, fuck... beg, his request, Tig yanked him up by his shoulders. Flame couldn't stop the hiss that flew from his lips when Tig slipped out of him with no finesse. He couldn't stop Tig's manhandling either, when he was spun around and pushed unceremoniously to his knees behind his couch.

Fuck, I have missed this. There was just something about being with a man who could toss him around as if he wasn't six foot two that did it for him.

Tig only allowed himself a moment to enjoy Flame's tightness after he came before he pulled his still semi-hard cock out of the man's hole. He glanced at Flame's cock as it jutted out from his jeans when he pushed the man down onto his knees. The desire to wrap his lips around that hard shaft was strong but he wasn't done with the man's ass yet.

Flame didn't speak when he looked up into Tig's eyes. He knew his hunger, his desperation, was clear in his gaze as he watched Tig get undressed.

His shirts never survive our encounters. The thought flittered across Flame's mind and made him grin.

Tig saw Flame's grin and knew it had nothing to do with the fucking he had just received. He also knew that if the man was still grinning after that pounding then he was just going to have to fuck him harder to wipe that grin right off his face.

"You want to cum?"

Flame's grin turned into a smirk when he answered. "For a Detective, you ask stupid questions."

Flame only had a brief chance to catch Tig's raised eyebrow before the cop grabbed him crudely by the back of his head. There was no chance to resist and barely a chance to take a breath before Tig stuck his cum covered cock into his mouth.

"Smartass." Tig fisted Flame's hair and thrust harshly between Flame's lips. "Guess you won't be cumming for a while if fucking your tight ass won't get you there."

Flame groaned around Tig's cock at the man's words. All it would take is a touch to send him over the edge into bliss but Tig denying him that satisfaction was its own kind of bliss.

"You're not going to cum until I've fucked you on every surface in the place." Tig's words were so soft they were almost a whisper. "Even if you beg," Tig continued speaking as he leisurely plunged into Flame's mouth.

There was no rush to cum again. No frantic need to get off like the last time Flame's lips were wrapped around his cock. Right now, Tig was just enjoying Flame's oral talents that were keeping him hard.

"You're not cumming until I've fucked your tight ass all over this apartment."

Flame moaned. He couldn't help it. He was just too turned on not to make noise and when Tig pulled out of his mouth and pulled him to his feet, he didn't resist. Tig manhandled him again, making him whimper, toward the kitchen table.

"You're a fucking tease, Tigger." Flame complained halfheartedly.

"If I was a tease," Tig pushed Flame's bare chest flat over the fake wood of the kitchen table. "I wouldn't let..." Tig thrust into Flame again and pulled out. "You..." Thrust, in then out. "Cum..." Thrust, in then out. "At..." Thrust, in then out. "All."

Every time Tig thrust, regardless of the leg lock Flame used to counter the motion, regardless of how he pushed his ass back to meet each assault, the kitchen table moved closer to the wall. Tig fucked him over his kitchen table just as roughly as he fucked him over his couch. Flame loved every fucking minute of it. Words of 'more' and 'harder' came on panted breaths until he felt Tig empty himself in his ass again.

"Holy shit." Flame rested his sweaty face against the smooth surface of his kitchen table.

Both of them were panting hard and Flame was sure that his cock was about to have an aneurysm. It hurt so bad that he wasn't above begging for relief. He was just about to do so when Tig forced him to stand on his wobbly legs. It wasn't until he felt Tig's hands running down his shoulders that he realized his arms were also aching.

"I'm not done with you yet," Tig growled in Flame's ear even though he knew it was going to take him some time before he could cum again. His cock was still semi-hard and he knew that as long as he didn't allow himself to go totally limp, that he'd be able to fuck Flame again. Whether he would get off again was doubtful but that didn't mean he couldn't fuck.

"I'm gonna stroke out," Flame mumbled as he leaned back into Tig's sweaty chest. The soft sound of the handcuffs being released mingled with their panting breaths. "If I don't cum soon," Flame finished his sentence while his aching arms were released. "Like right now."

Flame turned around and Tig pulled his hips back from Flame's erection. He grabbed Tig's hand but his attempt to place it on his almost purple cock was thwarted when Tig pressed his body forward. Chest to bare chest, cock to bare cock, their hands were trapped between them. When they touched, Tig claimed his mouth in another hungry kiss.

Flame's body took control as Tig took control of his mouth. He thrust against their sweaty skin to get the extra friction his cock needed to cum but no sooner did the contact occur, it was over.

"You so fucking suck," Flame grumbled when Tig stepped out of his reach.

"I do." Tig winked and Flame couldn't stop his heart from fluttering at seeing this new playful side of Tigger Flint. "And, if you're lucky, I will."

Flame groaned again at the thought of Tig's kiss swollen lips wrapped around his throbbing cock.

"Shower. Now." Tig ordered when Flame groaned. When the man didn't move, he held up the cuffs he had just removed. "Do I need to use these again?"

Tig's threat was an empty one and they both knew it. Flame enjoyed being handcuffed just as much as Tig enjoyed cuffing him.

Instead of replying, Flame pushed away from his kitchen table on wobbly legs and led the way to his bathroom. Tig fucked him again in the shower but still didn't touch his cock that was aching for the man's hand. Flame was sure Tig hadn't cum again while they fucked under the warm spray and he was strangely relieved. He wanted them to cum together. Preferably, in his bed. And that is just what happened when Tig led them to Flame's bed after their shower.

CHAPTER 18

THE thought of leaving Flame's bed briefly entered Tig's mind but he dismissed it quickly. His body was just too satiated to move. Tig was comfortably numb. So relaxed, that he didn't even realize his hand had settled on Flame's hip.

Flame lay on his back next to Tig. The sheets on his bed were soaked with sweat from both of them. A puddle of cum as it leaked from his very sore ass joined the mess. He knew he should get them up and change the sheets but was just too relaxed to bother. Plus, he had a feeling that the minute he said something, Tig would bolt again and he was enjoying listening to the man's soft breathing next to him. Enjoying it too much, if he were truly honest, so he couldn't be bothered to care about his sheets.

Tig's breathing evened out and Flame knew the cop had drifted off to sleep. The hand resting on his hip felt good, felt right, and it was that touch that made Flame realize he was in trouble. This was only supposed to be a hook-up, nothing more, and he was sure that was how Tig was going to view the last few hours of fucking.

He turned his head to look at the man who was stirring up unrealistic emotions. Tig had strong features and the slight cleft in his chin made Flame want to lick, suck, and nibble on it again. He squashed the idea. His eyes roamed down Tig's neck to his shoulder. Flame studied the dark black ink that started at Tig's collarbone and ran over his bicep before ending mid-forearm. The tattoo was more random Goth than tribal like his own but it seemed to fit the man.

Flame wanted to roll onto his side so he could do a closer study of Tig's body but he feared waking him. He wanted to study the Prince Albert which had made him see stars, with his hands. He already knew what the metal felt like on his tongue, down his throat, in his ass, and even as satiated and sore as he was, he wanted to feel it again.

Shit! Flame mentally cursed because he knew feeling Tig's cock again wasn't all he wanted from the cop. Flame forced himself to stop looking at Tig, stop thinking about what the man was making him feel, and closed his eyes.

His nap did not last long when he was awakened by Tig. Tig had rolled onto his side, facing Flame, and threw an arm across Flame's waist. Flame wasn't used to having another man sleep in his bed and the sudden intimate touch caused Flame's eyes to pop open and stare at Tig.

Tig was still asleep but now that the man was lying on his side, Flame could study his PA. As he looked at the hooped metal that pierced through Tig's piss slit, it was as if the man felt his scrutiny. Tig's cock grew hard as he watched and he resisted the temptation to reach out and stroke him.

"You watching me sleep?" Tig's voice was graveled from sleep. "Thought I fucked you enough to crash."

"I'm watching something." Flame smiled as he lifted his gaze to Tig's and reached out to wrap his hand around the man's hardening length.

"You're insatiable." Tig grinned and it made Flame's heart flutter again.

Only with you, Flame kept the thought to himself.

Instead, he pushed Tig onto his back and rolled on top of him. His own cock was hard again and he took them both into his hand while bracing his weight on his forearm next to Tig's head.

"Yeah. I am," Flame whispered against Tig's lips at the same time Tig groaned from his touch.

Tig enjoyed Flame's lazy kiss and stroking of their cocks together. Both were relaxed, gentle, comfortable, with no rush to get off. Flame's weight on top of him felt good. Too good, and he couldn't remember the last time he had enjoyed such a sensual pleasure of a man lying on top of him. Not that he was really trying to. The tender, persistent tug of Flame's hand moving over their silky skin together started the slow climb toward their mutual orgasm. The pressure built and the soft butterfly kisses they shared added to their pleasure until they both tumbled over the edge into bliss.

"Fuck," Tig's soft curse caressed Flame's lips.

"Yeah," Flame agreed with a whisper as he laid his head against the side of Tig's neck. He never wanted to move and he knew it wasn't because of the orgasm he had just had.

I am so screwed, Flame almost muttered aloud.

"What?" Tig asked against the side of Flame's head.

Fuck, he almost heard me! Flame lifted his head and gave Tig a shy grin. "Nothing."

Tig's hands caressed Flame's back, hips, and ass in languid circles until he became aware of his actions and stilled them. He gazed up into Flame's eyes and almost lost himself in their blue depths. What he saw in Flame's return gaze made his stomach flip-flop. That unexpected feeling was followed by one of panic.

Flame felt the change in Tig's body even though Tig remained still beneath him. The look he was enjoying, as Tig returned his steady gaze, shifted and Flame knew that whatever brief connection they had felt was gone.

"What?" It was Flame's turn to ask and he hoped Tig would explain why his behavior had changed.

"What time is it?" Tig asked to avoid answering Flame.

Flame glanced at his night table before replying, "5:40."

"You working today?"

Flame was caught off guard by Tig's question. He was sure the man was going to use work as an excuse to bolt from the intimate moment they found themselves sharing even though he knew it wasn't really an excuse because Flame knew Tig worked weekdays.

"Yeah. Not until eight, though."

"I need to be in at seven," Tig turned his head to look at Flame's alarm clock.

Flame took advantage of his exposed neck and twirled his tongue over Tig's thick jugular vein. He knew at any moment that Tig was going to roll him off, get dressed, and leave. It was the last thing he wanted Tig to do.

"If I don't leave now, I'll be late." Tig pushed on Flame's hips to move him back to the side of the bed he had been lying on. The loss of Flame's weight, his heat, made Tig want to pull the man back on top of him.

Son of a bitch, Tig mentally cursed himself. *I'm getting too used to this. Too attached.* He ran his hands over his face and hoped that Flame took the movement as one of trying to wake up and not what it really was. Frustration at having to leave. *This is a hook-up. Nothing more, nothing less.* Tig reminded himself and knew it was a fucking lie. How his feeling for Flame had morphed from hatred to something more, he didn't know but the disappointment on Flame's face told him he wasn't the only one whose feelings had shifted. Drastically.

"You know where the shower is," Flame said when Tig sat up and threw his legs over the side of the bed. It wasn't what he wanted to say but he bit his tongue.

"I'll just shower at home. Need clean clothes for work anyway." *And I want to smell you on my skin for as long as I can.* Tig reached for Flame's discarded shirt to clean off the drying cum on his stomach and abs.

"Alright."

Flame dressed in a pair of sweat pants and watched Tig redress, sans dress shirt again, before he walked the cop to the door. Tig opened the door and Flame tried not to feel disappointed that their time together was over.

I'm turning into a fucking chick. The thought had barely crossed Flame's mind when Tig turned around in his doorway. Tig pulled him in close, flush to his body, and gave him a deep sensual kiss goodbye.

Tig's lips lifted in a wry smile at the look of surprise on Flame's face when he pulled away and turned to leave again. *Why did I do that? This was a God damned hook-up for Christ's sake!* No matter what he tried to tell himself, he knew he was lying about what this was between him and Flame. That scared the fucking shit out of him. *Don't look back. Just leave. Treat it like a one off.* Too bad they were already past that point.

"Bradley's on Friday?" Flame couldn't help but ask. He knew it sounded too much like asking for a date but he couldn't resist. Dating Tig was something he wanted to do. Badly.

Tig stopped next to his car door and looked back at Flame. The light from inside the apartment was framing him but Tig didn't need the light to see the man's features, his pierced nipples, or his tribal ink.

Tig ignored his body's reaction to the invitation and forced himself to say, "We're not dating, Flame." He wasn't sure which one of them he was trying to remind or convince.

But we could be, Flame thought but instead countered. "Then what's the harm in getting a drink somewhere we can both be ourselves for a change?" Flame paused. "No one we work with goes there," Flame continued and Tig could hear how badly he wanted to take him out.

Tig could think of no argument to refuse Flame's offer. *Not that you want one.* "Okay. Text me." Tig replied and got into his car.

Flame watched Tigger leave as the first rays of the sunrise colored the sky in violets, pinks, and peach. He did nothing to mute his excitement about his date on Friday with Tigger as he closed his apartment door and got ready for work.

Flame's shift on Thursday was brutal. Between his sore ass, his aching body, and the sheer volume of calls they had, he was exhausted. Coffee was his best friend but even that wasn't doing shit for him. It was like he was suddenly immune to the caffeine pick-me-up. The few and too far between cat naps he was able to grab between calls did nothing to help either. They had just returned from another motor vehicle accident on I-275, the third MVA of the shift, when Brostowski called him out on his tired ass.

"You hit that shit after you left last night?"

Nope. It hit me. Flame didn't want to talk about his night, especially not with his best friend. Why John suddenly gave a shit, cared, about his sex life, he didn't know but he didn't have the energy to try and figure it out.

"So, *she* rock your world or were you rocking *hers?*"

Flame frowned. Even as tired as he was, he heard the emphasis his friend put on the female words and his irritation rose.

"Why the fuck do you care?" Flame snapped, his tiredness fueling his irritability. "Don't you watch enough porn? Or is it suddenly just my dick exploits you're interested in?"

Flame stormed past his friend without waiting for an answer. He had no idea what was up with John but he was too tired to figure it out let alone care. Thankfully,

Brostowski didn't follow him and was smart enough to leave him alone for the rest of their shift.

Thursday and Friday went by so slowly that Tig felt like he was standing still. He tried to tell himself that it wasn't because he was excited and anticipating meeting Flame at Bradley's. But he knew that was the reason, and as much as he wanted to deny that Flame's invite for drinks wasn't a date, he couldn't.

Tig hadn't been on a real date in so long that he couldn't recall the last one. Hit and runs, fuck and ducks, hook-ups with no expectations aside from busting a nut . had become such the norm that Tig felt trepidation at being reminded there could be anything else.

The only distraction from his thoughts about Flame, be they the memories of how the man's tight ass sucked his cock in deep or their upcoming date, had been the Cortez case. Alister's undercovers had moved quickly once they established their foothold with the John squad. They hadn't moved far enough up the food chain in the last week to actually see Cortez but they had been able to verify the pink 'Dumbo' shit was tied to the dealer. It was a step forward, if a small one and a good sign for their case that the man was trying to change his product to throw them off.

Tig was sure Pat noticed his tired ass on Thursday but his partner didn't comment on it, for which Tig was grateful. By Friday, Tig was recuperated from his fuckfest with Flame. Recuperated and looking forward to a repeat that night.

"Guns & Hoses?" Pat asked as they were shutting down their computers for the day.

"Sure. I have time for a few."

"Hot date tonight?" Pat raised an inquiring brow.

"Something like that." Tig couldn't stop the grin that graced his face.

"About time." Pat slapped him on the back and left it at that as they exited the station.

We still on for tonight?

It was the first text from Flame since he had sent his 'guarantee' text to the man two nights ago and Tig smiled.

"Your date?" Pat asked when they sat at the bar in Guns & Hoses and Tig's phone made a noise.

"Not sure if I'd call it a date," Tig replied and knew he was lying to his partner. If he admitted it was an actual date then he chanced Pat's questions about it on Monday.

"Uh huh," Pat grunted and took a swig of his beer. "You need to get out more. You work too much."

Tig glanced at his partner before reminding him, "You work just as much as I do."

"Yeah, but I have Mary to go home to every night." Pat grinned. "You should get you something like that."

Something like that, Tig repeated in his mind and it struck him that it was a strange way for Pat to say he needed a steady woman in his life.

"Gonna answer that?" Pat nodded toward Tig's phone.

"Yeah."

Be there by nine, Tig sent to Flame.

Good. Can't wait to see your hot fucking body again, Flame's reply was instant and Tig was glad he had the forethought to keep his screen shielded from Pat. *Don't want to just see it either.* Flame's second message came through before Tig could even reply to the first. Damn the man's words for making his cock twitch.

"Shit," Tig muttered and tried to shift on his stool to adjust himself without making it obvious to his partner.

"That good huh?" Pat smirked without looking at him.

"Yeah," Tig replied before he thought better of it.

"Good." Pat finally looked at him and it was with a smile. "Make it something then you both can come to dinner."

Again, Tig was struck by his partner's weird phrasing of words but he had no time to dwell on them. Pat killed his beer and slapped him on the back.

"Have a great date."

Tig barely had the chance to say "thanks" before Pat headed toward the door. Tig took his time finishing his beer before leaving Guns & Hoses so he would have plenty of time to get ready to meet Flame at Bradley's. To get ready for his *date* with Flame at Bradley's, his mind corrected him and he didn't argue with it for once.

Flame was impatient to see Tig. His impatience displayed itself by the text messages he couldn't stop himself from sending the man.

You dance? If not, you can just stand there while I move my body against you to the beat.

Flame waited for an answer and after a few minutes of not receiving one, he texted again.

You will feel the bass as I pull your hips to mine and press my hard cock into yours. 'Cause I *will* be hard as I grind against you like we are fucking on the dance floor.

Flame hit send and momentarily wondered if he was going too far teasing Tig. That apprehension disappeared when he recalled the smutty texts Tig had sent him a few days ago. *Turnabout is fair play*, Flame grinned to himself and only waited a moment before sending another text.

I'd fuck you in the club or maybe let you fuck me on the dance floor. Would it make you hot knowing all those men would be watching us fuck?

Flame gave Tig time to reply and refused to be discouraged when his phone remained silent.

Bet you'd like that. I would. Pounding into your ass or have you slam into mine as dozens of people watched.

"Fuck!" Flame cursed in his empty bathroom. His texts to Tig had him rock hard and he didn't fight the urge to do something about it. He wrapped his hand around his hard prick and began to stroke while his other hand typed another text.

I can feel myself buried deep in you while all those eyes watch me take your tight ass. Watch me as I wrap my hand around that pierced cock while you thrust into my fist for relief.

Flame's hand sped up as his mind was flooded with the visual inspired by his words.

But... I don't think I will give it to you. No...you made me wait.

Flame visualized fucking Tig on the dance floor of Bradley's in front of dozens of gay men. All of them wishing they were the ones pounding into Tig's hard body. His orgasm slammed through him, up his pulsating cock, over his hand to cover his chest and sink. Panting for breath, he tapped his screen that had gone into sleep mode. There was still no reply from Tig and he hoped his words had riled the man as much as they riled him. Flame grinned again to himself before sending one last text before stepping into his shower.

Are you waiting now? For round two? I am.

CHAPTER 19

THE first time Tig heard the tone that indicated an incoming text message, he was shaving. By the time he had started the shower, his phone went off a few more times. He resisted the temptation to check his phone. There was no doubt that it was Flame, and no doubt the man wasn't canceling based on the way his phone was blowing up.

Fucker is probably sexting. Tig grinned as he stepped under the spray. He was curious about Flame's texts especially if they were sex related. Would they be as raunchy as the ones he had sent the man? *God, I hope so!*

No extra time was spent in his shower. He made sure he was cleaned and ready for Flame to fuck him because he had no doubt that he would be the one getting fucked tonight. And, surprisingly, he had no problem with that. In fact, he was strangely looking forward to feeling Flame's thick cock buried in his ass again. Tig ran the towel over his body as he picked up the cell to see what Flame had texted him.

Are you waiting now? For round two? I am.

"Fuck," Tig hissed after reading the flood of texts that Flame had sent him. Yeah, he was waiting now and impatient to see the man.

How Flame had pegged him as an exhibitionist, he didn't know but his cock was ignoring the orgasm he had just had in the shower. As he dressed, he tried to force away the visions Flame's texts caused to flood his mind. It was a useless endeavor. By the time he was ready to leave, his cock was rock hard, rip-roaring, and ready for the firefighter he was meeting at Bradley's. The way he was feeling, he'd be lucky to make it through a single drink before he mauled the man on the dance floor. That thought made him grin as he got into his car and headed toward Ybor.

Flame sat on a stool, paying minimal attention to the pseudo stream that ran across the bar top in front of him. His gaze kept returning to the entrance as he waited for Tig to join him in Bradley's. The bar was crowded which was typical for a Friday night, but he still had a clear line of sight to the front door. Absentmindedly, he spun his beer bottle between his hands.

Tig had never replied to his sex texts and that caused him a level of nervousness that he was unaccustomed to feeling. Add that to not asking a man on a date before, *ever,* and it was amazing he wasn't a total wreck while he waited for Tig to show. Flame's phone vibrated on the bar in front of him and he was sure he looked desperate as he grabbed it.

Here. Where R U?

At the bar by the pool table, Flame typed back and tried to ignore the feeling of relief that flooded him at realizing Tig had actually showed up for their date.

Tig read Flame's reply and clipped his phone back onto his hip. He scanned the crowd as he made his way further into the bar. A wall of people parted and there was Flame sitting at the bar nursing a Bud Light.

Something else we have in common besides fucking ass. The thought flittered across Tig's mind while he made his way closer to the man.

"Drink?" Flame asked when Tig came close and rested his hand on his lower back.

"Yeah," Tig leaned closer. "But you promised me dancing."

Flame's cock got hard at the reminder of what he had promised to do to Tig on the dance floor.

"I did," Flame didn't hesitate in replying or standing from his stool.

Tig didn't resist when Flame's hand sought out his and latched on. He allowed himself to be dragged back to the dance area of the club.

"What are you drinking?" Flame asked because even though they always ran into each other in Guns & Hoses, he never paid any mind to what the man drank.

"One of those will work," Tig nodded to the bottle of Bud Light Flame was holding.

Flame gave Tig a nod before he flagged down the twink bartender who was dressed so minimally he would get nailed for indecency outside the bar. Their beers arrived and Flame finally turned back to Tig, focusing all of his attention on the man and waiting for him to speak.

Tig looked Flame over from head to toe while taking a sip of his beer and had to bite back a moan. The firefighter was dressed in black denim jeans, that he had seen before, and a navy muscle shirt that did nothing to hide his nipple piercings let alone the tribal tattoos that were obviously not just on his arms. He couldn't help but lick his lips at the sight. Flame was fucking hot. Sex on a God damned stick.

"So, got a dance fetish?" Tig asked to break the silence and felt stupid for his question.

Flame sensed that Tig was uncomfortable. He could totally relate. This wasn't some random hook-up just to get off. They had already been there and done that. This was getting to know one another outside the bedroom and it was fucking weird to say the least.

"I like to dance." Flame smiled and leaned closer. "Do you?"

Tig's body reacted when Flame leaned into him. The closeness of the man did things to him but he didn't have a chance to analyze those things before Flame spoke again.

"You never answered my texts."

Because they turned me on too much and I was fighting the urge to beat off, again. Tig fought another moan.

"I dance." Their beer bottles were forgotten on the bar as Afrojack blasted through the club and Tig took Flame's hand, pulling him toward the dance floor.

I think it's time to let you know
The way I feel when you take hold
One single touch from you, I'm gone
Still got the rush when I'm alone
I think it is time I let you know
Take all of me, I will devote
You set me free, my body's yours
It feels the best when you're involved

They entered the mass of bodies that were already dancing under the flashing laser lights. Neither man tried to keep any distance between them as the music seemed to sink into their bodies, their souls.

Tig groaned when Flame grabbed his hips so they could grind to the beat. He draped his arms over Flame's shoulders and moved his body to the music in sync with Flame. They fit together like a hand in a glove and Tig pushed away the thoughts that told him it shouldn't feel so good. That *Thomas Flame* shouldn't feel so damned good. Physically or otherwise.

Flame reveled in Tig grinding against him and chanced looking into the man's eyes. Purple, pink, and white lights illuminated his face and made Flame feel those fucking butterflies again. Flame pulled Tig close and sang along with the song as he breathed in Tig's scent.

> *Baby, baby, can't you see?*
> *That I'm giving all of me*
> *So, it's up to you now*
> *We could let time pass away*
> *I'll make an excuse to play*
> *But, it's up to you now*

Tig held Flame. They were bumping and grinding groins, getting them both beyond aroused when Flame started singing to the song Tig had not been paying any attention to. The words to the song, the words Flame whispered against his skin, were sinking deep.

> *Just wanna fulfill your needs*
> *While you're taking over me*
> *So, what do you want now?*
> *Take a picture, make a show*
> *'Cause nobody has to know*
> *All the ways that we get down*

Flame's breath whispered the words hotly against his ear while they danced. Tig knew the man was just singing to the song but there was a part of him, deep inside, that knew Flame meant every God damned word he was singing.

Flame couldn't think of a better song to breathe into Tig's ear. It was strange how hip-hop could be so fucking appropriate. And it definitely was where he was concerned when it came to Tigger Flint. Sometime over the last two weeks, his feelings toward the man he had always hated had shifted. Drastically. Hate was the furthest emotion he felt. Now he felt…what? Something more than like but less than love. Lust, want, and desire, were all good words to describe how he now felt about Tig. But they didn't encompass the emotions that were broiling within him. He wanted more. Not just more sex but more of everything and for some reason, his gut was telling him that Tig was the man he could have it with.

The words Flame parroted from Afrojack, whispered into Tig's ear as they were practically vertically fucking on the dance floor, hit him hard. They hit him deep and he knew they meant something even if they were just the lyrics of a fucking hip-hop song. It wasn't just the words themselves but the way Flame sang them that told Tig it wasn't just a song for a hook-up that Flame was trying to seduce him with.

He didn't need seducing from Flame and that should have worried him. Surprisingly, it didn't. Flame kept singing to him, his breath hot against Tig's ear, as their bodies rocked to the sexual beat and thump of the bass. Tig could do nothing but enjoy the man he held and he didn't fight the feeling.

The song changed and Tig allowed Flame to turn him. They never missed a beat as Flame pressed the front of his body along the back of Tig's. Flame's hands held Tig's waist, pulling Tig's ass back against his jean encased hard on. Tig's arms rose up and back to pull Flame's head closer to his shoulder. His extra few inches of height were perfect for Flame's lips to kiss his neck and lick the trails of sweat that soaked into his shirt collar. Tig moved his ass in sync with Flame and felt, more than heard, the man moan before he dropped his arms and turned in Flame's embrace.

Tig was killing him. Just. Fucking. Killing. Him. When the cop turned in his arms, still grinding against him to the beat, Flame couldn't stop himself from consuming his mouth. There was nothing gentle about the kiss. Flame poured all of his lust and hunger for Tig into the kiss.

"Fuck," Tig breathed against Flame's lips when they finally came up for air. "You're fucking killing me." Tig echoed Flame's thought.

Flame nodded his agreement. *Glad it's not just me.*

"Let's get a drink." Flame forced himself to pull away. "Before you make me blow my load like some fucking teenager." Flame wasn't embarrassed to admit what Tig did to him. He could feel that Tig was just as hard, on the same edge as he, but this was *supposed* to be a date.

"Yeah," Tig agreed and adjusted himself with no shame. "Good idea."

Tig allowed Flame to turn him again, toward the bar, and he enjoyed the way Flame's hands remained on his hips as they left the dance floor. He knew Flame was right about them getting a drink. They both needed to calm down before they embarrassed themselves in their jeans. Tig could already feel the wet spot his leaking cock was causing in his boxer briefs and knew it wouldn't take much stimulation if he wasn't wearing his jeans to turn that spot into a puddle of cum. Hell, as it was, he was fighting the urge to drag Flame into the restroom for a repeat of the last time they were here.

Flame ordered them two fresh beers. The ones they had been drinking still sat on the bar when they walked up but since they had left them unattended, they could just stay there. He leaned into Tig's back as he accepted his beer from the bartender at the same time Tig accepted his.

Fuck, he feels good. Flame enjoyed his body pressing against Tig's again for a moment before forcing himself to step back.

Tig turned to lean back against the bar and made himself take a swig of his beer so that he didn't pull Flame against him again. Flame stood close, not touching, but close enough that the other men in the bar would know that they were together. They didn't speak as they watched each other drink but just when Tig was about to break their silence, he was practically assaulted by an interruption.

"T!" A body pushed between them and Flame had to step back to avoid being shoved out of the way. "Haven't seen you in a while, baby." Arms snaked around Tig's shoulders before he could stop them. "Come home with me tonight. I want this again." Tig stopped the hand that was about to grope him.

Flame watched as a good looking blonde tried to climb up Tig's body. The guy was smaller than both he and Tig but not scrawny like a twink. He was built like a runner or a swimmer and Flame couldn't help but wonder how Tig hadn't broken the guy in bed with his rough fucking. He also wondered if the guy was really the type

Tig was into for hook-ups. The blonde guy just looked too fragile.

If he is, what the hell is he doing with me? Flame pushed aside the thought, and the spike of jealousy that followed quick on its heels.

Tig untangled the arm that was still wrapped around his neck. His eyes never left Flame's and he didn't miss the flash of emotion that passed over the man's face. Irritation then anger before Flame stared daggers at the guy who was rubbing against Tig's hip and begging for a repeat hook-up. Tig wasn't sure how he felt about the daggers that Flame was shooting at his hook-up from a few weeks ago. He wanted to be annoyed because Flame knew how the game was played but instead, Flame's sudden anger just made his cock harder.

"Not tonight," Tig finally freed himself from the clingy grasp of the guy whose name he couldn't even remember. "I'm busy."

"Awww," No-name tried to wrap his arms around Tig again. "Be busy with me."

Flame heard the interaction even though the music in this part of the bar was loud. His eyes hadn't left Tig's after his initial glance at the guy who wedged himself between them. The fact that Tig's gaze remained locked on his muted some of the irrational jealousy he felt. Deep down, he knew that he had no right to feel jealous over Tig's past conquests but that didn't stop the green-eyed monster from rising. The look on Tig's face wasn't one that indicated he needed to be rescued. No, it was one that begged patience. Still, Flame's desire to make his claim on Tig flared.

"He said he's busy." Flame leaned into the side of No-name and Tig. "With me," he finished when the guy glanced at him.

Flame expected Tig's previous hook-up to at least step back if not totally take the hint and leave. What he didn't expect was for the man to turn and press his body against him.

"Ohhh," No-name looked him over from head to toe. "Yum." The guy licked his lips like he could already taste Flame's cock.

Flame couldn't help smirking at the guy's reaction to him before he returned his gaze back to Tig. Tig was watching him closely but his expression remained unchanged.

"Who's your friend T?" No-name placed a hand on each of their chests. "Maybe you could both be busy with me." No-name pushed his hips into their groins.

Tig broke his eye contact with Flame as his old hook-up made the offer. He wasn't surprised the guy offered. Flame and he were similarly built and he knew how much his own body had turned the guy on the last time they had hooked up but did he really want to share Flame?

Flame tried to read Tig when the cop's eyes shifted to the man who was grinding his hips into them to the beat of the music. It didn't appear that Tig was surprised by the offer but Flame didn't think it was because he had already had a threesome with the man before. Tig just had the look of someone who expected such an offer from such a slut. Flame shifted his attention back to the blonde haired man. He was several inches shorter than Flame and as he allowed his eyes to really look at the guy, realized he was just the type that Flame would pick up for a one off.

Why am I not surprised that Tig would do the same? Flame smirked.

Tig saw Flame smirk at his previous hook-up who was trying to take them both back to his bed. He wasn't sure if the smirk was one of amusement or disdain. His plans for the night with Flame hadn't included a third party. Hell, just the two of them were enough to set the sheets on fire. They didn't need any extra entertainment to accomplish that. But, if that is where Flame wanted to take their date, Tig knew he would follow.

No-name dragged his hands down both of their chests until each palm rested over the bulges in their pants. He had no idea that it wasn't his teasing or his offer that had the men so aroused.

"Umm," No-name licked his lips slowly again and looked between Tig and Flame. "You like the idea!"

Flame's smirk turned into a grin when Tig raised an inquisitive brow. It seemed Tig was leaving the decision up to him. This wasn't what he planned for their date but the slight uplift of Tig's mouth into a partial grin told him that Tig was game for whatever he wanted to do. They would be fucking before the night was over, third or not. Flame leaned into Tig and ducked his head to whisper in his ear.

"Is he worth me wasting my time when I could be buried in you instead?"

Tig turned his head and licked his way up Flame's neck before he nipped his earlobe. "You'll be buried in me regardless." Tig felt the hot air of Flame's breathy groan caress his neck.

"Whatever you want to do is fine by me." Flame pulled slightly back to look into Tig's eyes. There was no doubt the hunger he saw there was for him and him alone. "I want you." Flame leaned back in to whisper against Tig's ear. "But the thought of you tearing his ass up…"

Tig chuckled at Flame's words and the press of the firefighter's groin against his other hip. He turned his head, raised his hand to Flame's nape, and gave the man a hungry kiss before pulling back and placing his mouth next to his ear again.

"Both of us tearing that ass up."

Another groan escaped Flame as he pulled back from Tig and looked over the man who would be *their* hook-up for the night.

"Fuck, that's hot!" No-name said as he rubbed against them again like a bitch in heat.

Flame and Tig shared a knowing smile before Flame called for his tab. Moments later, tab cashed out, Flame turned back to the guy who was grinding his hard prick against their hips.

"Let's go," Flame pushed the guy off of them and turned him toward the door. He took Tig's hand as they followed the trim waist and tight ass of Tig's previous hook-up from the bar.

CHAPTER 20

IN the parking garage, Tig climbed into Flame's jacked up F-150. They hadn't talked much after getting the hook-up's address. Tig only vaguely remembered the drive to New Port Richey the first time he met the cute blonde bottom.

"You okay leaving your Camaro here?" Flame asked as he started his truck and put it into reverse.

"Not really," Tig replied but continued when Flame put the truck back into park. "But your truck has more room."

Tig gave Flame a wicked grin that almost made Flame forget what he was going to say. If they were going to leave a vehicle in the Ybor parking garage it should be his truck and not Tig's classic car.

"Let's take your car." Flame killed the engine while he tried not to think about why Tig wanted to have more room on the drive to New Port Richey.

Tig leaned over the console when Flame killed the truck. His hand went to the hard outline of Flame's prick between his legs while he gave the man a kiss. He had intended the kiss to be gentle and reassuring, of what he didn't know, but Flame's reaction to his contact was fierce.

The second Tig's hand touched his aching hard-on and Tig's lips brushed his own, he was overwhelmed by a hunger for the cop. One hand pressed Tig's palm harder against his erection as his other grasped the back of Tig's head, fisting his hair, and forced their mouths to connect viciously. He pushed his hips up into the rough touch he was encouraging at the same time he thrust his tongue between Tig's lips, between his teeth, and tried to touch the man's tonsils.

Flame's response to his touch almost caught Tig off guard. Almost. The fact that Flame was just as hungry for him as he was for Flame made Tig's stomach do that flip-flop shit again but he didn't care. Couldn't care as the taste of Flame flooded his senses. Tig wasn't even aware when they both fumbled to free Flame from his jeans but when his hand wrapped around the velvet hardness of Flame's shaft, they both moaned into the fevered kiss at the contact.

"Shittt," Flame hissed and jerked up into Tig's fist when he broke the kiss.

Tig didn't grant Flame a reply. He wanted to taste the man too desperately, didn't want to waste his mouth on anything other than the feeling of Flame's cock on his tongue. Tig gave Flame's lower lip a nip before he abruptly pulled his face away and dropped his head into Flame's lap.

"Fuuuuuck!" Flame had no chance to stop Tig, not that he wanted to, when the man wrapped his lips around his cock.

His hips thrust up again roughly of their own accord and his hands dropped to tightly fist Tig's light hair. The hot wet heat of Tig's mouth, along with the manual stroke of his tight grip, was more than Flame could take. Three solid, deep thrusts and Flame's back arched, his legs tensed, feet pushing against the floorboard next to the trucks pedals, and he came down Tig's throat with a shout.

There had been no time to warn Tig and no time to be embarrassed about how quickly Tig had gotten him off. His balls had been begging to be emptied since he first laid eyes on the man in Bradley's. All Flame could do was pant, fight to catch his breath, as he waited for the glittery stars of his orgasm to fade from in front of his eyes.

Tig swallowed Flame down, swallowed his load, until the man had no more to give him. The first taste of Flame's release and the tight grip that pulled his hair was enough to send him over the edge into his own orgasm. He hadn't creamed his jeans since middle school but it was too late to worry about it now as he panted through his nose, refusing to remove his mouth from Flame just yet.

As Flame panted above him, Tig enjoyed the feeling of the man's fingers running through his hair. No longer did he suck Flame's semi-hard cock. Instead, he just relished the residual taste and the weight of Flame's prick in his mouth. The slight tug on his head forced Tig to let go of his prize and he sat up to look at Flame. Flame's face was flushed with that post orgasmic look that made almost any man sexy as fuck and Tig appreciated him in the dim lights of the parking garage.

Tig looked almost as satisfied as Flame felt but it wasn't the cocky expression he was used to seeing on the face of the man who made him lose control. No, it was an expression of satisfaction from giving another pleasure and it changed how Tig normally looked. Changed for the better. If Tig hadn't already been pulling the strings of Flame's heart, the current gaze the man gave him would have been a fierce tug. Flame brought his hand down from where he had been brutally gripping Tig's hair just moments before and caressed Tig's cheek with his thumb.

Tig leaned into Flame's tender touch as his hand moved from his temple and traveled over his cheek before tracing his cock swollen lips. He did not even realize he was doing it. The touch said more than words and that touch should have scared the shit out of him. It didn't. It felt too good and that fact alone should have sent him into a panic. Should have had him high tailing his ass out of Flame's truck as fast as he could but instead it relaxed him and he sat back up.

"What are we doing Flame?" Tig murmured, repeating the question he had asked the man a week before.

Flame had let his hand slide over Tig's face when he pulled away and sat back up in the passenger seat. He knew what Tig was asking him. He also knew Tig wouldn't appreciate his answer if he replied honestly. To avoid the question for as long as he could, Flame tucked himself back into his jeans before looking at Tig. He was surprised to see the growing wet spot at Tig's groin but he didn't spend anytime enjoying that Tig had gotten off just from giving him a blowjob.

The cop was staring out the windshield as if he was absorbed by the sight of the concrete wall of the parking garage. Tig didn't look freaked out, or have any expression so dramatic. He just looked lost, and maybe confused. Flame could relate. He was confused by his own growing feelings for Tig, but they made him feel too fucking good to question his sanity about them.

"I don't know Tig," Flame finally replied even though it felt like a lie. *I'm falling for you,* he wanted to say. *And I think you feel the same.* Flame wanted to voice his thoughts but just continued. "What do you want to do?"

Tig knew that Flame's question wasn't referring to where they were going to end up for the night but he took it that way regardless. He just couldn't contemplate any other options at the moment. Not couldn't, wouldn't.

"I'll meet you at you're place." Tig reached for the handle of the truck door.

"Tig." Flame reached out and touched Tig's arm.

Tig paused and looked back at Flame. The look on Flame's face echoed everything that Tig was feeling and he couldn't help but smile.

"Meet you there." Tig gave Flame a nod before he exited the truck.

His pants were still wet, sticky, and uncomfortable as he walked down a level to his Camaro but he didn't feel it. All he felt was the anticipation that came with being in Flame's arms again.

Flame was waiting at the garage exit when Tig drove down the ramp. They paid their parking fees and pulled out onto 15th Avenue. Neither man gave any thought to the blonde hook-up in New Port Richey that they were blowing off.

Tig followed Flame into his apartment and turned when the man closed and locked his front door. The frantic hunger he had felt was diminished but certainly not gone when Flame turned his steel blue gaze in his direction. It was a look that Tig had never seen before.

Hatred, anger, disgust, as well as hunger, lust and want were all expressions Tig could recognize on Flame's face. But the one that was focused on him, like a laser of a S.W.A.T. sniper scope, was new. It made his stomach do that flip-flop shit for the second time tonight and his chest tightened uncomfortably in anticipation.

Flame turned to the man who had somehow gotten under his fucking skin to the point that his heart ached like he was having a heart attack. He didn't question why he was feeling this way toward Tig. He didn't want to analyze his feelings. They felt too right to doubt with over thinking that was sure to make him question his sanity for being with Tig. He just wanted to feel. Feel more. Emotionally. Physically. Damn the consequences.

Flame stepped up to Tig where the man stood next to his leather couch and wrapped his arms around the cop's waist. He never took his eyes off of Tig's penetrating hazel gaze. If Flame would have allowed himself to analyze what was happening between them at all, he would have recognized his feelings being reflected back at him.

"What are we doing Flame?" Tig repeated and hoped that Flame would give him an answer that would confirm that this thing between them was nothing more than just sex, just another hook-up.

That's not what you want to hear, a small voice admonished Tig in his mind.

Flame leaned in and placed a soft kiss on Tig's lips and the man melted against him. There was no tongue, no teeth, offered in the kiss before he pulled away. He was mildly surprised by Tig's passivity.

"Whatever you want, Tig." Flame's hands caressed Tig's back while he held him close. He didn't stop Tig when the man snuggled his neck and wrapped his arms around his waist.

Tig moved his head to rest against Flame's neck. *That's what I am afraid of.* Tig sighed at Flame's reply that ghosted on his lips. *I don't know what I want.*

"I don't know what I want."

Tig's words drifted up from where his mouth was pressed into Flame's neck. Flame was sure that Tig had not meant for him to hear the reply but he could not stop his own from escaping his lips.

"I do," Flame whispered into Tig's hair. "Let me show us both."

Flame had expected Tig to react, tense, or at least reply with a hint of the frantic hunger that was the gist of their last two encounters. However, Tig just leaned back enough to look into Flame's eyes.

Tig realized he had spoken aloud when Flame replied to his thought. He heard the reply and surprised himself by not being self-conscience at admitting he was at a loss. When he leaned back to look at Flame, he saw nothing but honest affection. Affection and a trace of fear that his offer may be rejected. As nervous and uncertain as his feelings were making him, Tig had no thoughts or intentions of rejecting Flame.

"Okay." Tig stared into Flame's eyes which returned his gaze as if they were piercing his soul. "Show us."

The nervousness and the trepidation that Flame was unaware he even felt dissolved with Tig's words. He leaned in once more and gave Tig another soft kiss before he took them both to bed.

"Good weekend?" Pat's voice pulled Tig from his thoughts of Flame when his partner sat down at the desk across from him.

Tig had spent the remainder of Friday night and most of Saturday afternoon in Flame's bed before they rejoined the world of the living. They had sex, they fucked, and did everything and anything in between with each other. But in the end, it wasn't just fucking to get off that they'd accomplished. No. At some point the intimacy they shared with one another had become more important than blowing a load. Hot, harsh, frantic touches turned into soft, tender caresses and Tig couldn't deny how those touches made him feel. He couldn't deny how much he wanted to experience them again.

When he finally forced himself to leave Flame's apartment, he hated himself for doing so. But Flame had to work on Sunday and Tig knew if he had stayed, Flame wouldn't be worth a shit when he showed up for his shift.

Tig realized he hadn't answered his partner so he replied with a grin, "Yeah."

"Good." Pat smiled. "You look relaxed for a change." Tig didn't know how to reply to Pat's comment so he said nothing while he booted up his PC. "Whatever they're doing for you," Pat paused until Tig raised his head and met his gaze. "Keep letting them do it." Pat winked.

Tig knew the look he gave Pat was one of confusion with a tinge of panic. Pat O'Brian had been his partner for the last four years and Tig couldn't ask to be paired up with a better cop. The man was sharp as a whip and intelligent as fuck when it came to breaking a case. They had become friends outside of the office to the point where Pat's wife, Mary, insisted on Tig's attendance at dinner on at least one Sunday a month.

Pat never stuck his nose into Tig's personal life, for which he was more than grateful, and respected the fact that Tig wasn't a kiss and tell type of guy. Tig never felt like he couldn't share his sexual preference with his partner but he just never saw a reason to do so. But Pat's comments last week, along with those now, had Tig thinking his partner knew that he preferred men and was giving him the hints to tell him. If that was the case, Pat seemed okay with it. But if Pat was being discreet because he respected Tig or he was unsure of his assumption, now was not the time to discuss it.

Tig continued to stare at Pat as his partner grinned back at him. "I plan to," Tig finally said and offered his own smile.

"Good." Pat nodded and turned to his computer.

Tig watched his partner for a few more minutes and resisted the urge to interrogate Pat about what he thought he knew. He had just started checking his email when Pat spoke again.

"Is it serious?"

Tig's head shot up from his monitor to look at his partner. Pat was still focused on his own computer screen and didn't even acknowledge him. He was sure Pat had caught his movement. Tig gave Pat's question some serious thought before he answered. If his partner would have asked him about a relationship a week ago, he would have laughed off the prospect and question. Of course, Pat wouldn't have asked him a week ago. In fact, Pat had never asked him about a potential relationship, *ever*, so that should have told Tig something. Tig didn't need that *something* to tell him what he now had with Flame had turned into a relationship. But was it serious?

"Yeah," Tig replied and didn't look away from his partner. "Maybe." Tig paused. "I think we want it to be."

"Good," Pat repeated without looking away from his monitor. "It's about fucking time."

Tig didn't reply but instead focused on his own emails. Or at least pretended to focus because his mind was suddenly consumed by thoughts of what a relationship with Thomas Flame could mean for him and the rival that his heart was falling for.

CHAPTER 21

THANKFULLY, Flame's shift on Sunday wasn't as hectic as his last shift at the station. It wasn't as uncomfortable as his last shift either but that was more than likely due to lack of aches in his body and the fact that Brostowski had called in sick. The thought of how his body didn't hurt like it had during his last hellacious shift and the reason why made him think of Tig. Not that he needed any excuse to think of the cop. The disappointment Flame had felt when Tig insisted on leaving after they killed a pizza and a few beers the night before had faded.

As he remembered holding Tig in his arms while the cop attempted to leave, Flame realized that Tig didn't want to leave as much as Flame wanted him to stay. In hindsight, Flame could appreciate Tig's leaving in order to ensure Flame wouldn't be tired for his shift. Still, that didn't mean Flame wouldn't have sacrificed sleep for more time with Tig.

He resisted the urge to text Tig. Even after the night and day they had spent together getting to know one another, more than just fucking each other's brains out. Flame still wanted more. He knew he had fallen hard for Tigger and knew that he should be freaked out by the feelings that were coursing through him but he wasn't. Flame had always rolled with the punches. Embraced what he was feeling full force and even though he knew that he was risking a heartbreak beyond repair, he was still on board with going balls to the walls with his emotions toward Tig.

"Hey, Brostowski need a hangover day or what?" Johnson's voice shattered Flame's self-analysis and thoughts about Tig.

"Dunno." Flame shrugged. "Haven't talked to him since last shift."

Johnson grunted as if he didn't believe Flame and Flame realized that his claim was genuinely unbelievable since everyone knew the two of them spoke every day.

"Whatever, man." Johnson chuckled and headed toward the station kitchen.

Flame understood the man's doubt. John Brostowski and he had been thick as thieves since the first day they met and it was expected that they would know what was what with each other. But after Flame verbally flayed John on the last shift when the man was giving him shit about his hook-up, Flame hadn't heard from him. Flame couldn't remember the last time he had gone twenty-four hours, let alone seventy-two, without talking with his best friend.

"Fuck," Flame muttered under his breath as he pulled his phone off his hip.

He knew he had snapped at John on their last chaotic shift but the man's innuendos about the *woman* he had been with who wore his ass out had shattered his last nerve. Had his best friend only been giving him shit because he was dog ass tired, Flame would have blown it off. But that wasn't the case. John had been acting weird since the last flag football game and the insinuations he had made had pissed Flame off. Regardless, that didn't stop the thread of worry from creeping into him.

You okay, man? Thought you'd be here today.
Flame texted his best friend.

Just needed a break.

Flame stared at John's reply and couldn't make
any sense about what it meant. *Break from what?* Flame
couldn't help but wonder.

You OK? Flame sent and after several seconds,
received a reply after several more.

*Yeah, I'm good. G&H tomorrow for Willis's
bachelor party?*

Sure. What time?

Usual.

K. CU then. Flame replied and tried not to over
think the strange behavior that his best friend had been
displaying for the last two weeks.

Flame had just sat down with his beer at the table
in Guns & Hoses that his firehouse usually claimed when
the door to the bar opened. He expected to see John but
instead, his eyes landed on one very rumpled and sexy
Tigger Flint. He started to stand from his seat before he
remembered where they were. The flash of desire in Tig's
eyes upon seeing him matched his own and he almost
didn't care where they were. Almost.

He had resisted texting Tig since they parted ways
on Saturday. There was nothing that he could say that
wouldn't make him sound needy, clingy, and like a girl
so he didn't send a text at all. Not that he hadn't wanted

to and his only consolation from feeling guilty was that Tig hadn't texted him either.

Tig's eyes landed on Flame the moment he walked through the door as if the man were a magnet and he was nothing more than a pile of iron shavings. The spark of desire that ignited when his gaze met Flame's was unmistakable and stirred something deep within Tig. His heart sped up and did the flip-flop shit he was starting to associate with Flame.

He felt slightly guilty for not texting Flame since he'd last seen the firefighter. His unexpected, almost uncontrollable feelings for the man had stilled his fingers every time he opened up their message history. They were so far beyond the hook-up stage, past the fuck buddy label that Tig was at a loss when it came to texting Flame. Tig allowed himself the pleasure of drinking in Flame's hot body while he and Pat made their way to their usual spots at the bar.

As Flame watched Tig and his partner take seats at the bar, he couldn't help but wonder if the lack of texts from Tig was for the same reasons he hadn't sent any himself. They had a connection. A connection that was more than just wanting to fuck each other senseless. That much Flame was sure of after all the time they spent with each other, outside of fucking, over the weekend.

"You're not gonna start any shit are you?"

Pat's voice pulled his gaze away from Flame, and Tig cursed himself for staring at the man he was enamored with to the point of distraction. When he whipped his gaze away from Flame to reply, the look on Pat's face gave him pause. Pat's normal expression of defensive aggression, distain over the ongoing feud between him and Flame, was not present. Instead, Tig was greeted with a smirk that was more curious than anything else. Tig didn't know what to make of his partner's expression since the man was always more than willing to start shit with Flame if he came within range. Just like Tig used to do.

"I never start shit," Tig grinned and accepted his beer from Shelley.

"Yeah," Pat snorted and took a sip of his beer. "If you say so."

Flame drank his beer and watched Tig from the corner of his eye. It did not escape his notice that Tig had been looking at him while he and his partner made their way to the bar. Tig was talking to O'Brian but Flame saw his eyes look in his direction several times. The thought that he was a distraction to the cop made Flame grin and he pulled out his phone.

*Gonna be here long? I don't work tomorrow. *wink** Flame hit send and continued to watch Tig from the corner of his eye.

Pat had been telling him about his daughter's plans to visit when Tig's phone dinged on his hip. He was willing to ignore the sound that indicated he had a text message but apparently Pat wasn't.

"You gonna check that?"

Tig glanced at Pat and was about to reply that it could wait when his partner spoke again.

"Go ahead. Could be your hottie." Pat winked.

Tig pulled his phone from his hip and wasn't surprised to see the text from Flame. He glanced in the man's direction before typing his reply.

I do. Tig reminded Flame that he had to work in the morning and hit send just as the bar door opened to reveal Flame's best friend, that asshole Brostowski, walking in. *And you seem to have company anyway.*

Flame caught sight of John just as his phone vibrated twice. He glanced at the screen while John was grabbing his beer and quickly typed his reply.

Rather have your company. Later?

John plopped down across from Flame at the table before Tig replied but Flame was already halfway through typing up another follow up message.

Won't tire you out too much. Promise.

"That your *girl?*" John asked as Flame hit send on his text message to Tig. Flame was going to ignore John's tone but it seemed John didn't want to be ignored. "I just don't get you, man." Flame frowned at his best friend. "We tell each other everything so what's your deal? I am supposed to be your *best* friend." John was frowning and staring daggers at Flame when Jacobs and the rest of the crew walked in.

"Bring us a round, Shell. And keep them coming! Willis is tying the knot!" Jacobs called out to Shelley.

The arrival of the rest of Flame's co-workers saved him from having to answer John. It didn't save him from the occasional frown John sent his way though.

Tig heard the firefighter call out to Shelley and knew that Flame wouldn't be leaving anytime soon. Bachelor parties never ended early. Fire and police bachelor parties were especially notorious for continuing to all hours of the night. Tig tried not to let his disappointment that he wouldn't likely be seeing Flame tonight kill his mood. He focused on his conversation with Pat as Guns & Hoses filled up with more firemen for their party.

Flame bought several shots for the groom-to-be but only saluted his co-worker with his beer. He didn't want too get to drunk and have to leave his truck at the bar for the night.

It's not your truck or drunk driving that's keeping you somewhat sober. It's the chance to see Tig later.

Just thinking about the cop had Flame checking his watch again. He had been here for over two hours and figured that was long enough for appearance sake. *Time to take a leak and bail so I can spend time with Tig.*

Flame was washing his hands when John entered the restroom. He hid his disappointment that it wasn't Tig. Flame didn't want to argue with his best friend but by the look on John's face, he knew he wasn't going to avoid the confrontation.

"What the hell is your problem, John?" Flame conveyed his annoyance through his tone as he turned his back to the sink and faced John.

"You are!" John stepped in front of him. Flame prepared to defend himself against the smaller man if John decided to get physical with his anger. "I'm your best fucking friend, Flame, and you couldn't tell me?"

Flame blinked at John as his friend poked him in the chest. He didn't kiss and tell so he couldn't fathom why John was so pissed off all the sudden.

"I have no idea what the hell you are talking about." Flame played dumb.

"I'm talking about this." John fisted the front of Flame's tee shirt and pushed into him right before he crashed his lips viciously onto Flame's mouth.

Flame was so shocked by his best friend's oral attack that he couldn't do anything but brace his hands on the sink behind him. John pressed his whole body into

Flame as Flame's eye went wide. It was then that the bathroom door opened and Flame saw Tig over John's shoulder.

Time stood still. Flame saw the look of shock on Tig's face before anger made an appearance then quickly morphed into hurt. Time seemed to resume when Tig turned on his heel and let the bathroom door close in his wake. The sound of the door bumping shut snapped Flame out of his shocked stupor. He shoved John away roughly by the shoulders. John staggered and by the time he caught his balance, Flame was half way out the bathroom door trying to catch Tig.

"I saw you!" John yelled as Flame was still halfway through the door. "I saw you with that asshole in Ybor!" John pushed Flame out of the bathroom and between Flame's own momentum and the shove from behind he had to throw his hands out to avoid face planting into the wall opposite of the door.

"Tigger Flint? Really Flame?" John continued to yell, oblivious to the heads that turned in their direction. Flame pushed off the wall and turned to face his best friend's anger as John continued. "Of all the people you could choose to…"

Flame didn't give John a chance to finish the sentence before he shoved his friend back into the restroom.

"Tigger Flint? Really Flame?"

The sound of his name spit out so venomously from Brostowski's mouth caused Tig to turn back toward the hallway where the restrooms were located. His head wasn't the only one that turned toward the firefighters. Tig was trying to decide if he should intervene or not when Pat appeared at his side.

"What the hell did you do?" Pat asked as his eyes roamed over the rest of the firemen. They were outnumbered if Tig and Flame got into another brawl but Pat was pretty sure that wouldn't happen.

"I didn't do shit," Tig replied angrily. Pat spared his partner a glance when Brostowski's next words drifted across the now silent crowd.

"Of all the people you could choose to…"

Pat winced at the words and the power behind Flame's shove that sent Brostowski flying back into the men's room. The two firefighters never argued or came to blows. At least not that Pat had ever seen in Guns & Hoses. Usually, that behavior was reserved for Tig and Flame.

"Shit."

Tig heard Pat curse before his partner stormed off toward the two firefighters who had disappeared into the bathroom. Tig wasn't sure if he should follow or not. But knowing that Pat could end up outnumbered or even hurt trying to break up Flame and Brostowski, made up his mind.

"Stay. Put." Tig ordered over his shoulder at the firemen who had gathered for the bachelor party. Every single one of them looked as shocked as Tig felt as he stormed down the hallway after his partner. When he opened the bathroom door, chaos was ensuing in the small space.

"How could you fuck that asshole?" Brostowski yelled as Flame held him down on the floor and landed a punch to his ribs. Tig flinched before tensing at the words.

"Shut up, John." Flame was trying to fend off John's angry attacks.

"You're gay!" John managed to flip onto his stomach under Flame's bulk. "You couldn't fucking tell me? Six years, Flame. I'm your best fucking friend!" John bucked up, trying to throw Flame off.

Pat was trying to pull Flame off his best friend but wasn't getting the leverage he needed to break up the wrestling match on the floor.

"Shut. Up. John." Flame panted and landed another punch to John's kidney as he pushed his friend's head down into the tiled floor.

There was no room for Tig to get into the fray and try and break up the fight. The bathroom was just too small. Flame straddled Brostowski's thighs and was using his weight to pin down the fireman while he landed another punch.

"Knock it off. Both of you!" Pat yelled at the firemen. "Break it up!" Pat was pulling on Flame's tee shirt and trying to get into position to head lock Flame and pull him off.

"It should have been me!" Brostowski yelled as he tried to buck Flame off again.

John's words shocked Flame enough that he relaxed his hold on his best friend. That moment of shock, that pause in the pressure he was applying to hold John down, was just enough for John to buck Flame off. Flame flailed and fell back into Pat. Pat was caught off balance and Flame careened into him, almost knocking him on his ass. There was no room for Pat to fall but Tig instinctively reached out to catch his partner.

"Son of a bitch!" Pat grunted when Tig caught him.

John was attempting to scramble out from under Flame when Flame lunged at his best friend again. "What the fuck..." Flame yelled and Tig was sure the whole bar could hear the yelling match between the friends.

Pat shot forward and wrapped his arm around Flame's neck to pull him back. Flame had no choice but to allow himself to be yanked backward and up to his feet. Pat was shorter than Flame and in the small space, he had no choice but to press into Tig. Flame's back was arched in an uncomfortable position as Pat held him in a choke hold but he wasn't fighting the cop.

"I'm in love with you, asshole." John panted out as he stood. "Have been for years." John turned around and stared at Flame. "Should have been me you came out of the closet for."

Pat glanced over his shoulder at Tig and Tig met his gaze without flinching.

"Let him go, Pat." Tig's voice was flat and cold when he nudged his partner so he could open the door. Pat let Flame go and both men stepped forward to give Tig room.

Flame could do nothing but stare in shock at his best friend. Stare at the man he thought he knew inside out. A man he didn't know at all. The sucking noise of the bathroom door closing broke Flame out of his shock from hearing his best friend's declaration of love. Flame glanced over his shoulder at the closed door then back at John. No words came to his mind to say as his thoughts began to spin out of control. Not only was he outed to John but Tig's partner, Pat. Hell, after all the yelling in the bathroom, they were both probably outed to the whole fucking bar.

Shit, Flame felt the first tendrils of panic start when he realized the scope of the confrontation with John. He could only hope that the fallout from John's outburst wouldn't cause a catastrophe between Tig and his partner as he opened the bathroom door to leave.

"Flame, wait." John stepped forward and Flame looked over his shoulder. "Don't leave. Let's talk."

"I have nothing to say to you right now, John."

Flame stepped out of the bathroom and was greeted by the shocked, silent stares of his fellow fireman. He could deal with them later. Right now, he searched for Tig but wasn't surprised that the man was nowhere to be found.

CHAPTER 22

ANOTHER text message came through Tig's phone and he ignored it just like he ignored the plethora of calls he had been dumping into his voicemail for the last week. Pat had not commented on the information about his sexual preferences that was exposed in the incident at Guns & Hoses. In fact, Pat's behavior toward him hadn't changed at all. Tig wasn't sure if he was relieved or not that they hadn't discussed it.

"You should answer that," Pat said softly across their desks. Tig didn't even bother to look up from the file he was browsing. "Your phone has been blowing up all week. Talk about it or at least listen."

Tig frowned but recognized that his partner never gave away that he knew it was a man, knew it was Thomas Flame, who was setting off his phone several times a day.

"There's nothing to talk about." Tig flipped another page of the report he was pretending to read.

"There is and you know it."

"Drop it, Irish."

"Alright." Pat leaned back in his chair and stared across their desks. "Guns & Hoses after work then."

Tig finally glanced up with a frown and was greeted by Pat's raised brow daring him to say no. He had been avoiding the bar just like he had been avoiding Flame's messages. But by the look on his partner's face, he wasn't going to get away with avoiding it again today.

"Fine," Tig grumbled and tossed the file onto his desk.

Flame sat alone in Guns & Hoses and glanced at his phone. Again. The fallout from the guys at the station wasn't nearly as bad as Flame had expected it to be. He only hoped that the same could be said for Tig.

Tig froze just inside the door to Guns & Hoses when he saw Flame sitting alone at the firefighters table. It caused Pat to walk into him. Pat pushed him and he had no choice but to walk to their spot at the bar.

Flame tracked Tig and his partner as they crossed the bar. After the initial eye contact, Tig refused to look at him. He wanted to get up and go over to talk to the man but instead he just took another swig of his beer. After about fifteen minutes, Flame stood and walked over to the juke box.

"Miserable," Pat mumbled under his breath just loud enough for Tig to hear him. "Stubborn." Pat muttered again and Tig finally shot him a glance. "Both of you." Pat shook his head disgustedly.

Tig didn't bother to answer. He was too focused on ignoring Flame and the pain that was making his chest ache. It was ridiculous when he thought about it. Years of hating one another then two frantic weeks of fucking like rabbits, and what should have never started was over. It shouldn't hurt so fucking bad.

"For you, I'm sure," Pat snorted and tilted his head toward the juke box causing Tig to tune into the music that filled the bar.

And now I know who you are
It wasn't that hard
Just to figure you out
Now I did, you wonder why
I like the freckles on your chest
And I like the way you like me best
And I like the way you're not impressed, while you put me to the test

Tig grunted and killed his beer. *Fucking Flame and his music that always hit the nail on the head.* Tig didn't even glance at his ex-lover while Nickleback's words hit too close to home. He stood from the bar and said nothing to Pat before he walked out.

"What's the status from Miller?" Tig looked away from his computer and met Pat's disapproving gaze. He knew his partner thought he should at least listen to what Flame had to say even if Pat hadn't said as much. Tig was also pretty sure Pat was getting sick of hearing his phone go ape-shit all day.

"Tip came in and the Lt. is calling a meeting to schedule another raid," Pat replied but looked like he wanted to say something else entirely.

"When?"

"Later today probably. We should be hitting another lab by the end of the week."

"If we're lucky, Cortez will be there this time"

"Yeah, if we're lucky," Pat agreed.

Flame avoided John as much as he was able during their shifts. When he was forced to interact with his former best friend, he was stoically professional. He said nothing more than the job required. The one and only time John had tried to talk to him, he didn't even reply. He just turned his back and walked away. Everyone at the station felt the tension between them but their co-workers were all smart enough to stay out of the shit storm between the friends.

Flame had nothing to say to John after the shit he pulled at Guns & Hoses that caused Tig to shut him out. Every call he made to Tig was dumped into voicemail and every text he sent went unanswered. His choices for contacting the man he had fallen for were getting down to showing up at the police station to corner him.

Flame had been spending almost all of his free time at Guns & Hoses in hopes that he would run into Tig there again, even after he saw him there a few days ago and played the song he hoped would at least get Tig to talk to him. Flame even made a few trips to Bradley's but Tig hadn't made an appearance there either. He supposed he should be relieved that Tig wasn't out on the prowl again so soon but he wasn't. He even considered camping out on the man's doorstep but that idea was a bust since he didn't even know where the cop lived.

If he would just answer my texts.

Flame fumed at his helplessness at being unable to reach Tig. He just wanted to talk to the man to explain John's kiss and that the words his best friend spoke meant nothing to him. He lifted the weights again to work out his frustration while he wracked his brain for a way to get Tigger Flint to at least listen to what he had to say.

When the tones of another call blared overhead, Flame was forced to push all thoughts of Tig out of his mind. Maybe after fighting the fire they were being summoned to battle, he would come up with something. As he finished buckling on his bunker jacket and put his helmet on his head, he sincerely hoped that would be the case.

Tig stood behind Miller and next to two other S.W.A.T. team members by the side door of the warehouse they were about to raid. This was the first tip for a meth lab that was not located in a house or an apartment. It boded well for them and the chances were high that Cortez would be inside.

Miller held up his hand and counted down. Three. Two. One. The S.W.A.T. team member to Tig's left pulled back the battering ram and slammed it into the metal door when Miller's finger for 'one' closed into his fist. The second S.W.A.T. team member tossed a flash bang through the opening before all four of them charged through the door. Other teams breached the warehouse at the same time but Tig was only focused on his goal. Find the lab and catch Cortez if he was present.

The four man team that Tig was attached to entered the warehouse in a rush. Shelves filled with boxes and crates littered the floor providing plenty of cover for any of Cortez's men who might be defending the lab. And defend it they did. Shots were fired from both sides throughout the warehouse as they advanced.

At some point, Tig got separated from Miller and the rest of the S.W.A.T. team. He followed a perp that was fleeing deeper into the building and paused when he came to a corner. A glance around the wall revealed the meth lab they had been tipped off about. The quick glance had shown Tig the beakers and vacuum tubes of the lab setup and also gave him a glimpse of the man they had been trying to nail for months. In the brief look that Tig had, Cortez was collecting drugs and money into a large duffle. A shot fired and hit the wall next to where Tig's head had been a moment before. Tig squatted down and moved around the corner with his gun raised.

"TPD!" he identified himself and shot at the movement out of the corner of his eye on pure instinct. The shot took down the lackey he had been chasing but not before the asshole returned fire. Twice. The first shot hit Tig in his vest. The second didn't.

Tig felt the searing pain of the bullet just under his collarbone next to the strap over his shoulder that secured his vest. However, that didn't stop Tig from advancing on Cortez as the asshole was trying to escape through a side door.

Tig fired two warning shots, missing Cortez on purpose, before the drug dealer turned to face him with his gun raised. Tig only had a moment to be thankful that he wore a vest before Cortez fired. Agonizing pain ripped through Tig's thigh as he returned fire. Tig squeezed off three shots and they formed a perfectly circular pattern in the middle of Cortez's chest. But not before the drug dealer got off another shot. The shot wasn't aimed at Tig. It was aimed at the lab setup.

Tig fell to the floor, ducked and covered his head moments before the table that was lined with the meth lab beakers and tubes exploded. He didn't see the fireball that caused the table to fly through the air toward him. Tig saw nothing before he was hit by a crushing weight and his world went black.

Flame and the rest of Tampa Fire Rescue pulled up to the scene of a warehouse ablaze. The fire sprouted from the roof of one corner of the building while he jumped down from the rig and grabbed an axe from the side compartment of the engine. When he turned around, he noticed the Tampa Police Department's S.W.A.T. team mulling around the outside of the warehouse.

The memory of the last fire he responded to when S.W.A.T. was present made him think of Tig. He instinctively scanned the cops before he shook off thoughts of Tig and made his way toward his Captain. Before he could reach his commander for orders, he was intercepted. Patty O'Brian grabbed his arm and spun him around so they faced one another. All of the dread Flame felt at thinking Tig could be present returned.

"Tig's inside," O'Brian told him and his face conveyed all the worry that suddenly consumed Flame.

Flame fought the urge to run into the burning beast before him. It wouldn't help Tig if he ran blindly into the warehouse that was enveloped in fire.

"Where did he go in?" Flame asked O'Brian impatiently.

"There," Pat pointed to the side door that was closest to the blaze.

"How many others?" Flame forced himself to ask professionally.

"Three were with him. All checked in."

"Alright." Flame began to move away but Pat stopped him again.

"Bring him out, Flame." Flame gave Patty O'Brian a curt nod before turning away.

"John! With me!"

Flame didn't wait to see if his best friend followed. Out of habit, Flame had called for John to back him up as he entered the belly of the beast that was eating the warehouse one timber at a time.

The black smoke was thick when Flame entered through the battered door that S.W.A.T. had opened only an hour ago. That smoke did not deter Flame's forward momentum as it bellowed past him. He gave no thought to if John was behind him while he trailed his hand along the crate packed shelving. No flames had reached this section of the warehouse yet but Flame knew it was only a matter of time.

Warehouse fires were like hay bales just waiting for a lit match. There was no telling what type of combustibles the boxes and crates around them held. Fire wasn't their only concern. In fact, when it came to warehouse fires, heat was a larger threat than fire. Sometimes all it took was the increase of temperature to cause something to explode. All of this filtered through Flame's subconscious as he ventured deeper into the building toward the source of the fire.

Somehow he knew and his gut screamed that Tig was close to the point of ignition. He knew that he had to reach the man, the man who had captured his heart, before it was too late.

I won't be too late, Flame swore to himself before he made a mental promise to Tig. *I'll get you out of here even if you never talk to me again.*

Flame rounded a corner and only briefly paused when he caught sight of a body lying under a large piece of metal. He rushed forward and knelt next to the prone form. Instant recognition slammed into him as he looked down at Tig's unconscious body.

"John! Help me!"

With John's help, they freed Tig from under the weight of the metal slab that had previously been the meth lab tabletop. Flame pulled off his mask, not having a care for the toxic smoke that surrounded them, and leaned down close to Tig's face. Tig looked dead but Flame refused to believe it.

"Tig!" Flame shook Tig's shoulder to rouse him.

There was no response and it was then that Flame noticed the blood that still flowed freely over Tig's Kevlar vest. Fire wasn't Tig's main threat, Flame realized. He had been on enough scenes to recognize a gunshot wound to understand what he was looking at on Tig.

"Shit!" Flame cursed again before looking back at John.

"Put your mask back on!" John yelled at him, his voice muffled by the plastic facemask of his rebreather. "I'm clearing the room. Stay here."

"Hurry. He's been shot" Flame updated John before he pulled his mask back over his face.

Flame knew it was standard procedure to clear a room and wait for your partner even if you found a victim. As he watched John moved away, Flame applied pressure to Tig's wound. Tig didn't even flinch at what was sure to be a painful touch and Flame had to fight down another wave of panic that battered against him like a tidal wave. He was looking over Tig's body for more injuries when he noticed the pool of blood under Tig's thigh that couldn't have been caused by the metal table that had slammed into him.

Fuck! "John, we need to go!" Flame called out.

"Another one here."

Flame glanced in the direction of John's voice and saw his friend lifting a body in the classic fireman's carry. Flame wasted no time hefting Tig onto his shoulder in the same manner. Both firemen carried their burdens back the way they came and out of the blaze.

Ambulances were waiting when Flame exited the warehouse with Tig over his shoulder. As the EMT's approached, Flame tore his face mask away.

"Gunshot wound. Possibly two." Flame laid Tig down onto the waiting stretcher and stepped back to let the EMT and medic do their jobs.

"Two GSW's," the medic said as the EMT placed a oxygen rebreather mask over Tig's face. "Pulse fast and thready, respiratory rate slow and shallow, BP dropping." The medic rattled out Tig's vitals as she started a large bore IV. "Not looking good. Let's roll." The medic nodded to the EMT and the EMT slammed the doors of the unit closed before heading toward the driver's side.

"What hospital?" Flame called out to the EMT as the guy was climbing into the cab of the ambulance.

"Tampa General."

The door to the ambulance closed and they pulled away, lights flashing, just before Flame's Captain called out to him. Flame only allowed himself a moment more to stare after the departing ambulance before jogging over to over to his superior for the next order to do the job he loved.

The first thing Tig became aware of was an annoying beeping noise. It was constant and he just wished it would stop. His eyes were heavy but the urge to open them was strong. He knew he was likely in the hospital but even that knowledge was not enough to force his eyes open. Tig gave up trying. His body would let him open his eyes when it was good and ready and he knew there wasn't a damned thing he could do to speed up the process.

The warehouse fire was brutal. So brutal that it was two hours after the end of his shift before they killed the beast and were able to return to the station. Flame had only one thing on his mind while he stripped out of his bunker gear. Tig. He had just put his helmet on the hook above his gear when a hand landed on his shoulder.

"Flame," John said softly and Flame felt his friend try to turn him around.

Flame tensed. He didn't want to deal with the uncomfortableness that his best friend now represented. All he wanted to do was get to Tampa General and check on Tig.

"He'll be okay," John offered quietly and Flame allowed his head to drop to his chest and a sigh whooshed out of him. "Go on." John dropped his hand from Flame's shoulder and when Flame turned around, his friend was walking away.

The sound of beeping awoke Tig right before he was assaulted by the smell of smoke. The scent made him think of Flame before he forced his rapidly beating heart to calm.

The monitors above Tig's head increased their beeping, indicating Tig's increased heart rate, and Flame sat forward in concern. He resisted the urge to touch Tig and hold his hand for comfort. Instead, he just leaned closer to the bed Tig rested upon.

Tig once more forced his eyes to open. The desire to prove that the smoke he smelled was not real, that he wasn't dying in the warehouse fire, was strong. Strong enough that his eyelids cracked open and he was assaulted by what he was sure were the dim lights of a hospital room.

Flame held his breath while he watched Tig's eyes flutter open. He wasn't sure what he was expecting once Tig was awake but he hoped that Patty O'Brian could keep the rest of the cops out of the room long enough for him to find out.

Tig finally forced his eyes fully open, his gaze resting on the ceiling. The incessant beeping and the white pockmarked ceiling titles were enough to confirm he was in the fucking hospital. He hated hospitals. Just the thought of being in the hospital seemed to remind his body that there was pain to be felt. His shoulder burned and his thigh ached, both reminding him that Cortez shot him. Shots that his body decided to stop. Tig realized that Flame was keeping vigil by his bedside and was surprised to see the firefighter instead of his partner. Flame seemed to be holding his breath while he waited for Tig to say something.

"You're okay," Flame's low voice told him when he groaned. "Let me get the nurse for more pain meds."

Tig turned his head and his eyes landed on a much disheveled Flame. The firefighter stopped half way to standing when their eyes met.

"What are you doing here?" Tig croaked out. His voice was scratchy, felt raw, and it hurt to talk but he needed to know.

"Where else would I be?" Flame sat back down and gave Tig a weak smile before he stopped himself from reaching out to touch Tig's hand.

Tig just stared at Flame. The man was a sight for sore eyes. Maybe it was his close call with death but he couldn't think of a better view to wake up to. He berated himself for ignoring the man's attempts at contact over the last week and swore to himself that he would never do it again if Flame gave him another chance.

"You pulled me out," Tig croaked again. It was more a statement than a question when Flame picked up the small cup of ice water next to his bed.

"I did." Flame moved the bendy straw to Tig's lips and he took a drink. Flame pulled the cup away and finally gave into the urge to take Tig's hand.

They stared at one another for a long moment, royal blue eyes meeting hazel green as emotions were conveyed without words.

"But if that is what it is going to take to get you to talk to me when we have a misunderstanding in the future," Flame smiled as his thumb caressed Tig's knuckles. "I can't say I recommend that approach."

Tig watched the smile that spread across Flame's lips and didn't stop the one that graced his own. It took Tig's drug addled mind a moment to comprehend Flame's words but after he did and before he could breathe a sigh of relief that he'd have a second chance with the man, he spoke with hesitation.

"The future?"

"Yeah." Flame gave him another sip of water before he leaned closer to the hospital bed that Tig was trapped upon. "The future."

Tig turned his hand so he could thread his fingers with Flame's. The flip-flop shit he felt around Flame assaulted his heart again. The feeling was uncomfortable, a tightening in his chest, and caused the heart monitor to increase its beeping. Still, he didn't want the feeling to stop.

"What are we doing Flame?" Tig grinned as he asked the question that had almost become a pick-up line for the man.

"Whatever we want, Tig."

Tig nodded at Flame's response, his smile never faltering, and the smile only got wider when Flame lifted his hand and placed a promising kiss on his knuckles. "You and me and nobody else."

"I'm good with that." And Tig was.

ABOUT THE AUTHOR

Brenda is unlike most authors since she only began writing a few years ago. Her first book *Fates*, an adult fantasy, was published in 2010. Her love for reading fantasy, paranormal, and contemporary erotic romance has caused her to discard her Bachelor's degrees in management and marketing in order to write full time. She is an Amazon and ARe best-selling author.

Brenda resides in Tampa, FL when not attending conventions and is a volunteer with the Tampa Bay Sisters of Perpetual Indulgence. She is also an active member in organizing the Florida Leather Fetish Pride weekend and an associate member of the Tampa Leather Club.

She would love to hear from you! Visit her on the following:

Website: www.bcothernbooks.com
Facebook: Brenda Cothern Books
Facebook Fan Page: Brenda Cothern Books, Inc.
Goodreads: Brenda Cothern
Smashwords: BCothernBooks
Google+: Brenda Cothern Books
Twitter: BCothernBooks

For signed digital autograph, please send her a request through Authorgraph! A personalized autographed PDF for the book will be signed and sent to you!
http://www.authorgraph.com/authors/BCothernBooks

If you enjoy this book, please show your support by giving it stars and/or writing a review on the various online sites such as Amazon or Goodreads.

To read the first chapter of EVERY book she has written or will write, please visit the preview section of her website.

www.BCothernBooks.com

I would like to acknowledge and thank MLR Press (www.mlrbooks.com) for compiling the below information on the various support groups.

THE TREVOR PROJECT

The Trevor Project operates the only nationwide, around-the-clock crisis and suicide prevention helpline for lesbian, gay, bisexual, transgender and questioning youth. Every day, The Trevor Project saves lives though it's free and confidential helpline, its website and its educational services. If you or a friend is feeling lost or alone call The Trevor Helpline. If you or a friend are feeling lost, alone, confused or in crisis, please call The Trevor Helpline.

You'll be able to speak confidentially with a trained counselor 24/7.

The Trevor Helpline: 866-488-7386

On the Web : http://www.thetrevorproject.org/

THE GAY MEN'S DOMESTIC VIOLENCE PROJECT

Founded in 1994, The Gay Men's Domestic Violence Project is a grassroots, non-profit organization founded by a gay male survivor of domestic violence and developed through the strength, contributions and participation of the community. The Gay Men's Domestic Violence Project supports victims and survivors through education, advocacy and direct services. Understanding that the serious public health issue of domestic violence is not gender specific, we serve men in relationships with men, regardless of how they identify, and stand ready to assist them in navigating through abusive relationships.

GMDVP Helpline: 800.832.1901

On the Web: http://gmdvp.org/

THE GAY & LESBIAN ALLIANCE AGAINST DEFAMATION/GLAAD EN ESPAÑOL

The Gay & Lesbian Alliance Against Defamation (GLAAD) is dedicated to promoting and ensuring fair, accurate and inclusive representation of people and events in the media as a means of eliminating homophobia and discrimination based on gender identity and sexual orientation.

On the Web: http://www.glaad.org/

GLAAD en español:

http://www.glaad.org/espanol/bienvenido.php

SERVICEMEMBERS LEGAL DEFENSE NETWORK

Service members Legal Defense Network is a nonpartisan, nonprofit, legal services, watchdog and policy organization dedicated to ending discrimination against and harassment of military personnel affected by "Don't Ask, Don't Tell" (DADT).The SLDN provides free, confidential legal services to all those impacted by DADT and related discrimination. Since 1993, it's in house legal team has responded to more than 9,000 requests for assistance. In Congress, it leads the fight to repeal DADT and replace it with a law that ensures equal treatment for every service member, regardless of sexual orientation. In the courts, it

works to challenge the constitutionality of DADT.
SLDN Call: (202) 328-3244
PO Box 65301 or (202) 328-FAIR
Washington DC 20035-5301
e-mail: sldn@sldn.org
On the Web: http://sldn.org/

THE GLBT NATIONAL HELP CENTER

The GLBT National Help Center is a nonprofit, tax exempt organization that is dedicated to meeting the needs of the gay, lesbian, bisexual and transgender community and those questioning their sexual orientation and gender identity. It is an outgrowth of the Gay & Lesbian National Hotline, which began in 1996 and now is a primary program of The GLBT National Help Center. It offers several different programs including two national hotlines that help members of the GLBT community talk about the important issues that they are facing in their lives. It helps end the isolation that many people feel, by providing a safe environment on the phone or via the internet to discuss issues that people can't talk about anywhere else. The GLBT National Help Center also helps other organizations build the infrastructure they need to provide strong support to our community at the local level.
National Hotline: 1-888-THE-GLNH
(1-888- 843-4564)
National Youth Talkline
1-800-246-PRIDE (1-800-246-7743)
On the Web: http://www.glnh.org/
e-mail: info@glbtnationalhelpcenter.org

Printed in Great Britain
by Amazon